Also by Matt Haig

The Last Family in England
The Dead Fathers Club
The Possession of Mr Cave
The Radleys
The Humans
Humans: An A-Z
Reasons to Stay Alive

For Children

The Runaway Troll
Shadow Forest
To Be A Cat
Echo Boy
A Boy Called Christmas
The Girl Who Saved Christmas

MATT HAIG

CANONGATE

Canongate Books Ltd, 14 High Street, Edinburgh EH1 1TE

www.canongate.co.uk

1

British Library Cataloguing-in-Publication Data
A catalogue record for this book is available on request from the British Library

ISBN 978 1 78211 861 9
Export ISBN 978 1 78211 862 6

Typeset in Minion 11/14 pt by Palimpsest Book Production Ltd,
Falkirk, Stirlingshire

Printed and bound in Great Britain by Clays Ltd, St Ives plc.

For Andrea

I often think of what Hendrich said to me, over a century ago, in his New York apartment.

'The first rule is that you don't fall in love,' he said. 'There are other rules too, but that is the main one. No falling in love. No staying in love. No daydreaming of love. If you stick to this you will just about be okay.'

I stared through the curving smoke of his cigar, out over Central Park where trees lay uprooted from the hurricane.

'I doubt I will ever love again,' I said.

Hendrich smiled, like the devil he could be. 'Good. You are, of course, allowed to love food and music and champagne and rare sunny afternoons in October. You can love the sight of waterfalls and the smell of old books, but the love of people is off limits. Do you hear me? Don't attach yourself to people, and try to feel as little as you possibly can for those you do meet. Because otherwise you will slowly lose your mind . . .'

PART ONE

Life Among the Mayflies

I am old.

That is the first thing to tell you. The thing you are least likely to believe. If you saw me you would probably think I was about forty, but you would be very wrong.

I am *old* – old in the way that a tree, or a quahog clam, or a Renaissance painting is old.

To give you an idea: I was born well over four hundred years ago on the third of March 1581, in my parents' room, on the third floor of a small French château that used to be my home. It was a warm day, apparently, for the time of year, and my mother had asked her nurse to open all the windows.

'God smiled on you,' my mother said. Though I think she might have added that – should He exist – the smile had been a frown ever since.

My mother died a very long time ago. I, on the other hand, did not.

You see, I have a condition.

I thought of it as an illness for quite a while, but illness isn't really the right word. Illness suggests sickness, and wasting away. Better to say I have a condition. A rare one, but not unique. One that no one knows about until they have it.

It is not in any official medical journals. Nor does it go by an official name. The first respected doctor to give it one, back in the 1890s, called it 'anageria' with a soft 'g', but, for reasons that will become clear, that never became public knowledge.

*

5

The condition develops around puberty. What happens after that is, well, not much. Initially the 'sufferer' of the condition won't notice they have it. After all, every day people wake up and see the same face they saw in the mirror yesterday. Day by day, week by week, even month by month, people don't change in very perceptible ways.

But as time goes by, at birthdays or other annual markers, people begin to notice you aren't getting any older.

The truth is, though, that the individual hasn't stopped ageing. They age exactly the same way. Just much slower. The speed of ageing among those with anageria fluctuates a little, but generally it is a 1:15 ratio. Sometimes it is a year every thirteen or fourteen years but with me it is closer to fifteen.

So, we are not immortal. Our minds and bodies aren't in stasis. It's just that, according to the latest, ever-changing science, various aspects of our ageing process – the molecular degeneration, the cross-linking between cells in a tissue, the cellular and molecular mutations (including, most significantly, to the nuclear DNA) – happen on another timeframe.

My hair will go grey. I may go bald. Osteoarthritis and hearing loss are probable. My eyes are just as likely to suffer with age-related presbyopia. I will eventually lose muscle mass and mobility.

A quirk of anageria is that it does tend to give you a heightened immune system, protecting you from many (not all) viral and bacterial infections, but ultimately even this begins to fade. Not to bore you with the science, but it seems our bone marrow produces more hematopoietic stem cells – the ones that lead to white blood cells – during our peak years, though it is important to note that this doesn't protect us from injury or malnutrition, and it doesn't last.

So, don't think of me as a sexy vampire, stuck for ever at peak virility. Though I have to say it can feel like you are stuck for ever when, according to your appearance, only a decade passes between the death of Napoleon and the first man on the moon.

One of the reasons people don't know about us is that most people aren't prepared to believe it.

Human beings, as a rule, simply don't accept things that don't fit their worldview. So you could say 'I am four hundred and thirty-nine years old' easily enough, but the response would generally be 'are you mad?'. 'Or, alternatively, death.'

Another reason people don't know about us is that we're protected. By a kind of organisation. Anyone who does discover our secret, and believes it, tends to find their short lives are cut even shorter. So the danger isn't just from ordinary humans.

It's also from within.

Sri Lanka, three weeks ago

Chandrika Seneviratne was lying under a tree, in the shade, a hundred metres or so behind the temple. Ants crawled over her wrinkled face. Her eyes were closed. I heard a rustling in the leaves above and looked up to see a monkey staring down at me with judging eyes.

I had asked the tuk-tuk driver to take me monkey spotting at the temple. He'd told me this red-brown type with the near bald face was a rilewa monkey.

'Very endangered,' the driver had said. 'There aren't many left. This is their place.'

The monkey darted away. Disappeared among leaves.

I felt the woman's hand. It was cold. I imagined she had been lying here, unfound, for about a day. I kept hold of her hand and found myself weeping. The emotions were hard to pin down. A rising wave of regret, relief, sorrow and fear. I was sad that Chandrika wasn't here to answer my questions. But I was also relieved I didn't have to kill her. I knew she'd have had to die.

This relief became something else. It might have been the stress or the sun or it might have been the egg hoppas I'd had for breakfast, but I was now vomiting. It was in that moment that it became clear to me. *I can't do this any more.*

There was no phone reception at the temple, so I waited till I was back in my hotel room in the old fort town of Galle tucked inside my mosquito net sticky with heat, staring up at the pointlessly slow ceiling fan, before I phoned Hendrich.

'You did what you were supposed to do?' he said.

'Yes,' I said, which was halfway to being true. After all, the outcome had been the one he'd asked for. 'She is dead.' Then I asked what I always asked. 'Have you found her?'

'No,' he said, as always. 'We haven't. Not yet.'

Yet. That word could trap you for decades. But this time, I had a new confidence.

'Now, Hendrich, please. I want an ordinary life. I don't want to do this.'

He sighed wearily. 'I need to see you. It's been too long.'

Los Angeles, two weeks ago

Hendrich was back in Los Angeles. He hadn't lived there since the 1920s so he assumed it was pretty safe to do so and that no one was alive who would remember him from before. He had a large house in Brentwood that served as the headquarters for the Albatross Society. Brentwood was perfect for him. A geranium-scented land of large houses tucked behind high fences and walls and hedges, where the streets were free from pedestrians and everything, even the trees, looked perfect to the point of sterile.

I was quite shocked, on seeing Hendrich, sitting beside his large pool on a sun-lounger, laptop on knee. Normally, Hendrich looked pretty much the same, but I couldn't help notice the change. He looked *younger*. Still old and arthritic, but, well, better than he'd done in a century.

'Hi, Hendrich,' I said, 'you look good.'

He nodded, as if this wasn't new information. 'Botox. And a brow lift.'

He wasn't even joking. In this life he was a former plastic surgeon. The back story was that after retiring he had moved from Miami to Los Angeles. That way he could avoid the issue of not having any former local clients. His name here was Harry Silverman. ('Silverman. Don't you like it? It sounds like an ageing superhero. Which I kind of am.')

I sat on the spare lounger. His maid, Rosella, came over with two sunset-coloured smoothies. I noticed his hands. They looked old. Liver spots and baggy skin and indigo veins. Faces could lie easier than hands could.

'Sea buckthorn. It's crazy. It tastes like shit. Try it.'

The amazing thing about Hendrich was that he kept thoroughly of the times. He always had done, I think. He certainly had been since the 1890s. Centuries ago, selling tulips, he'd probably been the same. It was strange. He was older than any of us but he was always very much in the current of whatever zeitgeist was flowing around.

'The thing is,' he said, 'in California, the only way to look like you are getting older is to look like you are getting younger. If you can move your forehead over the age of forty then people become very suspicious.'

He told me that he had been in Santa Barbara for a couple of years but he got a bit bored. 'Santa Barbara is pleasant. It's heaven, with a bit more traffic. But nothing ever happens in heaven. I had a place up in the hills. Drank the local wine every night. But I was going mad. I kept getting these panic attacks. I have lived for over seven centuries and never had a single panic attack. I've witnessed wars and revolutions. Fine. But I get to Santa Barbara and there I was waking up in my comfortable villa with my heart going crazy and feeling like I was trapped inside myself. Los Angeles, though, is something else. Los Angeles calmed me right down, I can tell you . . .'

'Feeling calm. That must be nice.'

He studied me for a while, as if I was an artwork with a hidden meaning. 'What's the matter, Tom? Have you been missing me?'

'Something like that.'

'What is it? Was Iceland that bad?'

I'd been living in Iceland for eight years before my brief assignment in Sri Lanka.

'It was lonely.'

'But I thought you wanted lonely, after your time in Toronto. You said the real loneliness was being surrounded by people. And, besides, that's what we are, Tom. We're loners.'

I inhaled, as if the next sentence was something to swim under. 'I don't want to be that any more. I want out.'

There was no grand reaction. He didn't bat an eye. I looked at his gnarled hands and swollen knuckles. 'There is no *out*, Tom. You know that. You are an albatross. You are not a mayfly. You are an albatross.'

The idea behind the names was simple: albatrosses, back in the day, were thought to be very long-living creatures. Reality is, they only live to about sixty or so; far less than, say, the Greenland sharks that live to four hundred, or the quahog clam scientists called 'Ming' because it was born at the time of the Ming dynasty, over five hundred years ago. But anyway, we were albatrosses. Or albas, for short. And every other human on earth was dismissed as a mayfly. So called, because of the short-lived aquatic insects who go through an entire life cycle in a day or – in the case of one sub-species – five minutes.

Hendrich never talked of other, ordinary human beings as anything other than mayflies. I was finding his terminology – terminology I had ingrained into me – increasingly ridiculous.

Albatrosses. Mayflies. The silliness of it.

For all his age and intelligence, Hendrich was fundamentally immature. He was a child. An incredibly ancient child.

That was the depressing thing about knowing other albas. You realised that we weren't special. We weren't superheroes. We were just *old*. And that, in cases such as Hendrich, it didn't really matter how many years or decades or centuries had passed, because you were always living within the parameters of your personality. No expanse of time or place could change that. You could never escape yourself.

'I find it disrespectful, to be honest with you,' he told me. 'After all I've done for you.'

'I appreciate what you've done for me . . .' I hesitated. What exactly had he done for me? The thing he had promised to do hadn't happened.

'Do you realise what the modern world is *like*, Tom? It's not like the old days. You can't just move address and add your name to the parish register. Do you know how much I have had to *pay* to keep you and the other members safe?'

'Well then, I could save you some money.'

'I was always very clear: this is a one-way street—'

'A one-way street I never asked to be sent down.'

He sucked on his straw, winced at the taste of his smoothie. 'Which is life itself, isn't it? Listen, kid—'

'I'm hardly that.'

'You made a choice. It was your choice to see Dr Hutchinson—'

'And I would never have made that choice if I'd have known what would happen to him.'

He made circles with the straw, then placed the glass on the small table beside him in order to take a glucosamine supplement for his arthritis.

'Then I would have to have you killed.' He laughed that croak of his, to imply it was a joke. But it wasn't. Of course it wasn't. 'I'll make a deal, a compromise. I will give you the exact life you want – any life at all – but every eight years, as usual, you'll get a call and, before you choose your next identity, I'll ask you to do something.'

I had heard all this before, of course. Although 'any life you want' never really meant that. He would give me a handful of suggestions and I'd pick one of them. And my response, too, was more than familiar to his ears.

'Is there any news of her?' It was a question I had asked a hundred times before, but it had never sounded as pathetic, as hopeless, as it did now.

He looked at his drink. 'No.'

I noticed he said it a little quicker than he normally would. 'Hendrich?'

'No. No, I haven't. But, listen, we are finding new people at an incredible rate. Over seventy last year. Can you remember when we started? A good year was five. If you still want to find her you'd be mad to want out now.'

I heard a small splashing sound from the swimming pool. I stood up, went to the edge of the pool, and saw a small mouse, hopelessly swimming along past a water filter. I knelt down and scooped the creature out. It scuttled away towards the perfectly manicured grass.

He had me, and he knew it. There was no way out alive. And even if there was, it was easier to stay. There was a comfort to it – like insurance.

'Any life I want?'

'Any life you want.'

I am pretty sure, Hendrich being Hendrich, he was assuming that I was going to demand something extravagant and expensive. That I would want to live in a yacht off the Amalfi Coast, or in a penthouse in Dubai. But I had been thinking about this, and I knew what to say. 'I want to go back to London.'

'London? She probably isn't there, you know.'

'I know. I just want to be back there. To feel like I'm home again. And I want to be a teacher. A history teacher.'

He laughed. 'A history teacher. What, like in a high school?'

'They say "secondary school" in England. But, yes, a history teacher in a high school. I think that would be a good thing to do.'

And Hendrich smiled and looked at me with mild confusion, as if I had ordered the chicken instead of the lobster. 'That's perfect. Yes. Well, we'll just need to get a few things in place and . . .'

And as Hendrich kept talking I watched the mouse disappear under the hedge, and into dark shadows, into freedom.

London, now

London. The first week of my new life.

The headteacher's office at Oakfield School.

I am trying to seem normal. It is an increasing challenge. The past is trying to burst through.

No.

It is already through. The past is always here. The room smells of instant coffee, disinfectant and acrylic carpet, but there is a poster of Shakespeare.

It is the portrait you always see of him. Receding hairline, pale skin, the blank eyes of a stoner. A picture that doesn't really look like Shakespeare.

I return my focus to the headteacher, Daphne Bello. She is wearing orange hoop earrings. She has a few white hairs amid the black. She is smiling at me. It is a wistful smile. The kind of smile no one is capable of before the age of forty. The kind that contains sadness and defiance and amusement all at once.

'I've been here a long while.'

'Really?' I say.

Outside a distant police siren fades into nothing.

'*Time*,' she says, 'is a strange thing, isn't it?'

She delicately holds the brim of her paper cup of coffee as she places it down next to her computer.

'The strangest,' I agree.

I like Daphne. I like this whole interview. I like being back here, in London, back in Tower Hamlets. And to be in an interview for an ordinary job. It is so wonderful to feel, well, *ordinary* for once.

15

'I have been a teacher now for three decades. And here for two. What a depressing thought. All those years. I am so old.' She sighs through her smile.

I have always found it funny when people say that.

'You don't look it,' is the done thing to say, so I say it.

'Charmer! Bonus points!' She laughs a laugh that rises through an entire two octaves.

I imagine the laugh as an invisible bird, something exotic, from Saint Lucia (where her father was from), flying off into the grey sky beyond the window.

'Oh, to be young, like you,' she chuckles.

'Forty-one isn't young,' I say, emphasising the ludicrous number. *Forty-one. Forty-one. That is what I am.*

'You look very well.'

'I've just come back from holiday. That might be it.'

'Anywhere nice?'

'Sri Lanka. Yes. It was nice. I fed turtles in the sea . . .'

'Turtles?'

'Yes.'

I look out of the window and see a woman with a gaggle of schoolkids in uniform head onto the playing field. She stops, turns to them, and I see her face as she speaks unheard words. She is wearing glasses and jeans and a long cardigan that flaps gently in the wind, and she pulls her hair behind her ear. She is laughing now, at something a pupil is saying. The laugh lights up her face, and I am momentarily mesmerised.

'Ah,' Daphne says, to my embarrassment when she sees where I am looking. 'That's Camille, our French teacher. There's no one like her. The kids love her. She always gets them out and about . . . Al fresco French lessons. It's that kind of school.'

'I understand you've done a lot of great things here,' I say, trying to get the conversation back on track.

'I try. We all try. It's sometimes a losing battle, though. That's my only concern about your application. Your references are amazing. And I've had them all checked . . .'

I feel relieved. Not that she has checked the references, but that there had been someone who had picked up the phone, or emailed back.

'. . . but this isn't a rural comprehensive in Suffolk. This is London. This is Tower Hamlets.'

'Kids are kids.'

'And they're great kids. But this is a different area. They don't have the same privileges. My concern is that you've lived a rather sheltered life.'

'You might be surprised.'

'And many students here struggle hard enough with the present, let alone with history. They just care about the world around them. Getting them engaged is the key. How would you make history come alive?'

There was no easier question in the world. 'History isn't something you need to bring to life. History already *is* alive. We are history. History isn't politicians or kings and queens. History is everyone. It is everything. It's that coffee. You could explain much of the whole history of capitalism and empire and slavery just by talking about coffee. The amount of blood and misery that has taken place for us to sit here and sip coffee out of paper cups is incredible.'

'You've put me right off my drink.'

'Oh, sorry. But the point is: history is everywhere. It's about making people realise that. It makes you understand a place.'

'Right.'

'History is people. Everyone loves history.'

Daphne looks at me doubtfully, her face retreating into her neck as her eyebrows rise. 'Are you sure about that?'

I offer a small nod. 'It's just making them realise that everything they say and do and see is only what they say and do and see because of what has gone before. Because of Shakespeare. Because of every human who ever lived.'

I look out of the window. We are on the third floor and have quite a view, even in the grey London drizzle. I see an old Georgian building I have walked past many times.

'That place, that place over there. The one with all the chimneys? That used to be an asylum. And over there' – I point to another, lower brick building – 'was the old slaughterhouse. They used to take all the old bones and make porcelain from them. If we had walked past it two hundred years ago we'd have heard the wails coming from the people society had declared mad on one side and the cattle on the other . . .'

If, if, if.

I point to the slate terrace rooftops in the east.

'And just over there, in a bakery, on Old Ford Road, that's where Sylvia Pankhurst and the East London suffragettes used to meet. They used to have a big sign, painted in gold, saying "VOTES FOR WOMEN" that you couldn't miss, not far from the old match factory.'

Daphne writes something down. 'And you play music, I see. Guitar, piano *and* violin.'

And the lute, I don't say. *And the mandolin. And the cittern. And the tin pipe.*

'Yes.'

'You put Martin to shame.'

'Martin?'

'Our music teacher. Hopeless. He's hopeless. Can barely play the triangle. Thinks he's a rock star, though. Poor Martin.'

'Well, I love music. I love playing music. But I'd find it a hard thing to teach. I've always found it hard to talk about music.'

'Unlike history?'

'Unlike history.'

'And you seem up to speed with the current curriculum.'

'Yes,' I lie, easily. 'Absolutely.'

'And you're still on the young side of things.'

I shrug, and make the kind of face I think you are meant to make.

'I'm fifty-six so forty-one is young, trust me.'

Fifty-six is young.

Eighty-eight is young.

One hundred and thirty is young.

'Well, I am quite an *old* forty-one.'

She smiles at me. She clicks the top of her pen. Then clicks it again. Each one is a moment. The first click, the pause between the click, and the second click. The longer you live, the harder it becomes. To grab them. Each little moment as it arrives. To be living in something other than the past or the future. To be actually here.

Forever, Emily Dickinson said, is composed of nows. But how do you inhabit the now you are in? How do you stop the ghosts of all the other nows from getting in? How, in short, do you live?

I am drifting away.

It has been happening a lot recently. I had heard about this. Other albas had spoken about it. You reached the mid-point of your life, and the thoughts got too much. The memories swell. The headaches grow. The headache today isn't so bad, but it is there.

I try to concentrate. I try to hold on to that other now, a short few seconds ago, where I was enjoying the interview. Enjoying the feeling of relative ordinariness. Or the illusion of it.

There is no ordinary.

Not for me.

I try to concentrate. I look at Daphne as she shakes her head and laughs, but softly now, at something she doesn't disclose. Something sad, I feel, from the sudden glazing of her eyes. 'Well, Tom, I am quite impressed by you and this application, I must say.'

Tom.

Tom Hazard.

My name – my original name – was Estienne Thomas Ambroise Christophe Hazard. That was the starting point. Since then I have had many, many names, and been many, many things. But, on my first arrival into England, I quickly lost the trimmings and became just Tom Hazard.

Now, using that name again, it feels like a return. It echoes in my head. *Tom. Tom. Tom. Tom.*

'You tick all the boxes. But even if you didn't you'd be getting the job.'

'Oh, really. Why?'

She raises her eyebrows. 'There's no other applicant!'

We both laugh a little at that.

But the laugh dies faster than a mayfly.

Because then she says, 'I live on Chapel Street. I wonder if you know anything about that?'

And, of course, I do know about that, and the question wakes me like a cold wind. My headache pulses harder. I picture an apple bursting in an oven. I shouldn't have come back here. I should never have asked Hendrich for this to happen. I think of Rose, the last time I saw her, and those wide desperate eyes.

'Chapel Street. I don't know. No. No, I'm afraid I don't know.'

'Don't worry.' She sips her coffee.

I look at the poster of Shakespeare. He seems to be staring at me, like an old friend. There is a quote below his image.

We know what we are, but know not what we may be.

'I have a feeling about you, Tom. You have to trust your feelings, don't you?'

'I suppose so,' I say, though feelings were the one thing I had never trusted.

She smiles.

I smile.

I stand up, and head to the door. 'See you in September.'

'Ha! September. September. It will fly by. Time, you see. That's another thing about getting older. Time speeds up.'

'I wish,' I whisper.

But she doesn't hear, because then she says, 'And children.'

'Sorry?'

'Children are another thing that seem to make life go faster. I have three. Oldest is twenty-two. Graduated last year. Yesterday she was playing with her Lego; today she's collecting the keys to her new flat. Twenty-two years in a blink of an eye. Do you have any?'

I grip the door handle. This is a moment, too. And inside it, a thousand others come painfully alive.

'No,' I say, because it is easier than the truth, 'I don't.'

She seems, for a brief moment, a little awkward. I think she is about to comment on this but instead she says, 'See you soon, Mr Hazard.'

I step out into the corridor that smells of the same disinfectant, where two teenagers lean against the wall, staring down at their phones as devoutly as old priests with prayer books. I turn back to see Daphne looking towards her computer.

'Yes. See you soon.'

As I walk out of Daphne Bello's office, and out of the school, I am in the twenty-first century but also the seventeenth.

As I walk the mile or so to Chapel Street – a stretch of betting shops and pavements and bus-stops and concrete lampposts and half-hearted graffiti – I am almost in a trance. The streets feel too wide. And when I get to Chapel Street I discover what I of course know: the houses that had once been there no longer are, replaced by ones built in the late 1800s, tall and red-bricked and as austere as the time of their design.

At the corner, where I had known a small deserted church, and a watchman, there is now a KFC. The red plastic throbs like a wound. I walk along with my eyes closed, trying to sense how far

21

along the street the house had originally been and I come to a stop after twenty or so steps. I open my eyes to see a semi-detached house that bears no physical relation to the house I had arrived at all those centuries ago. The unmarked door is now a modern blue. The window reveals a living room complete with a TV. Someone is playing a video game on it. An alien explodes on the screen.

My headache pounds and I feel weak and I have to step back, almost as if the past is something that could thin the air, or affect the laws of gravity. I lean back against a car, lightly, but enough to set off the alarm.

And the noise is loud, like a wail of pain, howling all the way from 1623, and I walk briskly away from the house, then the street, wishing I could just as easily walk away from the past.

London, 1623

I have been in love only once in my life. I suppose that makes me a romantic, in a sense. The idea that you have one true love, that no one else will compare after they have gone. It's a sweet idea, but the reality is terror itself. To be faced with all those lonely years *after*. To exist when the point of you has gone.

And my point, for a while, was Rose.

But after she was gone so many of the good memories were clouded by the last. An end that was also a terrible beginning. That final day I had with her. Because it is this day, the one where I headed to Chapel Street to see her, that has defined so many over the centuries.

So . . .

I was standing outside her door.

I had knocked and waited and knocked again.

The watchman, who I had passed at the corner of the street, was now approaching.

'It is a marked house, lad.'

'Yes. I know that.'

'You must not go in there . . . It is unsafe.'

I held out my hand. 'Stand back. I am cursed with it too. Do not get any closer.'

This was a lie, of course, but an effective one. The watchman stepped back away from me, with considerable haste.

'Rose,' I said, through the door. 'It's me. It's me. Tom. I just saw Grace. By the river. She told me you were here . . .'

It took a while, but I heard her voice, from inside. 'Tom?'

It had been years since I had heard that voice.

'Oh, Rose, open the door. I need to see you.'

'I can't, Tom. I am sick.'

'I know. But I won't catch it. I have been around many plague sufferers these last months and I have had not so much as a cold. Come on, Rose, open the door.'

She did so.

And she was there, a woman. We were the same age, near enough, but now she looked like she was nearing fifty, while I still seemed a teenager.

Her skin was grey. Sores patterned her face like territories on a map. She could hardly stand up. I felt guilty that I had made her leave her bed but she seemed pleased to see me. She talked, semi-coherently, as I helped her back into bed.

'You look so young, still . . . You are still a young man . . . a boy, almost.'

'I have a little line, in my forehead. Look.'

I held her hand. She couldn't see the line.

'I am sorry,' she said. 'I am sorry I told you to leave.'

'It was the right thing. Just my existence was a danger to you.'

I should also say, in case it needs saying: I don't know for sure that the words I write were the words that were actually spoken. They probably weren't. But this is how I remember these things, and all we can ever be is faithful to our memories of reality, rather than the reality itself, which is something closely related but never precisely the same thing.

Though I am absolutely sure, word for word, she then said: 'There is a darkness that fringes everything. It is a most horrid ecstasy.' And I felt the horror of her horror. That, I suppose, is a price we pay for love: the absorbing of another's pain as if our own.

She drifted in and out of delirium.

The illness was taking further hold, almost by the minute. She was now the opposite of me. While for me life stretched out towards an almost infinitely distant point in the future, for Rose the end was now galloping closer.

It was dark in the house. All the windows had been boarded up. But as she lay on the bed in her damp night clothes, I could see her face shining like pale marble, the red and grey patches colonising her skin. Her neck was swollen with egg-sized lumps. It was terrible, a kind of violation, to see her transformed like this.

'It's all right, Rose. It's all right.'

Her eyes were wide with fear, almost as if something was inside her skull, slowly pushing from behind.

'Soft, soft, soft . . . All will be well . . .'

It was such a ridiculous thing to say. All was not going to be well. She moaned a little. Her body writhed in pain.

'You must go.' Her voice was dry.

I leaned over and kissed her brow.

'Careful,' she said.

'It is safe.' In truth, I didn't know for certain if that was true. I thought it was, but couldn't know it, having only lived forty-two years on earth (and looking little more than the sixteen Rose first thought I was). But I didn't care. Life had lost its value in the years away from her.

Even though I hadn't seen Rose since 1603 the love was still there, exactly as strong, and now it was hurting. It was hurting more than any physical pain could try to.

'We were happy, weren't we, Tom?' The faintest echo of a smile was on her face now. I remembered walking past Oat Barn carrying heavy pails of water, on some long-lost Tuesday morning, content in our chatter. I remembered the joy of her smile and her body, when it had writhed from pleasure not pain, and of trying to be quiet so her sister wouldn't wake. I remembered long walks back from Bankside, dodging the stray dogs and slithering in mud, comforted by nothing but the thought that she would be at the end of the journey home, and be the point of it.

All those times, all those talks, all that *everything*, reduced to the simplest most elemental truth.

'We were . . . I love you, Rose. I love you so much.'

I wanted to hold her up and feed her a rabbit pie and some cherries and make her well again. I could see she was in so much pain that she just wanted to die now but I didn't know what that would mean. I didn't know how the world would stay together.

There was also something else I wanted. An answer that I hoped dearly she would have.

'Sweetheart, where is Marion?' I asked.

She stared at me a long time. I readied myself for some terrible news. 'She fled . . .'

'What?'

'She was like you.'

It took a moment to sink in.

'She stopped growing old?'

She spoke slowly, between sighs and coughs and whimpers. I told her she didn't have to say anything, but she felt she had to. 'Yes. And people started to notice when the years went by and she didn't change. I told her we would have to move again and it troubled her greatly, and Manning came to us—'

'Manning?'

'And that night she ran, Tom. I ran after her yet she had vanished. She never came back. I have no idea where she went or if she is safe. You must try to find her. You must try to look after her . . . Pray, be strong now, Tom. You find her. I shall be fine. I shall be joining my brothers . . .'

I had never felt weaker, and yet I was ready to give her anything, even the myth of my strength and future happiness.

'I will be strong, my Rose.'

Her breath was a weak draught. 'You will.'

'Oh, Rose.'

I needed to keep saying her name and for her to keep hearing it. I needed her to keep being a living reality.

We are time's subjects, and time bids be gone . . .

She asked me to sing to her. 'Anything in your heart.'

'My heart is sad.'

'Sing sadly, then.'

I was going to grab my lute but she just wanted my voice, and my unaccompanied voice was not something I was particularly proud of, even in front of Rose, but I just sang it for her.

Her smiles, my springs that makes my joys to grow,
Her frowns the Winters of my woe . . .

She smiled a soft, troubled smile and I felt the whole world slipping away, and I wanted to slip with it, to go wherever she was going. I did not know how to be me, my strange and unusual self, without her. I had tried it, of course. I had existed whole years without her, but that was all it had been. An existence. A book with no words.

'I will look for Marion.'

She closed her eyes, as if she had heard the final thing she had wanted to hear.

She was as grey, now, as a January sky.

'I love you, Rose.'

And I searched her mouth, and the line between her pale, blistered lips for the slightest curve, the slightest response, but she was still now. The stillness was terrifying. Motes of dust were the only things moving.

I pleaded with God, I asked and begged and bargained, but God did not bargain. God was stubborn and deaf and oblivious. And she died and I lived and a hole opened up, dark and bottomless, and I fell down and kept falling for centuries.

London, now

I still feel weak. My head throbs. I walk. I think it will help ease the memories of Chapel Street. I walk to the antidote: Hackney. Well Lane. Now called Well Street. The place where Rose and I first lived together, before the years of misery and separation and plague took over. The cottages and stables and barns and pond and fruit orchards are long gone. I know it isn't healthy to walk around no longer familiar streets, looking for memories that have been paved over, but I need to see it.

I keep walking along. These must be among the busiest streets in Hackney. Buses and shoppers bustle past. I pass a phone shop and a pawnbroker's and a sandwich bar. And then I see it, on the other side of the road – the spot where we must have lived.

It is now a windowless red-brick building, with a blue and white sign outside. HACKNEY PET RESCUE SERVICES. It is depressing to feel your life erased. The kind of depressing that requires you to rest against a wall near the cash machine, causing you to apologise to the old man guarding his PIN number, explaining that you don't want to rob him, and deal with his stare as if he still isn't sure.

I watch a man with a Staffordshire terrier leave the building. Then I realise what I can do. How I can make a little peace with my past.

I can cross the street and go inside.

Every other dog in the place is barking. But this one is just lying in its undersized basket. It is a strange grey creature with sapphire eyes. The dog, I feel, is too dignified for such modern garishness, a wolf out of its time. I related.

The dog has an untouched chew toy beside him. A bright yellow rubber bone.

'What breed is it?' I ask the dog shelter volunteer (name badge 'Lou'). She scratches the eczema on her arm.

'He's an Akita,' she says. 'Japanese. Pretty rare. Bit like a husky, isn't he?'

'Yes.'

This is the spot, as far as I can tell. This kennel, this one with this beautiful, sad-looking dog inside, is where the room used to be. The room we slept in.

'How old is he?' I ask Lou.

'Pretty old. He's eleven. That's one of the reasons it's been hard to find a home for him.'

'And why is he in here?'

'He was picked up. He was living on a balcony to a flat. Chained up. Horrid state. Look.' She points at a red-brown scar on his thigh where there is no hair growing.

'A cigarette burn.'

'He looks so depressed.'

'Yep.'

'What's his name?'

'We never knew his name. We call him Abraham.'

'Why?'

'The tower block where we found him was called Lincoln Tower.'

'Ah,' I said. 'Abraham. It suits him.'

Abraham stands up. Comes over to me and stares up with those light blue eyes, as if trying to tell me something. I hadn't intended to get a dog. That hadn't been part of today's plan. And yet, here I am, saying, 'This is the one. I'd like to take him home.'

Lou looks at me in surprise. 'You don't want to see the rest?'

'No.'

I notice the blotched skin on Lou's arm – crimson and sore – and in my mind it was that cold winter's day, in Dr Hutchinson's waiting room, amid the other patients, as I nervously waited for a diagnosis.

London, 1860

There was a blizzard. After a relatively mild and inconsequential spell, during the previous few days in January the temperature had fallen sharply. It was the coldest I had known London to be since 1814, the year of Napoleon jokes and financial scandal and the last Frost Fair, when market traders had sold their wares on the frozen Thames.

As then, to be outside meant to be almost unable to move your face. You could almost feel your blood start to freeze. I could hardly see during my two-mile walk to Blackfriars Road, and my path was guided by the lampposts, those elegant black wrought-iron streetlamps that once seemed so modern. Blackfriars Road was the location of the hospital where Dr Hutchinson was working at the time, the London Cutaneous Institution for Treatment and Cure of Non-infectious Diseases of the Skin. Quite a catchy name, by Victorian standards.

Of course, I didn't have a disease of the skin. My skin caused me no irritation. I had no rashes. There was nothing wrong with my skin other than that it was two hundred and seventy-nine years old, yet looked centuries younger; but then my whole body felt centuries younger. If only my mind could have felt thirty as well.

The reason I had contacted Dr Hutchinson was because of his work discovering and researching a similar, albeit opposite, affliction known as 'progeria'.

The word is derived from the Greek words 'pro', meaning not only *before* but also *early*, and 'geras', which means *old age*. Premature old age. That's what it is, essentially. A child is born and when they are still a toddler strange symptoms begin to emerge. These symptoms become more startling as the child ages.

The symptoms include those associated with ageing: hair loss, wrinkled skin, weak bones, prominent veins, stiff joints, kidney failure and often loss of eyesight. They die at a young age.

These ill-fated children have always existed. Yet the illness was never recognised until Dr Hutchinson first described it, in relation to a six-year-old boy who was losing his hair and suffering skin atrophy.

So, I was reasonably optimistic on my way to see him. If anyone could help me, he could. You see, I had, in truth, been struggling recently. I had spent most of the last two hundred years searching London and the rest of the country, looking for Marion, occasionally thinking I had seen someone who looked like her, then making a fool of myself. I remember, in particular, the beating I'd received from a drunken cobbler in York on the Shambles, who believed I was propositioning his wife, by asking her when she was born. I played music whenever I could get paid for it, moving on and changing my identity whenever anyone got suspicious. I had never accumulated wealth. The money I had made had always floated through like a draught, being spent on rent and ale.

There were many times I had lost all hope in my search. A search not just for a lost person, but for that other thing I had lost – meaning. For a point. It occurred to me that human beings didn't live beyond a hundred because they simply weren't up for it. Psychologically, I mean. You kind of *ran out*. There wasn't enough self to keep going. You grew too bored of your own mind. Of the way life repeated itself. How, after a while, there wasn't a smile or gesture that you hadn't seen before. There wasn't a change in the world order that didn't echo other changes in the world order. And the news stopped being new. The very word 'news' became a joke. It was all just a cycle. A slowly rotating downward one. And your tolerance for human beings, making the same mistakes over and over and over and *over* again, began to fade. It was like being stuck in the same song, with a chorus you had once liked but now made you want to rip your ears off.

Indeed, it was often enough to make you want to kill yourself. I sometimes thought about putting this desire into action. For years after Rose died, I would often catch myself in apothecaries, contemplating a purchase of arsenic. And recently I was back in that state. Standing on bridges, dreaming of non-existence.

And I possibly would have gone through with it, were it not for the promises I had made to Rose and my mother.

I just didn't like my condition.

It made me lonely. And when I say lonely, I mean the kind of loneliness that howls through you like a desert wind. It wasn't just the loss of people I had known but also the loss of myself. The loss of who I had been when I had been with them.

You see, in total, there had been three people I had properly loved in life: my mother, Rose and Marion. Of those, two were dead, and one was alive only as a possibility. And without love as an anchor, I had drifted. I had gone to sea, on two different voyages, drowning myself in drink, driven only by the determination to find Marion, and hopefully also myself in the process.

I walked through the blizzard. I was hungover. It took a lot to make me hungover, but I was always sure to put in the effort. The city seemed only half there, because of the snow, as if I was walking inside one of Monet's fuzzy depictions of London, which he was soon to paint. There was no one about, except outside the Christian Mission where men in ragged, ill-fitting suits and flat caps waited for food. They were so still, so quiet, so despondent, stiff with cold.

There was a very good chance, I realised, that my journey would be wasted. Yet what could I do? I was quite desperate to see Dr Hutchinson, for if anyone in the world could tell me about my condition I was sure it would be him.

I had no idea if he would even be there, given the weather.

As soon as I arrived a nurse, Miss Forster, assured me that Dr Hutchinson was *always* here.

'Never missed a day's work in his life, I'd dare say,' Miss Forster told me, as I am sure she had told many before. She looked so pristine and white with her immaculate cap and apron that she seemed to have been something made by the blizzard itself. 'You are lucky today,' she said. 'Everyone in London seems to want to speak to Mr Hutchinson about their ailments.' She studied me, trying to work out exactly what kind of skin complaint I had.

I followed Miss Forster up three flights of stairs and I was told to wait in a well-furnished room, full of expensive high-backed chairs with red velvet seats and damask wallpaper and a stately wall clock. 'He's still seeing someone,' she told me, in the kind of reverential whisper you'd use in church. 'You might have to wait a fair time, Mr Cribbs.'

(I was now Edward Cribbs, in honour of a former Plymouth drinking buddy.)

'Waiting's my speciality,' I said.

'Very good, sir,' she said earnestly, and then left me. I remember sitting in that room with people whose faces were colonised by terrible blotches and rashes.

'Awful out, isn't it?' I said to one woman, with a livid purple rash covering her face.

(One thing that has remained constant, across four centuries, has been the desire for a British person to fill a silence with talk of the weather, and whenever I have lived there I was no exception to this rule.)

'Oh yes, sir,' she said, but didn't expand on this.

Eventually, the door I was waiting beside opened and out came a male patient. He was well dressed, like a dandy, but his face was covered in rough, raised blotches like a microscopic mountain range.

'Good day,' he said to me, smiling as broadly as his face allowed, clearly having experienced some miracle (or the promise of one).

There was that quiet lull unique to waiting rooms and the clock ticked away the silence until it was my turn.

I entered the room and the first thing I noticed was Dr Hutchinson himself. Jonathan Hutchinson was a very impressive-looking man. Even in the ultimate era of impressive-looking gentlemen, he was formidable. He was tall and smart and had a long beard. The beard, in particular, earned admiration. Neither Greek philosopher nor shipwrecked castaway, this was something very carefully thought out and pre-planned, the beard getting narrower and wispier as it descended until it reached a thin white line, a tail that faded imperceptibly into nothing. It may have been the intense nature of the morning that made me see in that beard a metaphor for mortal existence.

'Thank you for agreeing to this meeting,' I said, and instantly regretted it. It made me sound desperate.

Dr Hutchinson checked his pocket watch. He would do this a few times more, during this meeting. He probably wasn't really bothered about the time. It just seemed like a habit. It was quite a common one, actually. The way people check smartphones today.

He stared at me. He picked up a letter from his desk. It was the one I had written. He read excerpts back to me.

'*Dear Dr Hutchinson*' – his voice was rich and dry, like port – '*I am a great admirer of your work, and happened upon an article you had written on the subject of the new disease you discovered, whereby the body ages before its time . . . I myself have a strange condition, one similar in nature, though – if anything – even more unfathomable . . . it appears to me that you are the only man in all of Christendom who might be able to give me an explanation and thereby put a lifetime's mystery to rest . . .*'

He carefully folded the letter and put it aside on his desk. Then he studied me carefully.

'Your skin is illuminated with health. It is the skin of a healthy man.'

'I am healthy. In body. Healthier than most people.'

'Where is your problem?'

'Before I speak I must have assurance that I can remain unidentified. That if you were to publish any findings that arise due to what you discover my name will not be found in any journals. This is of the utmost importance. Do I have that assurance?'

'Of course. Now, you have aroused my curiosity. Tell me what is your problem.'

And so I told him. 'I am old,' I said simply.

'I don't—'

'I am older than is meant to be.'

It took a second, but then he seemed to absorb it. His voice changed after that. Became a little less sure of itself. The question demanded to be asked, even though I could see he was scared to ask it. '*How* old?'

'Older than is possible,' I said.

'Possibility is everything that has ever happened. The purpose of science is to find out where the limits of possibility end. When we have achieved that – and we shall – there will be no more magic, no more superstition, there will just be *what is*. Once it was impossible that this globe we are on wasn't flat. It is not for science – and certainly not for medicine – to flatter our expectations of Nature. Quite the opposite.' He looked at me for a long time. Then he leaned forward and whispered something. 'Rotten fish.'

'I'm not sure I understand.'

He sat back, pursed his lips. There was a mournful look to him. 'No one sees the connection between rotten fish and leprosy, but it is there. If you eat too much rotten fish you will develop leprosy.'

'Oh,' I said. 'I didn't know that.'

(Of course, now, from the twenty-first century I can positively say that if you eat rotten fish you won't get leprosy, though I have lived long enough to know that in another two hundred years it may be proven that eating rotten fish actually does cause leprosy and that Dr Hutchinson was actually right about this. If you live long enough you realise that every proven fact is later disproved and then proven again. When I was little, the average person, outside the scientific community, still believed the Earth was flat because they walked around and that is what they saw. Then people began to finally get to grips with the idea that the Earth was spherical. But then the other day I was skimming through a copy of *New Scientist* magazine in WH Smith's and it was all about something called the 'holographic principle'. It's to do with string theory and quantum mechanics and how gravity acts like a hologram. So anyway, the mind-boggling bit is that the theory hints that the entire universe is just two-dimensional information on a cosmological horizon and that everything we think we see in three dimensions is really as much an illusion as a 3D movie, and it could all be a simulation. So really, the world (and everything) might be flat after all. And then again it might not be.)

'So tell me,' he said, reminding me of the question that was still in the air. A question that I knew had to be answered. 'How old are you?'

So I told him. 'I was born on the third of March, in the year fifteen eighty-one. I am two hundred and seventy-one years old.'

I expected him to laugh, but he didn't. He stared at me for a long, long time as snow flurries danced busily outside the window, as if to mirror my swirling mind. His eyes widened and he pinched his lower lip between his fingers. And then he said, 'Well. There. That settles the matter quite conclusively. Now I can set about and give you a diagnosis.'

I smiled. This was good. A diagnosis was precisely what I was after.

'But, for proper help, you will need to go to Bethlem.'

I remembered passing the place. Hearing the dull screams from inside. 'Bethlem Hospital? As in . . . Bedlam?'

'The very same.'

'But that's a place for lunatics.'

'It is an asylum, yes. It will give you the help you need. Now, please, I have more appointments today.'

He nodded to the door.

'But—'

'Please, I recommend that you visit Bethlem. It will help with your . . . delusions.'

The most fashionable philosopher at this time was the German Arthur Schopenhauer, who was still (just) alive. I had been reading a lot of him, which was probably inadvisable. Reading Schopenhauer when you felt melancholy was like taking off your clothes when you felt cold, but a line of his came back to me.

Every man takes the limits of his own field of vision for the limits of the world.

I had thought, in coming to Dr Hutchinson, I was coming to the man with the broadest field of scientific vision, the one most likely to understand my condition, and having this belief slip away felt like a kind of grief. The death of hope itself. I was beyond every field of vision. I was a kind of invisible man.

As a result, I became quite animated. I pulled a coin from my pocket.

'Look at this. Look at this penny. It is Elizabethan. Look. Look. My daughter gave it me when I had to go away.'

'That is an antique coin. I have a friend who has a silver coin from the reign of Henry the Eighth. A halfgroat, I think it is called. And I assure you, my friend was not born in the age of the Tudors. And that a halfgroat is rarer than a penny.'

'I am not deluded. I promise you. I have been alive for a long time. I was there when the British found Tahiti. I knew Captain Cook. I worked for the Lord Chamberlain's Men . . . Please, sir, you must tell me. Has someone else been to see you? A girl . . . a woman . . . talking of the same condition. Her name was Marion but she could have called herself something else. She might have been masquerading under another identity. In order to survive, we often need to—'

Dr Hutchinson looked worried now. 'Please, go. I see you are getting agitated.'

'Of course I am agitated. You are the only man who can help me. I need to understand myself. I need to understand why I am like this.'

I grabbed his wrist. His hand shrank away, as though my madness could be contagious.

'We are a stone's throw from the police station. If you don't see yourself out, I will call for help and the police will come and take you away.'

There were tears in my eyes. Dr Hutchinson clouded into a ghost of himself. I knew I had to leave. I knew I had to give up hope, for a little while at least. So I stood up and nodded and left without a single word more, and kept myself, and my history, a secret for another thirty-one years.

London and St Albans, 1860–1891

After that first meeting with Dr Hutchinson I slipped into a state beyond my usual grief and restlessness and anxiety and despair – one of not feeling anything at all. And when I felt nothing I almost became nostalgic for the grief; at least when you felt pain you knew you were still alive. I had tried to fight this, forcing myself into life and noise. I had gone, on my own, to a few of the new music halls, always sitting near the front, right in the heart of the noise and laughter, and I laughed or sang along, trying to feel some of the joy that filled the room. But I was immune.

So one baking hot August day in 1880 I walked from Whitechapel to St Albans. London was too much for me. Too many memories. Too many ghosts. It was time to be someone else again. I suppose the way I understand my life is as a kind of Russian doll, with different versions inside other versions, each one enclosing the other, whereby the life before isn't seen from the outside but is still there.

For years I thought the key was to keep building new shells on top of the old ones. To keep moving, to keep changing, to keep transforming into something else in the eyes of society.

St Albans wasn't far from London but it was far enough. It was as new a place to me as any place in England could be, and I found work as a farrier. People now think of the early 1880s being an industrial time of smoke and factories but, as with every age, it was a carousel of many periods at once. The past stays and echoes even as modernity roars ahead. It was still the age of the horse and cart, and blacksmiths were thriving as much as they had ever been.

But in St Albans, things became worse. I would sometimes lose myself completely, and just stare into the orange heat of the forge, hardly aware of myself – or anything at all. On occasion my manager, Jeremiah Cartwright, would elbow me or slap me on my back and tell me 'to climb down from the clouds'.

Once, when I was on my own, I took a desperate action in the pursuit of feeling. I pulled up my sleeve, took a searing piece of iron, curved into a horse-shoe from the flames, and pushed it against the top of my left forearm. I held it there, as my skin hissed and cooked beneath it, and I clenched my jaw and eyes tight, and contained the scream.

I still have that scar, like a half-smile, and I get a strange comfort when I look at it. Though it is another thing I have to be careful about. Another thing I have to conceal. A distinguishing mark, interfering with my anonymity.

It worked, I suppose. I felt the pain. It had come in and screamed through me, with mind-pulsing intensity. I had to exist, I realised, because for pain to be felt there must be a living presence – a *me* – to feel it. And there was a reassurance in that knowledge, that proof of my own reality.

But I still sought proof that I wasn't mad.

Then, one day, a thought occurred to me. The thought was this: maybe I did have the proof. I, myself, was the evidence, and time was the proof.

And so it was that I decided to take that evidence, one final time, to Dr Hutchinson.

London, 1891

Dr Hutchinson didn't know it was me. I mean, he wouldn't have recognised the name from the list of appointments because the last time he had seen me I was Edward Cribbs and now I was back, for the first time since my youth, with my true name again. Well, true first name. I was Tom. Not the Huguenot Hazard or the dull Smith but the rather more symbolic Winters.

It was a warm day – the fourth of June – and I had ridden into town on a horse-dragged cart that belonged (both the cart and the horse) – to my sullen boss Jeremiah.

The London Cutaneous Institution for Treatment and Cure of Non-infectious Diseases of the Skin was now called the London Skin Clinic, but otherwise everything was still much as I remembered it. The fine furnishings, the three flights of stairs. Even Dr Hutchinson's office was much as before, though somewhat more cluttered. His desk now overflowed with papers and open books, and his leather chair had a rip in it. It was still essentially the same place, but it looked like it had been hit by a whirlwind.

Dr Hutchinson, like most humans, had aged far ahead of his environment. His once distinguished beard was now wispy and grey and sparse. The whites of his eyes were yellowing and his hands were twisted with arthritis and spotted from time. And that rich plum voice now came with raspy intakes of breath. He was, in short, an ordinary human and time was doing its work.

'So, Mr Winters. Now, I don't seem to have any notes for you.' He hadn't looked up since I had entered the room. He just stared down at the chaos of papers on his desk.

'When I arranged the appointment I didn't give any information.'

And it was then that he looked at me. At first he noticed my unclean clothes and blackened hands, and might have wondered what a rough-dressed man like myself was doing in his office.

'I settled the payment downstairs,' I said, clearing my throat. 'I am now wondering if you recognise me.'

He looked up. His eyes met mine.

'The last time I came to see you I did so under the name of Edward Cribbs. Do you remember that name? Do you remember? You advised me to go to the lunatic asylum.'

The rasping of his breath grew louder. He stood up out of his leather chair and came over to me. He stood ten inches from my nose. He rubbed those aged eyes.

A whisper. 'No.'

'You remember, don't you? You do. I can see. Thirty-one years ago.'

He was out of breath, as if the realisation was a hill he had climbed. 'No. No, no, no. It can't be. It is an illusion. You might be Maskelyne or Cooke.' (Maskelyne and Cooke were the illusionist double act of the day, who'd just been doing a host of London shows.)

'I assure you it is I, sir.'

'I must have taken leave of my senses.'

It was depressing that he found it so much easier to question his sanity than my reality.

'No, sir, I assure you that you haven't. The condition I told you about, my condition, the condition of holding back the tide of years, the condition that sounds like a blessing but which is also a curse – is real. I am real. My life is real. This is very real.'

'You are not a ghost?'

'No.'

'You are not a spectre of my mind?'

'No.'

His hand reached out to touch my face.

'What was the day of your birth?'

'I was born on the third of March in the year fifteen eighty-one.'

'Fifteen eighty-one.' He repeated it not as a question but as something so incredible it needed saying before it could be absorbed. 'Fifteen eighty-one. Fifteen eighty-one. You were eighty-five years old when the Great Fire of London—'

'I felt its heat. Its sparks singed my skin.'

He stared at me in a new way, as if he was a palaeontologist and I was a fresh dinosaur egg, ready to hatch. 'Well, well, well. This changes everything. *Everything.*

'Tell me, are you the only one? Have you ever known anyone else like you? With this . . . condition?'

'Yes!' I said. 'There was a man I met once, during Captain Cook's second voyage. A man from the Pacific Islands. His name was Omai. He became the rarest of things – a friend to me. And also . . . my daughter Marion. I have not seen her since she was a girl. Her mother told me that she had inherited my condition. That she stopped ageing normally around eleven years of age.'

Dr Hutchinson smiled. 'This is a gigantic thing to comprehend.'

And I smiled too, and felt the soul-anchoring joy of being understood.

And this joy stayed inside me right up until Dr Hutchinson's body was found floating in the Thames thirteen days later.

London, now

I still have a headache.

Sometimes it is almost not there, while at other times that is all there is, and the pain always coincides with memories. It is less a headache and more a memory ache. A life ache.

No matter what I do, it never goes completely. I have tried everything. I've taken ibuprofen, drunk litres of water, had lavender-scented baths, lain in the dark, rubbed my temples in slow circles, slow-breathed, listened to lute music and the sound of waves on a beach, meditated, did a stress-relief yoga video course where I repeated the mantra '*I am safe, it's okay to let go*' about a hundred times until I felt terrified of my own voice, watched brain-dead TV, stopped drinking caffeine, turned the brightness down on my laptop, but still the headache stays, as stubborn as a shadow.

The one thing I haven't properly tried is sleep. I have a trouble with sleep that has been growing over the decades.

Last night I couldn't sleep so I watched a documentary about turtles. They aren't the longest-living species but they are one of them, and some turtles 'live to over one hundred and eighty'. I put that in inverted commas because mayfly estimates such as these always turn out to be underestimates. Just look at how wrong they were about sharks. Or, well, humans. My bet is that there is at least one turtle out there approaching her five hundredth birthday.

Anyway, the thing that was depressing me was that humans weren't turtles. Turtles have been around for two hundred and twenty million years. Since the Triassic period. And they haven't really changed that much. Humans, in contrast, have been around only a short while.

And you don't have to be a genius to switch on the news and conclude: we probably don't have long. The other human sub-species – such as the Neanderthals, the Denisovans in Asia, the casually named 'hobbits' of Indonesia – had proven crap at the long game and so, most likely, would we.

It is all right for the mayflies. It is all right if you know you only have another thirty or forty years. You can afford to think small. You can find it easy to imagine that you are a fixed thing, inside a fixed nation, with a fixed flag, and a fixed outlook. You can imagine that these things *mean something*.

The longer you live, the more you realise that nothing is fixed. Everyone will become a refugee if they live long enough. Everyone would realise their nationality means little in the long run. Everyone would see their worldviews challenged and disproved. Everyone would realise that the thing that defines a human being is *being a human*.

Turtles don't have nations. Or flags. Or strategic nuclear weapons. They don't have terrorism or referendums or trade wars with China. They don't have Spotify playlists for their workouts. They don't have books on the decline and fall of turtle empires. They don't have internet shopping or self-service checkouts.

Other animals don't have *progress*, they say. But the human mind itself doesn't progress. We stay the same glorified chimpanzees, just with ever bigger weapons. We have the knowledge to realise we are just a mass of quanta and particles, like everything else is, and yet we keep trying to separate ourselves from the universe we live in, to give ourselves a meaning above that of a tree or a rock or a cat or a turtle.

So here I am, with my head full of human fears and pains, my chest tight with anxiety, thinking about how much future I have in front of me.

I am lucky these days if I manage three hours of sleep. In the old days I used to take Quieting Syrup – a kind of cough mixture recommended by Hendrich – but Quieting Syrup contained morphine, and so they stopped making it when they prohibited opiates a hundred years ago. So now I have to make do with Beecham's Night Nurse, which never really hits the spot.

I should have gone to the doctor, of course, but I didn't. It was a rule of the Albatross Society. No doctors. Not for anything. And it was easy, after my guilt over Dr Hutchinson, to follow this through. I have wondered if it was a tumour, though I have never heard of an alba having a tumour. And obviously if I have one it would be very slow-growing. One that would give me at least an average human lifespan ahead of me. But no, the symptoms aren't even close.

Anyway, the headache is there with only one day to go before the new job. I drink some water and eat some cereal and then I take Abraham for a walk. He had spent the night eating the arm of the sofa but I don't want to judge him. He has enough issues already.

I suppose I needed a dog with problems, in order to think less about my own. Akitas were made for the Japanese mountains, so I knew that he was a comrade of sorts, someone made for more noble surroundings, reduced to the grime and pollution and concrete streets of east London. No wonder he pissed on the carpet and ate the sofa. This wasn't the life he'd asked for.

So we walk along, myself and Abraham, with all the exhaust fumes in our faces.

'There used to be a well here,' I tell him, as we pass a betting shop. 'And here, right here, that's where all the men used to play skittles after church on a Sunday.'

A teenage boy passes us, in turned-up trousers and an oversized 'The Hundreds' T-shirt, looking like an oblivious distant echo of a seventeenth-century London boy of his age in rhinegrave breeches

47

and overskirt. The boy looks up from his phone and glances at me with quizzical and disapproving eyes. To him I am just another loose-screwed London loner, talking to myself. Maybe he is going to be one of the pupils I will be teaching on Monday.

We cross over the road. We pass a lamppost with an advert tied to it. THE CANDLELIGHT CLUB. *Relive the Roaring Twenties at London's top speakeasy-themed cocktail bar.* My headache intensifies, and I close my eyes and a memory rises like a cough – playing 'Sweet Georgia Brown' at Ciro's piano bar in Paris, with a stranger's hand resting softly on my shoulder.

I am in the park now. I hadn't played the piano for years, I realise. I am fine with that, most of the time. I have long convinced myself that the piano is like a drug, seductive and strong, and it can mess you up, it can awaken dead emotions, it can drown you in your lost selves. It is a nervous breakdown waiting to happen. I wonder if I will ever play again. I unclip the lead from Abraham's collar and he stays by my side and looks up at me, confused, as if perplexed by the concept of freedom.

I relate.

As I stare around the park I see a man with a Bichon Frise discreetly scoop up shit with a plastic bag. A squirrel darts in jerky zigzags up the trunk of a beech tree. The sun climbs out from behind a cloud. Abraham trots away.

It is then that I notice her.

A woman sitting on a bench, reading, a short distance away. I recognise her, which itself is rare. I hardly pay much attention to what people look like any more. Faces blur into other faces. But I know instantly this is the woman I saw out of the window of Daphne's office. The French teacher. As then, she seems wholly herself. It takes a lot to be unique in a species of so many. She has style. I don't mean in what she is wearing (corduroy blazer, jeans, glasses), though that is perfectly fine. I mean in the easeful way in which she places the book down beside her on the bench and stares around at the park. In the way she puffs out her cheeks a little and blows and closes her eyes and tilts her head up to invite the sun. I look away. I am a man in a park looking at a woman. I could be anyone. It isn't 1832 any more.

But then, as I look away from her, she calls over.

'Your dog is lovely.' She has a French accent. The new French. Yes. It is definitely the same woman I had seen. She holds out the back of her hand for Abraham to smell. Abraham licks his gratitude, and even wags his tail.

'You're honoured.'

And then she looks up at me in a rather unsettling way. A little too long. I am not arrogant enough to believe I am so attractive it is difficult for her to turn away. In reality, I haven't had *those* sort of looks from anyone for at least a hundred years. In the 1700s, when I looked in my twenties and wore my grief like a scar, I was often the subject of long, lingering gazes, but not these days. No. She is looking at me for another reason. And that troubles me. Maybe she had seen me too, at the school. Yeah. That was probably it.

'Abraham! Abraham! Here, boy! Here!'

The dog pants his way to me and I clip on his lead and I walk away, even as I feel her eyes on the back of my neck.

At home, I start looking at lesson plans for the year sevens, and the first topic to appear on the dim-lit screen is 'Witch Trials in Tudor England', which I already know is integral to the syllabus.

I realise there is a reason I am doing this. Why I want to become a history teacher. I need to tame the past. That is what history is, the teaching and telling of it. It is a way to control it and order it. To turn it into a pet. But history you have lived is different to history you read in a book or on a screen. And some things in the past can't be tamed.

My brain suddenly hurts.

I rise and walk kitchenward and find myself making a Bloody Mary. Basic. No stick of celery. I play some music, simply because music sometimes helps. I resist Tchaikovsky's Sixth, and Billie Holiday, and my sea shanty Spotify playlist, and go for 'The Boys of Summer' by Don Henley, which was written yesterday (actually, 1984). I have liked this song ever since I first heard it – in Germany in the eighties. I don't know why. It always makes me think of my childhood, even though it was made centuries after it. It reminds me of the poignant French chansons Maman used to sing, the ones she chose after we had moved to England. The sad, nostalgic ones. And I think, as the headache continues, how the pain in John Gifford's head all that time ago must have been a whole infinity worse. And I close my eyes and feel those early memories come rolling back, with the power to thin the air.

Suffolk, England, 1599

This is what I remember. My mother sat beside my bed, singing in French and playing her cherrywood lute, her fingers running fast across the strings as if escaping something.

Normally, music was her escape. I never saw my mother more calm than when she was gently singing an *air de cour*, but this evening something was troubling her.

She was a beautiful singer, and always closed her eyes when she sang, as if songs were dreams or memories, but today her eyes were open. She was staring at me with that vertical crease in her forehead. It was the crease that always appeared whenever she thought about Father, or the trouble in France. She stopped playing. She set down the lute. A gift from the Duke of Rochefort, when I was still a baby.

'You do not change.'

'Maman, please. Not again.'

'There is not a hair on your face. You are eighteen now. But you still look much as you did five years ago.'

'Maman, I cannot help the way I look.'

'It is as though time has stopped for you, Estienne.'

She still called me Estienne at home, even if I was always Thomas in public.

I tried to hide my own worry and reassure her. 'Time hasn't stopped. The sun still sets and rises. Summer still follows spring. I have been working as hard as anyone my age.'

Mother stroked my hair. She could see only the child I still seemed to be.

'I don't want more bad things to happen.'

One of my earliest memories came to me: of her howling with grief and burying her face in a tapestry hanging in the hall of our vast home in France, on the day we found out my father had been killed by cannon-fire on a battlefield near Reims.

'I will be fine.'

'Yes. I know the money from thatching is good, but maybe you should stop working for Mr Carter. Everyone can see you, up on the Giffords' roof, thatching. And they talk. Everyone is talking now. It's a village.'

The irony was that, during my first thirteen years of life, I aged quickly. Not unnaturally quickly but certainly quicker than average. This was why Mr Carter had recruited me. I had been young, so he could pay me cheap, but I had been tall and broad and strong-armed for a thirteen-year-old. The trouble was, that after such fast development to suddenly slow to what seemed like no change at all must have made it more noticeable.

'We should have gone to Canterbury,' I said. 'Or London.'

'You know what I am like in towns.' She paused, reconsidered, smoothed her petticoat. I looked at her. It seemed wrong that my mother, who had lived most of her life in one of the finest houses in France, was reduced to living in a two-room cottage in a village full of suspicious minds in this faraway corner of England. 'Maybe you are right. Maybe we should—'

There was a sound outside. A terrible wailing.

I quickly put on my trousers and shoes and went to the door.

'No, son, stay inside.'

'Someone is hurt,' I told her. 'I had better see.'

I ran out, and the day was at that last point before night, after sunset, where the sky is a fragile finch-egg blue. There was enough light to see people doing what I was doing, rushing out of their cottages further along the lane, all trying to see what the commotion was.

I kept running. And I saw it.

Him.

John Gifford.

He was a long way off but he was easy to recognise. He was as large as a haystack. He was walking along with his arms hanging by his sides, in a strange fashion, as if they were dead things attached to him. He vomited, twice, violently, leaving rancid puddles on the lane, and then staggered forward.

His wife Alice and the three children followed, like panicking cygnets, letting out wails of their own.

By the time he had made it to the green the whole of Edwardstone seemed to be there. We could see the blood now. It was pouring out of his ears, and, after a cough, it streamed out of his mouth and his nose too, flowing into his beard. He fell to the ground. His wife was there, next to him, placing a hand over his mouth, and another over his ear, desperately trying to plug the flow of the blood.

'Oh John, oh Lord save you, John. Oh Lord . . . John . . .'

Some of the crowd were praying. Others were shielding their children from the sight, pressing their faces into their clothes. Most, though, were staring in grim fascination.

'Lucifer's work,' said wide-eyed Walter Earnshaw, the knife-grinder. He was standing next to me. Stinking of hops and what we would now call halitosis.

John Gifford was still now, lying face up, except for a shaking in his arms, which became less and less. And then he died, right there on the green, on the black, blood-sodden grass.

While Alice collapsed on top of him, the sudden grief convulsing out of her, the villagers just stood there, by and large, in a numb kind of silence.

It felt wrong, being witness to such private pain, so I turned away.

But, as I walked past the familiar faces, I saw the baker's wife, Bess Small, staring right at me with accusing eyes.

'Yes, Thomas Hazard, mind you stay away now.'

At the time the words confused me. But, not long after, I would remember them as a warning.

I turned, once, and saw John Gifford, still as a mound, his large dead hands shining, then I kept walking, watched by the moon, which stared from the sky like another horrified face.

London, now

'Witches,' I say, in the voice of a teacher. That is, a voice that isn't really heard.

So, this is the life I have chosen above all others. The life of a man standing in a room of twelve-year-olds ignoring him.

'Why do you think people four hundred years ago wanted to believe in witches?'

I survey the room. The faces are smirking or embarrassed or checking their phones or all three. It is 9.35 a.m. We are only five minutes into the lesson. It is going badly. The lesson, the day, the job. It is all going badly.

Maybe being a teacher wasn't a new beginning for me. Maybe it was just the newest in a line of disappointments.

I had – right up until Sri Lanka – spent eight years in the north of Iceland, ten miles north of the fishing village of Kópasker. I had wanted Iceland because before that I had spent a few years in Toronto. Toronto is the greatest and happiest city on earth, but despite that – maybe because of that – it made me unhappy, as I just lived in an apartment there, never seeing anyone. Once I went to watch the Blue Jays play baseball, but being surrounded by so many people who I knew I could never connect with was the thing that had made me want to go to Iceland. And all that living alone in Iceland had done was make me want an ordinary life.

But an ordinary life is not a guarantee of happiness. And, of course, this – being a teacher – was just a *pretence*. Maybe everyone was pretending *something*. Maybe every teacher and pupil at this school was pretending *something*. Maybe Shakespeare was right.

Maybe all the world *was* a stage. Maybe without the act everything would fall apart. The key to happiness wasn't being yourself, because what did that even mean? Everyone had many selves. No. The key to happiness is finding the lie that suits you best.

And, right then, staring at those smirking twelve-year-olds, I think: this is the wrong lie.

'Why did people believe in witches?' I repeat. Daphne walks along the corridor outside. She gives me a smile and two thumbs up as she passes by at a busy pace. I smile back, acting as if this is great fun and I am doing it well, like a natural, like someone who had done this before, many times, and not like the oldest of dogs learning a new trick.

I repeat my question.

'What made people want to believe in witchcraft?'

At first it looks like a girl on the front row is putting up her hand to answer, but it is just a yawn.

So I answer my own question. I try my best not to remember what this topic makes me remember. I try to cement over the cracks in my voice.

'People believed in witches because it made things easier. People don't just need an enemy, they need an explanation. And it's often useful, in unsettled times, where ignorance is everywhere, for people to believe in witches . . . Who do you think believed in witches?'

'Stupid people,' someone says. It is a mumble, hard to locate.

I smile. There are fifty-five minutes left of the lesson.

'You'd think so. But no. It was all kinds of people. Queen Elizabeth the First passed a law against them. Then the one after her – King James – he considered himself an intellectual and he even *wrote a book* about them. The first technology to lead to fake news wasn't the internet, it was the printing press. Books solidified the superstition. Almost everybody believed in witches. And there were witchfinders who travelled around the country, finding . . .'

There is a sudden sharp pain, an intensifying of the headache, radiating from my inner brain, causing me to hesitate, dangerously, mid-sentence.

The yawning girl on the front row now looks concerned. 'Are you all right, sir?'

'Yes, I've just got a bit of a headache. I'll be fine.'

Then someone else. Another girl, near the back: 'So how did they find out if someone was a witch or not? What did they do?'

And the question flaps around my head like a crow in a dark room.

What did they do?
What did they do?
What did they do?

Suffolk, England, 1599

My mother was, in the tradition of parents, quite a complicated and contradictory human being. Moralistic but a devout lover of pleasure (food, music, the aesthetics of nature). Deeply religious but seemingly as comforted by singing a secular *chanson* as by prayer. A lover of the natural world who was visibly anxious every time she left the castle. Fragile, but also tough and stubborn. I never knew how many of her oddities had sprung from grief and how many from her own inherent nature. 'There is not one blade of grass, there is no colour in this world that is not intended to make us rejoice,' my mother told me once, shortly after arriving in England. 'That is what Monsieur Cauvin says.'

I didn't like Monsieur Cauvin. Or Calvin, I should say. Because he seemed to be the source of all our problems. Well, he had been. But I had taken the baton. And our problems were getting worse now, quite quickly, and I knew – when they came and knocked on the door – that there was nowhere for us. Nowhere in the world where we could be safe.

The witchfinder, the 'pricker' as his job was known, was called William Manning. He was a tall solid square-faced man, from London. Thinning hair but broad-shouldered and strong, with thick butcher's hands. He was half blind, or appeared to be, on account of the cataract over his left eye. We never saw him arrive in the village, though I do remember waking to hear two galloping horses heading east past our house.

The rider of the other horse was the Justice of the Peace. I never knew him as anything other than Mr Noah. He was dressed in fine clothes and fancied himself a gentleman. He was also tall, but grey-skinned. Death-like. Cadaverous (a word I wasn't to pick up for another two hundred years or so).

We were county-level news now, though we had no accurate idea of our importance until the hard quick knock on the door.

William Manning grabbed my wrist. He had a tough grip. He pointed with his free hand to a small pink blotch on my skin, but was careful not to touch it.

'The devil's spot!' Manning said, with grim triumph. 'Mark there, Mr Noah.'

Mr Noah looked. 'I see it. Most sinister.'

I laughed. I was scared. 'No,' I told them. 'It's a flea bite.'

I still looked thirteen. They expected the obedience of a boy, not the insolence of a young man. Manning glowered at me. There was no other verb, then or now. But then his attention turned to my mother.

'Undress yourself,' he said, his voice quiet and stern. I hated him. Right then. I had never really known hate before. Only in the abstract, for the men who killed my father. But I had never known what they looked like. Hate needs a face.

'No,' I said.

My mother was confused. Then, when she understood, she said no and insulted them in French. Manning was an ignorant man, masquerading as a man of learning, and had no idea of the language she was speaking.

'Mark her. She speaks like a devil. She is invoking foul spirits.'

It was at this point that he asked for the door to be closed, as an assortment of villagers – including Bess Small herself, her face full of gleeful disapproval, standing next to poor Alice Gifford – were now there on our doorstep, excited by the unfolding drama. Mr Noah closed the door. I stood between Manning and my mother. Manning pulled out a dagger and held it at my throat.

Mother undressed. She cried. I felt my eyes warm up too. Fear and guilt. This was all my fault. The fault of my physical strangeness, of my body's inability to age.

'If you say another word, your witchmother will be killed right where she is, before you or Marbas can see it different.'

Marbas. The infernal spirit who could cure all diseases. I was going to hear the name a lot over the coming hours, as that nightmare day unravelled itself.

My mother was naked. There by the table and the tin pottage bowls. And I saw Manning's eyes feast on her, hating her for his own temptation. He stuck the tip of his dagger against her skin and pricked her, first on her shoulder, then her forearm, then near her navel. Little bulbs of blood.

'Look at the darkness of the blood, Mr Noah.'

Mr Noah looked.

The blood was blood colour. Because it was ordinary human blood. But Mr Noah saw something else in it, or imagined he did, as he was impressed by Manning's air of authority. 'Yes. It is most dark.'

People only see what they have decided to see. I have learned this lesson one hundred times over, but it was still new to me then. My mother winced every time that dagger touched her, but to Manning she was faking it.

'See her cunning? Mark the counterfeit of pain on her face. She has made some kind of trade, it would appear. The most unusual death of John Gifford appears to be the price of her son's eternal youth. Quite a malevolent trade.'

'We have nothing to do with John Gifford's death. I helped thatch his roof. That is all. My mother never even knew him. She stays in the cottage most of the time. Please, stop doing that!'

I couldn't watch any more. I grabbed Manning's arm. He hit the dagger handle against my head, then his other hand grabbed my throat and he repeatedly struck the handle in the same spot as my mother wailed and I thought my skull might smash open.

60

I was on the floor. Dazed and silent and wishing my body was as strong as an eighteen-year-old's body should have been.

And then he, Manning, spotted another flea bite, this time on my mother, near her belly button, like a little red moon above a planet.

'The same mark as on the boy.'

My mother trembled. Robbed of her clothes she could no longer speak.

'It's a flea!' I said, my voice pained and desperate and cracked. 'An ordinary flea bite.'

And I pressed my hands into the stone of the floor, to stand back up. But there came another stamp against the back of the skull.

And after that, everything went dark.

I sometimes repeat this in a dream. If I fall asleep on the sofa I remember that day. I remember the bulbs of blood on my mother's skin. I remember the people at the doorway. And I remember Manning and his foot, stamping down, jolting me awake through the distance of centuries.

You see, everything changed after that. I am not saying my childhood had been perfect before this point but now I often want to climb back into that time *before*. Before I knew Rose, before I knew what would happen to my mother, before, before, before . . . To cling to who I was, right at the beginning when I was just a small boy with a long name who responded to time and grew older like everybody else. But there is never a way into the before. All you can do with the past is carry it around, feeling its weight slowly increase, praying it never crushes you completely.

London, now

At lunch break I nip to the supermarket down the street and buy myself a pastrami sandwich, some salt and vinegar crisps and a small bottle of cherry juice.

There is a queue for the checkout assistant so I do what I normally resist and use the self-service checkout.

Like the rest of the day so far, it does not go well.

The disembodied female voice keeps telling me of an 'unidentified item in bagging area', even though the only items in the bagging area are the items I had just scanned.

'Please ask a member of staff to assist you,' she – the robot future of civilisation – adds. 'Unidentified item in bagging area. Please ask a member of staff to assist you. Unidentified item in bagging . . .'

I look around.

'Hello? Excuse me?'

There are no members of staff. Of course there aren't. There is, however, a group of teenage boys all wearing variations of the Oakfield uniform (white shirts, and a few green and yellow ties) all in the queue, holding drink cans and packets of food and looking in my direction. They say something, identifying me as a new teacher. And then there is some laughter. I feel the most familiar feeling of all: that I am living in the wrong time. And I stand there, just staring at the screen and listening to the voice, my head aching, and my soul slowly wondering if Hendrich was right. Maybe I shouldn't have come back to London.

As I walk along the corridor to the staff room I pass the woman with glasses. The one who I had seen in the park, reading. The French teacher Daphne had told me about. The one who had stared at me in that disconcerting way. She is wearing red cotton trousers and a black polo-neck and shiny patent flat shoes. Her hair is pulled back. A confident, civilised look. She smiles.

'It's you. From the park.'

'Oh yes,' I say, as if I was only just remembering at that moment. 'That was you. I'm the new history teacher.'

'How funny.'

'Yes.'

Her smile is also a frown, as though I confuse her. I have lived long enough to know this look. And fear it.

'Hello,' I say.

'Hello there,' she says, with a slight French accent. I think of the forest. My mother singing. I close my eyes and see a sycamore seed spiralling beneath a hard blue sky.

I feel a familiar sense of claustrophobia. Confinement. As if this world is never big enough to hide in.

And that is it.

I have to keep walking, as if I can also walk away from what she might be thinking.

After my first day teaching, I sit at home next to Abraham with his head on my lap. He is asleep, lost in dog dreams. He flinches and twitches, like a stuttering image, stuck between two moments. He whimpers a little. I wonder what memories he is reliving. I put my hand on him, stroking to soothe him. Slowly, the movement stops. He makes no sound but that of his breath.

'It's all right,' I whisper. 'It's all right, it's all right, it's all right . . .'

I close my eyes and I see the towering form of William Manning as clear as if he is in the room.

Suffolk, England, 1599

William Manning stared at the darkening sky, his expression severe. There was something theatrical about him, as if this was just a show. This was very much the nature of the times – this era of Marlowe and Jonson and Shakespeare – everything was theatre. Even justice. Even death. Especially that. We were nearly ten miles from Edwardstone but the whole village was there. You might imagine that in the sixteenth century witch trials were a regular occurrence. They were not, not really. They were a rare entertainment, and people came from miles around to watch and jeer and feel safe in a world where evil could be explained and found and killed.

Manning spoke to me, but also the crowd. He was an actor. He could have been one of the Lord Chamberlain's Men.

'Your fate will be decided by your mother. If she drowns, her innocence shall be shown, and you shall live. If she lives, and survives the stool, then you – as the progeny of a witch – will be sent to the gallows alongside your mother and dealt with there. Do you understand?'

I stood by my mother, on the grassy bank of the River Lark, with my legs and wrists in irons, just as hers were. She – dressed again – was shaking and shivering like a wet cat despite the warm day. I wanted to talk to her, to comfort her, but knew any communication between us would be seen as a plot or a plan to conjure malevolent forces.

Only when they pulled her closer to the riverbank, closer to the stool, did words burst out of my mouth.

'I'm sorry, Mother.'

'It's not your fault, Estienne. It's not your fault. I am sorry. It is mine. We should never have come here. We should never have come to this place.'

'Mother, I love you.'

'I love you too, Estienne,' she said, a sudden defiance bursting fast out of her, even as she cried. 'I love you too. You must be strong. You are strong, as your father was. I want you to promise: you must stay alive. Whatever happens. *You must stay alive.* Do you understand me? You are special. God made you this way for a purpose. You must find your purpose. Do you promise to live?'

'I promise, Mother. I promise, I promise, I promise . . .'

I watched as they fastened her into the wooden chair. She pressed her legs together, not wanting to part her knees, as a last futile defence. So two men took a leg each and pulled her into position, pressing her back against the seat. She wriggled and screamed as the metal strap was fixed across the seat.

I didn't watch as they raised her in the air. But when she reached the highest point Manning told the wild-haired man holding the rope to halt.

'Wait, wait there . . .'

And it was then I looked and saw my mother against that hard blue sky. Her head dropped and she looked down at me, and I can still see those terrified eyes all these centuries later.

'Start the ordeal,' said Manning, who had walked to the edge of the riverbank.

'No!'

I closed my eyes and heard the noise of the chair touching the water. And then I reopened my eyes. I watched her disappear, become a blur of green and brown, and then nothing at all. A rush of air bubbles rose to the river's surface. William Manning held his hand up and open, the whole time, telling the man who held that horribly slack rope to keep her under.

I looked at that large meaty red hand, a brute's hand, praying for the fingers to close. Of course, whatever happened, she would die. And yet still – even as my own life hung in the balance – I wanted her to emerge from the water alive. I wanted her to speak again. I couldn't imagine a world without her voice.

When they hoisted the chair and her dripping dead body out of the water there was an answer left as a secret in the river. Had she pushed the air out of her in panic or deliberately? Had she sacrificed her life for mine? I didn't know. I wouldn't ever know.

But she had died, because of me. And I stayed alive, because of her. And for years I regretted the promise I had made.

PART TWO

The Man Who Was America

London, now

Here I am.

I am in the car park. I have finished my second day at Oakfield School and am now in the process of unlocking my bicycle, which is attached to a metal fence next to the staff car park. I ride a bike because I have never trusted cars. I've ridden a bike now for a hundred years and I think they are one of the truly great human inventions.

Sometimes change is for the better, and sometimes change isn't for the better. Modern toilets with a flush are definitely a change for the better. Self-service checkouts are definitely not. Sometimes things are a change for the better and the worse at the same time, like the internet. Or the electric keyboard. Or pre-chopped garlic. Or the theory of relativity.

And a life is like that. There's no need to fear change, or necessarily welcome it, not when you don't have anything to lose. Change is just what life is. It is the only constant I know.

I see Camille head to her car. The woman who I had seen in the park. And the corridor, yesterday, where we hadn't said much. But I had felt claustrophobic and needed to walk away.

But now, there is no escape. She reaches her car. Puts the key in her lock as I struggle with mine. Our eyes meet.

'Hi there.'

'Oh, hi.'

'The history guy.'

The history guy.

'Yes,' I said. 'Just having a bit of trouble with the key.'

71

'You can have a lift if you want.'

'No,' I say, a bit too quickly. 'I'm . . . it's . . .'

(It doesn't matter how long you live. Small talk remains equally complex.)

'Nice to meet you again. I'm Camille. Camille Guerin. I'm French. I mean, that's my subject. Was also my nationality, too, though who lets nationality define them? Apart from idiots.'

I don't know why, but I say, recklessly, 'I was born in France.' This goes against my CV, and Daphne is mere metres away. *What am I doing? Why do I want her to know this?*

Another teacher – someone I hadn't been introduced to yet – walks out and Camille says 'See you tomorrow' to them and they return it.

'So,' she asks me, 'do you speak French?'

'Oui. But my French is a bit outdated . . . un peu vieillot.'

She tilts her head, frowns. I know this look. It is recognition. 'C'est drôle. J'ai l'impression de vous reconnaître. Where have I seen you? I mean, the park, but before then, I feel sure of it now.'

'It's probably a doppelgänger. I have the sort of face people confuse easily with other faces.'

I smile, still polite, but distant. This conversation can't really go anywhere but trouble. It isn't making my head feel any better either.

'I'm short-sighted. Hence the glasses. But I did a test once,' she says, now adamant. 'I came out as a "super-recogniser". It's a gift I have. The way my temporal lobe is wired. I was in the top one per cent, in terms of visual recognition. Strange brain.'

I want her to stop talking. I want to be invisible. I want to be a normal person with nothing to hide. I look away. 'That's wonderful.'

'When were you last in France?'

'A long time ago,' I say, doubting she is old enough to remember me from the 1920s. My bike is free now. 'See you tomorrow.'

'I will solve it,' she says, laughing, as she gets into her little Nissan. 'I will solve you.'

'Ha!' I say. Then, when her car door closes, I say, 'Shit.'

She beeps me as she passes, giving a fast wave. I wave back and I bike away and I think how easy it would be to just not turn up tomorrow. To talk to Hendrich and disappear again. But there is a part of me – a small but dangerous part – that is keen to know where she knew me from. Or, maybe, a small part that simply wants to be solved.

Later, at home, Hendrich calls.

'So, how is London?' he asks.

I am sitting at the little IKEA desk, staring at the Elizabethan penny I have been carrying around for centuries. I normally just keep it in the wallet, in its little sealed polythene bag, but now I have it out on the desk. I stare at the fading coat of arms, and remember Marion's fist tight around it. 'It's fine.'

'And the job? Are you . . . settling in?'

There is something about his tone that's annoying. Patronising. The way he said 'settling in' in a vaguely amused way. 'Listen, Hendrich, forgive me, but I have a headache. I know it's only brunch-time with you, but it's getting late here and I have to be up early preparing lessons tomorrow. I really would like to go to bed now if that's—'

'You're still getting the headaches?'

'Sometimes.'

'They're par for the course. We all get them towards our middle years. It's memory pain. You just need to be careful. Modern life doesn't help. Cut down on your screen time. Our eyes weren't made for artificial light. No one's eyes were made for that. It's all the blue wavelengths. Disturbs our circadian rhythms.'

'Right. Yes. Exactly. Our circadian rhythms. Anyway, I better go.'

Barely a second later: 'It could be seen as ungrateful, you know?'

'What could?'

'Your recent attitude.'

I place the coin back in the bag and seal it. 'It's not an attitude. There's no attitude.'

'I've been thinking a lot lately.'

'About what?'

'The beginning.'

'The beginning of what?'

'Of us. When I heard about the doctor. When I telegrammed Agnes. When she came to collect you. When I first met you. Eighteen ninety-one. Tchaikovsky. Harlem. Hot dogs. Champagne. Ragtime. All of that. I made every day your birthday. I *still* make every day your birthday. Or could do, if you weren't so obsessed with living the most mundane kind of life on offer. If you could get over your obsession with finding Marion.'

'She's my daughter.'

'And it's understandable. But look at what you've had. Look at the lives I have given you . . .'

I am in the kitchen now. I have the phone on speaker and am getting a glass of water. I drink the water down, taking big, continuous gulps, thinking of my mother, under the water, exhaling her last breath. Then, as Hendrich keeps talking I go and open up my laptop.

'I've basically been your fairy godmother, haven't I? You were Cinderella, shoeing horses or whatever you were doing, and now look at you. You can have the coach, the glass slippers, whatever you want.'

I log on to Facebook. I have set up a page for myself. It draws more suspicion *not* having a Facebook page than having one, so Hendrich was okay with the idea (even he, or the retired plastic surgeon he was currently playing, has one).

Obviously, the profile information is fiction. There isn't even an option to put 1581 as your year of birth, anyway.

'Are you listening to me?'

'Yes, Hendrich, I'm listening. I'm listening. You are my fairy godmother.'

'I'm just worried about you. Really worried, Tom. I've been thinking, ever since you came out here, there was something in your eyes. Something that worried me. A kind of yearning.'

I laugh a tired laugh. 'A yearning?'

And then I notice something.

I have a friend request on Facebook. It is her. Camille Guerin. I accept the request. Then – as Hendrich keeps talking – I find myself looking at her wall.

She updates in a mixture of French and English and emoji. She quotes Maya Angelou and Françoise Sagan and Michelle Obama and JFK and Michel Foucault. She has a friend in France who is raising money for Alzheimer's and she links to his donation page. She has written a few little poems. I read one called 'Skyscrapers' and another called 'Forest'. I like them. Then, hardly thinking, I click through her photos. I want to find out more about her, and how she might have known me. Maybe she was an alba. Maybe I had met her a *long* time ago. But no. A quick look through her pictures shows that in 2008, when she joined Facebook, she looked, well, a decade younger. She had looked in her twenties. She was also with a man. Erik Vincent. A frustratingly good-looking man. In one photo he is swimming in a river. In another he is wearing a running vest with a number on it. He is tagged in the pictures. In almost every profile pic up till 2011, and then there is nothing at all until 2014. I wonder what happened to Erik. I look back at the poem 'Forest' and realise it is dedicated to him. His profile page is no longer there.

I feel like I am not the only mystery to solve.

'You can't lay down an anchor, Tom. You remember the first rule, don't you, Tom? You remember what I told you, in the Dakota, you remember the first rule?'

In one photo, from 2015, Camille is just staring, sadly, out at the camera. She is out on a pavement café in Paris somewhere, a glass of red wine in front of her. This is the first photo of her in

75

glasses. She is wearing a bright red cardigan, which she is tucking in close around her. A colder evening than she imagined. Her mouth is a smile, but a forced one.

'The first rule,' I say wearily, 'is that you don't fall in love.'

'That's right, Tom. You don't. It would be a very foolish thing to do.'

'I don't mean to be rude but why are you calling? You know it helps, to get into the role.'

'Of a mayfly?'

'Yeah.'

He sighs. Makes a little throat-clearing growl sound. 'I once knew a tightrope walker. A mayfly. He was called Cedar. Like the tree. Strange name. Strange man. Used to work at the funfair on Coney Island. He was very good at tightrope walking. Do you know the way you can tell if a tightrope walker is any good?'

'How?'

'They're still alive.'

He laughs at his own joke before continuing. 'Anyway, he told me the secret to managing the tightrope. He said people were wrong when they said the secret was to relax and to forget about the drop below you. The secret was the opposite. The secret was *never to relax*. The secret was *never to believe you are good*. Never to forget about the *drop*. Do you understand what I am saying? You can't be a mayfly, Tom. You can't just relax. The drop is too big.'

I take the phone into the bathroom and piss quietly against the inside of the toilet bowl, avoiding the water. 'The drop. Right. I still don't understand why you are calling me, Hendrich.'

I look in the mirror and I notice something. Something wonderful and exciting, just above my left ear. A grey hair! This is my second. The first one I got in 1979. By 2100 I might have so many they could be noticeable. It gives me a thrill like no other when I notice such a change (hardly ever). I save the flush till later and leave the room, feeling happily mortal.

'I call you when I want to call you. And you answer. Or I will get worried. And you know that you don't want me to get anxious, because then I will have to do something. So, just remember your place. Remember how much the society has helped you. Okay, we'd have liked to have found your daughter. But remember everything else. Remember that before eighteen ninety-one you were lost. You had no freedom. You had no choice. You were just a confused grief-stricken man, who had no idea who he was. I gave you a map. I helped you find yourself.'

I still haven't found myself, I don't say. *I'm nowhere near.*

'Remember eighteen ninety-one, Tom. Keep it in mind.'

And when the phone call ends, I do what he instructs. As I click off Camille's photo I think back to 1891, I think of that moment when my life stopped being one thing and started being another, and I try to understand it. I try to work out if I sailed into a trap or into freedom, or if, maybe, it could have been both at once.

Skyscrapers

I
Like
The way
That when you
Tilt
Poems
On their side
They
Look like
Miniature
Cities
From
A long way
Away.
Skyscrapers
Made out
Of
Words.

Forest

I want you to
Slow down
I just want it all
To slow down;
I want to make a forest
Of a moment
And live in that forest
For ever
Before you go.

St Albans, England, 1891

Jeremiah Cartwright had read the sky and declared, with a dark seriousness, that it was going to rain later and that he must go for iron while it was still dry. He wouldn't be back for another hour. I was alone, by the forge, watching the metal as it glowed red, then orange. Yes, as in life, strike while the iron is hot, but not just any heat. You had to wait until the orange was starting to brighten, become that raw bright pink-yellow-orange. This was *forging heat.* The heat of change. The yellow quickly became white and as soon as it was white hot it was all over, so you had to watch and grab the moment before it was too late.

It was only when I took the metal and placed it over the anvil to begin to strike it that I realised someone was standing there.

A woman. A peculiar-looking woman.

I can still picture her, vividly, the way I first saw her. She looked about forty years old.

She was dressed in a long skirt and blouse, both black, and her face was shaded by a broad-brimmed hat. An outfit far too hot for the late June day, let alone for the hellish temperature of the forge. It took me a second, because of the shading over her face, to realise that she was wearing a jet-black silk eye patch over her left eye.

'Hello there. How can I help you?'

'You will find it is the other way around.'

'What do you mean?'

She shook her head. She was wincing a little from the heat of the place. 'No questions. Not just yet. Your curiosity shall be satisfied, I assure you. You must come with me.'

'What?'

'You can't stay here.'

'What?'

'I said: no questions.'

The next thing I knew she was pointing a small wooden pistol straight at my chest.

'Blazing fuck. What are you doing?'

'You have outed yourself to the scientific community. There is an institute . . . I haven't got time to explain this. But, if you stay here, you will be killed.'

The heat of the forge often made being in there a kind of delirium, a fever dream. For a moment, I thought this was a waking dream.

'Dr Hutchinson is dead,' she said. Her voice was composed, but there was a quiet force to it, as if not just stating a fact but an inevitable one.

'Dr Hutchinson?'

'Murdered.'

She let the word stay in the air, with nothing but the sound of the roaring fire for company.

'Murdered? Who by?'

She handed me a news item that had been cut out of *The Times*. *Doctor's Body Found in Thames*.

I skimmed the piece.

'You made a mistake. You should never have gone to see him about your condition. He had written a paper on you. On the condition. He had given it a name. Anageria. The paper would have, very possibly, been published. And that wouldn't do. Not at all. So, I am afraid the society had no other recourse. He had to die.'

'You killed him?'

Her face now shone from the heat. 'Yes, I killed him, to save lives. Now, come with me. There is a coach waiting outside. It is ready to take us to Plymouth.'

'Plymouth?'

'Don't worry, it is not to reminisce.'

'I don't understand. Who *are* you?'

'My name is Agnes.'

She opened up her handbag and pulled out an envelope. She handed it to me. I put down the mallet and took it. It had no name, no address, but its blue paper bulged with contents.

'What is this?'

'It's your ticket. And your identity papers.'

I was thrown. 'What?'

'You have lived long. You have a good survival instinct. But you have to leave now. You must come with me. There is a coach waiting. From Plymouth we head to America. You will find every answer you have ever wanted.'

And she walked out without another word.

Atlantic Ocean, 1891

Boats had changed.

I had been to sea before, but being at sea no longer felt like being at sea.

The progress of humanity seemed to be measured in the distance we placed between ourselves and nature. We could now be in the middle of the Atlantic, on a steam ship such as the *Etruria*, and feel as if we were sitting in a restaurant in Mayfair.

We were in first class. First class in those days really was first class, and you had to keep up appearances.

The woman, Agnes, had provided me with a suitcase full of new clothes and I was wearing an elegant cotton twill three-piece with a silk ascot tie. I was clean shaven. She had shaved me, with a razor blade, and as she did so I seriously contemplated the possibility that she was going to cut my throat.

From the restaurant window, we could see the lower decks, where crowds of people in second class and steerage were walking around in shabbier attire, the clothes I had been wearing last week, or were leaning against the rail and looking out to the horizon, with nothing but Ellis Island and American dreams awaiting them.

Of everyone I have ever met, I would say Agnes was the most difficult to put into words. She was an extremely rare concoction of forthright character, amoral habits and restrained manners. Oh, and she had the capacity for murder.

She was still in mourning black, Queen Victoria-style, and looked every part the upper-class lady. Even the eye patch seemed to have an elegance about it. Though her choice of drink – whisky – seemed a little eccentric.

Her name – her present name – was Gillian Shields. But she had been born Agnes Wade.

'Think of me as Agnes. I am Agnes Wade. Never use that name again but think of it always. Agnes Wade.'

'And think of me as Tom Hazard.'

She was born in York in 1407. She was older than me by more than a century. This managed both to trouble and to comfort me. I hadn't yet got to hear about all of her various identities over the years, but she revealed that in the mid-eighteenth century she had been Flora Burn, the famous pirate who had operated off the coast of America.

She had just ordered the chicken fricassee and I had ordered the broiled bluefish.

'Is there a woman in your life?'

I hesitated before answering, and she felt the abrupt need to qualify her question. 'Don't worry. I have no interest in you in that regard. You are too serious. I enjoy serious women, but prefer – when I partake – for a man to be as light as day. It was curiosity. There must have been someone. You can't live as long as you have lived without there being someone.'

'There was one. Yes. A long time ago.'

'Did she have a name?'

'She did. Yes. She had a name.' That was as much as I was going to give her.

'And no one since?'

'Not really. No. No. No one since.'

'And why was that?'

'It just was.'

'You've been nursing a broken heart?'

'Love is pain. It's easier not to.'

She nodded in agreement, and swallowed, as if my words had

a taste, and she looked away into the distance. 'Yes. Yes, it is. Love is pain.'

'So,' I said, 'you were going to tell me, why did you kill Dr Hutchinson?'

She looked around at the other diners, who were sitting stiff and upright in that overdressed upper-class way. 'Would you kindly not air accusations of murder in the dining room? You need to learn the art of discretion. Of speaking about a thing without actually speaking of it. Truth is a straight line you sometimes need to curve, you should know that by now. It is a true wonder you are alive.'

'I know but—'

Agnes closed her eyes. 'You need to grow up, do you understand? You are still a child. You may look like a man now, but you are still a wide-eyed boy and you need to become, quite urgently, a grown-up. We need to civilise you.'

Her attitude of indifference appalled me. 'He was a good man.'

'He was a man. That was all you really knew, wasn't it? He was a man. A doctor, seeking glory out of misery, whose best work was behind him. A man who had happily cast you aside and dismissed you previously. He was sixty-eight years old. He was frail. He was a skeleton in tweed. At best he had only a few years to live. Now, if he had stayed alive to publicise his findings, to make his name as the man who discovered anageria, then it would have led to far more harm. And deaths of people who not only have years to live, but centuries. It is called the greater good, surely you understand that? Lives are lost in order to save more lives. That is what the society is fighting.'

'The society, the society, the society . . . You keep talking about this society, but you haven't told me anything. I don't even know what it is called.'

'The Albatross Society.'

85

'Albatross?'

Our food arrived.

'Is there anything else I could do for you?' the smartly dressed, slick-haired waiter asked.

'Yes.' Agnes smiled. 'You could disappear.'

The waiter looked taken aback, and smoothed his moustache for comfort. 'Very well.'

I stared down at my exquisitely prepared fish and my stomach hungrily rumbled with the knowledge that I hadn't eaten like this in over a century.

'It is thought that albatrosses live a long time. And we live a long time. Hendrich Pietersen founded the society in eighteen sixty-seven as a means of uniting and protecting us – people like us – the "albatrosses" or "albas" – from outside threats.'

'And who is this Hendrich Pietersen?'

'A very old and very wise man. Born in Flanders but has been in America since it was America. He made money during the tulip mania and came to New York when it was still New Amsterdam. Traded furs. Built up his wealth. Amassed, ultimately, a fortune. He got into property. All kinds of things. He *is* America, that is who Hendrich is. He set up the society to save us. We are blessed, Tom.'

I laughed.

'Blessed. Blessed. It is a curse.'

She sipped her red wine.

'Hendrich will want to know that you appreciate the nature of the gift you have been given.'

'I will find that hard to do.'

'If you want to stay alive, you will do it.'

'I don't know if I actually care too much about staying alive, Agnes.'

'Not Agnes,' she whispered sharply. She looked around the room. 'Gillian.'

She took something out of her bag. Some Quieting Syrup cough mixture. She poured it into her whisky. She offered to do the same to mine. I shook my head.

'Do you understand how selfish you sound? Look at everyone else. Look around this dining room. Even better, think of all those émigrés in steerage. Most of them will be dead before they are sixty. Think of all those terrible illnesses we have known people to die from. Smallpox, cholera, typhoid, even plague – I know you are old enough to remember.'

'I remember.'

'That will not happen to us. People like us die in one of only two ways. We either die in our sleep aged around nine hundred and fifty, or we die in an act of violence that destroys our heart or brain or causes a profound loss of blood. That is it. We have immunity from so much human pain.'

I thought of Rose trembling with fever and delirious with pain as she was on that last day. I thought of the days and weeks and years and decades afterwards. 'There have been times in my life when shooting myself in the head seemed profoundly preferable to the blessing of existence.'

Agnes gently swirled the cocktail of whisky and Quieting Syrup in her glass. 'You have lived a long time. You must know by now that it is not just ourselves we endanger when our truth begins to surface.'

'Indeed. Dr Hutchinson, for instance.'

'I am not talking about Dr Hutchinson.' She swiped back faster than a cat. 'I am talking about other people. Your parents. What happened to them?'

I took my time, chewing on the fish, then swallowing, then dabbing the side of my mouth with a napkin. 'My father was killed in France due to his religion.'

'Ah. The Wars of Religion? He was a Protestant? A Huguenot?'

I nodded three times.

'And your mother?' Agnes's eye stared at me. She sensed that she had me. And she did, I suppose. I told her the truth.

'You see? Ignorance is our enemy.'

'No one is killed for witchcraft now.'

'Ignorance changes over time. But it is always there, and it remains just as lethal. Yes, Dr Hutchinson died. But if he had lived, if his paper was published, people would have come for you instead. And others.'

'People? What people?'

'Hendrich will explain. Don't worry, Tom. Your life is not in vain. You have a purpose.'

And I remembered how my mother had told me I needed one – a purpose – and as I ate the tender fish I wondered if I was on the cusp of finding it.

New York, 1891

'Look at her,' said Agnes, as we stood outside on the upper deck of the *Etruria*. '*Liberty Enlightening the World.*'

It was my first sighting of the Statue of Liberty. Her right arm raising that torch high into the air. She was a copper colour back then, and shone, and looked most impressive. She glowed in the sun, as we got closer to the harbour. She seemed vast – epic and ancient – something on the scale of sphinxes and pyramids. I had only been alive since the world had become smaller, more modest again. But I looked at the New York skyline and felt like the world was dreaming bigger. Clearing its throat. Getting some confidence. I put my hand in my pocket, held Marion's penny between my fingers. It was, as ever, a comfort.

'I've been up close,' said Agnes. 'It looks like she is standing still but actually she is walking. She is breaking out of the chains of the past. Of slavery. Of civil war. And she is heading towards liberty. But she is caught for ever in that moment of stopped time. Look, can you see? Stop looking at the torch and look at her feet. She's moving, but not moving. Heading towards a better future, but not quite there yet. Like you, Tom. You'll see. Your new life awaits.'

I stared up at the Dakota, a magnificent, ornate, seven-storey butter-cream stone building with elegant balustrades and a steep gable roof. I had a feeling of dizziness caused by that rare sense that things were moving fast, not just in my life but in the world. I had been in New York for a few hours now, and the feeling had not waned. There was something about New York in the 1890s.

Something exciting. Something so real you felt you could breathe it in. Something that made me feel again.

I paused for a moment on the threshold.

What would have happened if I had run away right then? If I had pushed Agnes away and disappeared into the park or sprinted fast along 72nd Street and somehow got away? But I was dizzy with it, I suppose, with all the novelty of the city. It was already making me feel more alive, after all those dead years of nothingness.

A statue of an American Indian – Agnes called him 'the watching Indian' – gazed solemnly down at us. In 1980, while on a job in São Paulo, I would watch the news of John Lennon's assassination on a small colour television screen. The footage was of that same building, where Lennon was shot. I wondered if the building itself had a curse, affecting all who passed through its doors.

Standing outside, I was nervous. But at least it was a feeling. I wasn't used to them recently.

'He will be testing you, even when he isn't testing you. It is all a test.' We climbed the stairs. 'He can read people – faces, movements – better than anyone I have met. Hendrich has developed, over the years, a seemingly unnatural *aptitude*.'

'An aptitude for what?'

Agnes shrugged. 'He just calls it aptitude. It's an aptitude for people. An understanding of people. Apparently, between the ages of five hundred and six hundred, your cerebral talents become heightened to a point beyond a normal human range. He has dealt with so many people, in so many different cultures, that he can read faces and body language with an astounding accuracy. He knows if he can trust people.'

We were there, in the French flat – we didn't use the word 'apartment' in America back then – on the top floor of the Dakota building, with Central Park spread beneath us.

'I try to pretend it's my garden,' said the tall lean bald sharp-suited man at the window. He held a cane, which he clutched tightly. As much for show as for his arthritis, which hadn't yet taken him over.

'It's a very impressive view,' I told him.

'Yes. And these buildings grow by the day. Please, sit down.'

Elegant was the word. There was an elegant Steinway piano and beside it an elegant, expensive-looking leather sofa. Standing lamps, a mahogany desk, a chandelier. Agnes made herself comfortable on the sofa and gestured to a chair near the desk. Hendrich was on the other side of the desk, but still standing, staring out of that window. She gave me a firm nod, to indicate that I had better sit right away.

Meanwhile Hendrich stayed staring at Central Park.

'How have you survived, Tom?' He turned to face me. He was old, I realised. If he had been an ordinary human – a 'mayfly' as Agnes called them, straight-faced – you would have guessed his age as seventy. In our days, right now, adjusting for inflation, you'd go higher. Eighty plus. He looked older then than I have ever known him to look.

'You have lived such a long time. And from what I hear you haven't been doing so in the best circumstances. What stopped you from jumping off a bridge? What drives you?'

I looked at him. His cheeks sagged and his eyes had so many bags under them he reminded me of a melting candle.

I didn't want to say the real reason. If Marion was alive I didn't want Hendrich knowing about her. I didn't trust anyone.

'Come on, we are here to help you. You were born in a château. You were made for fine things, Tom. We will restore you to that life. And to your daughter.'

I felt things contract around me. 'My daughter?'

'I read Dr Hutchinson's report. About Marion. Don't worry, we will search for her. We will find her, I promise you. If she's alive we will find her. We will find all of us. And as new generations emerge we will find them too.'

I was scared, but also, I confess, a little thrilled at the idea that I could get help in my search for Marion. I felt, suddenly, less alone.

There was a decanter of whisky on his desk. And three glasses. He poured a round of whisky without asking if we wanted one. As it happened, I did, to calm my nerves.

He read the label. 'Look at this. "Wexford Old Irish Malt Whiskey Liquor. A Taste of the Past." A taste of the past! When I was a young man, whisky didn't even exist.' His accent was hard to place. Not fully American. 'But I'm a good deal older than you.'

He sighed wistfully and sat down behind the vast mahogany desk.

'It's strange, isn't it? All the things that we have lived to see. In my case it's quite a list: spectacles, the printing press, newspapers, rifles, compasses, the telescope . . . the pendulum clock . . . the piano . . . Impressionist paintings . . . photography . . . Napoleon . . . champagne . . . semi-colons . . . billboards . . . the hot dog . . .'

He must have seen the confused look on my face.

'Of course, Agnes. The poor man has never had a hot dog before. We must take him to Coney Island. They have the best in the whole city.'

'They sincerely do,' said Agnes, who seemed to have lost a little of her sharpness around him.

'Is it food?' I asked.

'Yes.' He laughed, drily. 'It's a sausage. A special sausage. A Dachshund sausage. A special little frankfurter. It's heaven in a bun. It's what all of civilisation has been heading towards . . . If I'd have known, growing up in Flanders, that one day I would get to taste a *hot dog*. Well!'

It seemed strange. Had I been sent across the ocean – leaving a man dead behind me – to indulge in a conversation about sausages?

'Pleasure. That is the aim, isn't it? To enjoy *good things* . . . fine things. Food. Liquor. Art. Poetry. Music. Cigars.'

He took a cigar from his desk, along with a chrome lighter.

'Would you like a cigar?'

'I don't enjoy tobacco.'

He looked disappointed. Handed one to Agnes instead. 'It's good for the chest.'

'I'm fine,' I said, sipping my whisky.

He lit their cigars and said, 'The finer things. The sensual pleasures. There is no other meaning than that, I've discovered. There is nothing else.'

'Love?' I said.

'What about that?'

Hendrich smiled at Agnes. When the smile returned to me there was a menace to it. He moved the topic on. 'I have no idea why you took it upon yourself to visit a doctor about your condition. Maybe you thought, now superstitions like witchcraft aren't so prevalent, that it was a safe time to do so?'

'I thought it would help people. People like us. To have a medical explanation.'

'I am sure Agnes has already indicated why this was naïve.'

'A little, yes.'

'The truth is this: there is more danger now than there has ever been. The advances being made in science and medicine are not advances to be welcomed: germ theory and microbiology and immunology. Last year they found the vaccine for typhoid. What you won't know is that in pursuit of their research the inventors of the vaccine capitalised on the work of the Institute for Experimental Research in Berlin.'

'Surely a typhoid vaccination is a good thing?'

'Not when the research was conducted at the expense of us.' He clenched his jaw slightly, trying to keep his anger out of view. Agnes' stiff silence made me worry even more. Maybe there was a gun in his desk. Maybe this had been a kind of test and I had failed and now he was going to put a bullet in my head.

'Scientists' – he said the word as if it tasted of sulphur – 'are the new witchfinders. You know about witchfinders, don't you? I know you do.'

'He knows about witchfinders,' assured Agnes, blowing a thin stream of smoke towards the standing lamp.

'But what you don't know is that the witch trials never ended. It just goes by a different name. We are their dead frogs. The institute knows of us.' He leaned over the desk, dropping ash onto a fresh copy of the *New York Tribune*, his stare burning like the butt of his cigar. 'Do you understand? There are members of the scientific community *who do know about us.*' He sat back in his chair. 'Not many. But a few. In Berlin. They have no interest in us as human beings. Indeed, they don't even see us *as* human beings. They imprisoned two of us. Tortured them in the laboratory where they kept their guinea pigs. A man and a woman. The woman escaped. She is part of the society now. She still lives in Germany, in a village in the Bavarian countryside, but we got her a new life and name. She helps us when we need her. And we help her.'

'I didn't know this.'

'You're not meant to.'

I noticed that the park was cluttered with fallen trees.

A bird landed on the windowsill.

I didn't recognise it. Birds were different here. A small robust yellow creature with dull grey wings, it jerked its head towards the window. Then the other way. I never tired of the way birds moved when they weren't in flight. It was a series of tableaux rather than continuous movement. Staccato. Stuck moments.

'Your daughter could be in danger. We all could. We need to work together, you understand?'

'I do.'

'There is one last question I need to ask you,' Hendrich said, after a sip of whisky.

94

'Please do.'

'Do you want to survive? I mean, really? Do you want to stay alive?'

I had long asked myself this question. The answer was usually yes, because I didn't want to die while I still had a daughter, possibly still alive, and yet it was very difficult to say I wanted to survive. Ever since Rose, it had been a pendulum between the two possibilities. To be or not to be. But in that lavish apartment, with that yellow bird still on the ledge, the answer seemed clearer. From this height, with the hard blue sky and bold new city in front of me, I felt closer to Marion. America made you think in the future tense. 'Yes. Yes, I do want to survive.'

'Well, to survive we must work together.'

The bird flew away.

'Right,' I said. 'Right. Work together.'

'Don't look so worried. We are not a religious sect. Our aim is to stay alive, yes, but only so we can enjoy life. We have no gods here, save maybe Aphrodite. And Dionysus.' He looked wistful for a moment. 'Agnes, are you heading up to Harlem?'

'Yes. I'm going to see an old friend, and then sedate myself and sleep for a week.'

Light gleamed like a jewel on the decanter. The sight made Hendrich happy. 'Look! The sun is out. Shall we take a walk in the park?'

An uprooted maple tree was in our path.

'Hurricane,' Hendrich explained. 'Killed some people a few weeks ago, sailors mainly. The park keepers have been a bit slow to do the clear-up.'

I stared at the roots, spreading like tentacles. 'Must have been ferocious.'

Hendrich smiled at me. 'It was quite a show.'

He stared down at the scattered earth and leaves on the path.

'The immigrant experience. Right there. The wind comes and suddenly you're not in the ground any more. And your roots are out on show and looking strange and unfamiliar. But you've been uprooted before, right? You've uprooted yourself. You've had to, surely.'

I nodded. 'Many times.'

'It shows.'

I was trying to take this as a compliment. It was difficult.

'The trick is to stay upright. You know how to move and stay upright?'

'How?'

'You have to match the hurricane. You have to be your own storm. You have to . . .'

He stopped. His metaphor was running out of steam. I noticed how shiny his shoes were. I had never seen shoes like them.

'We are different, Tom,' he said eventually. 'We are not other people. We carry the past with us. We see it everywhere. And some-times that can be dangerous, and we need to help each other.' His hand was now on my shoulder, as if he was telling me something of the deepest importance. 'The past is never gone. It just hides.'

We walked slowly around the maple tree.

Manhattan rose out of the ground, ahead of us, like a new type of storm-proof forest.

'We have to be above them. Do you understand? For our future survival, we have to be selfish.'

We passed a couple wrapped up in overcoats, laughing at some secret joke. 'Your life is changing. The world is changing. It is ours. We just have to make sure most of the mayflies never know about us.'

I thought of a body floating along the Thames.

'But to kill Dr Hutchinson . . .'

'This is a war, Tom. It is an unseen war, but it is a war. We have to protect ourselves.'

He lowered his voice as two smart-suited men with identical moustaches rode by us on black bicycles. The bicycles had equal-sized wheels, which seemed a very modern development to me.

'Who is this Omai?' Hendrich whispered. His eyebrows raised like sparrow wings.

'Sorry?'

'Dr Hutchinson wrote about him. From the South Pacific. Who is he?'

I laughed nervously. It was strange having someone know your biggest secrets. 'He was an old friend. I knew him back in the last century. He came to London for a while, but he doesn't want to be found. I haven't seen him for over a hundred years.'

'Fine,' he said. 'Fine.'

Then Hendrich opened his jacket and pulled out two beige tickets from the inside pocket. He handed me one.

'Tchaikovsky. Tonight. The Music Hall. Hottest ticket in town. You need to see the bigger picture, Tom. All this time alive and you still can't see it. But you will, you will. For the sake of your daughter. For the sake of yourself. Trust me, you will . . .' He leaned in and grinned. 'And if not, well, you might find yourself out of time altogether.'

We sat in the plush red seats, and when the woman with the extravagant claret-red dress – puff-sleeved, high-necked, bell-skirted, ornately embroidered décolletage – next to Hendrich stood up and left for the restroom, he tilted his head towards me and surreptitiously pointed out a celebrity in attendance.

'Man on balcony . . . leaning over . . . next to the lady in the green dress. The one everyone is looking at while pretending they aren't.' I saw a genial rosy-skinned man with a round owlish face and a neatly trimmed white beard. 'Andrew Carnegie. Titan of industry. Richer than Rockefeller. More generous too . . . But, look, he's an old man. What's he got left? Another decade? Maybe a bit more? Yet every single piece of Carnegie steel in every railroad across this country will be there long after him. This hall, built with spare change, will be standing when he is six feet under the earth. That's why he built it. So his name will live long into the future. This is what the rich do. Once they know they can survive comfortably and their children can survive comfortably they set about working on their legacy. Such a sadness to that word, don't you think? Legacy. What a meaningless thing. All that work for a future in which they don't appear. And what is legacy, Mr Hazard? What is legacy but the most empty and mediocre substitute for what we have. Steel and money and fancy concert halls don't give you immortality.'

'We aren't immortal.'

He smiled. 'Look at me, Tom. I look the same age as him. But in reality I am younger than a baby. I'll still be here in the year two thousand.'

I risked offending him. 'But how do you feel inside? The thing that has always worried me is the idea of spending several lifetimes as an old man.'

And for a moment I thought I *had* offended him. I thought I had overstepped an invisible line. And maybe I had, but he just smiled at me and said, 'Life is life. So long as I can hear music and so long as I can still enjoy oysters and champagne . . .'

'So you aren't in pain?'

'I have some bone trouble, yes. It keeps me awake at night from time to time. And I am no longer entirely immune to colds and fevers. You will notice this as you get older. All those physical benefits of being an alba begin to fade. You catch things. You become more like them. The biological shield drops. But I am good with pain. Small price to pay for *being alive.*

'Life is the ultimate privilege, so I am among the most privileged people on the planet. You should be grateful too. You will still be here deep into the next millennium. Beyond me. Beyond Agnes.

You are a god, Tom. A walking god. We are gods and they are mayflies. You need to learn how to enjoy your *deific existence.*'

A frail-looking man with an intense expression and thinning hair walked towards the centre of the stage. He stood in front of the crowd and gave the semblance of a smile. The whole hall erupted in applause. He stayed there, silent, just staring out at us for a while. And then he – Tchaikovsky – turned towards the little lectern that was on the stage, picked up his baton and held it in the air. He paused a moment. It was like watching an old wizard with a wand, summoning the energy needed to cast the spell.

The hall fell silent. I had never heard a silence like it. The whole hall seemed to be holding its breath. It felt civilised and modern. It felt refined and tantalising all at once, like a polite collective pre-orgasm.

Time slowed, inside that moment.

Then the music began.

I hadn't enjoyed music for years. So I sat in my seat waiting, as always, for nothing at all.

After a blast of trumpets the violins and cellos were left on their own for a while, creating a noise that started small and tender, and rose to create a kind of symphonic storm.

And, yes, it did nothing at first. But then, somehow, it *got in.*

No. Not got in. That's the wrong way of putting it. Music doesn't get in. Music is already in. Music simply uncovers what is there, makes you feel emotions that you didn't necessarily know you had inside you, and runs around waking them all up. A rebirth of sorts.

There was such a yearning and energy to it. I closed my eyes. I could not describe here on the page how I felt. The very reason such music exists is because it is a language that couldn't be communicated in any other way. But all I can say is that I felt suddenly alive again.

As the trumpets and French horns and bass drum thundered in, it had such power my heart quickened and my mind felt dizzy. When I opened my eyes I saw Tchaikovsky with his baton, seemingly pulling the music right out of the air, as if music was something already in the atmosphere that you just had to locate.

Then, when it was all over, the composer seemed to deflate again. Even as the whole hall got to its feet and showered him with wave after wave of applause, and the odd roar of 'Bravo!', he gave the smallest of smiles and the smallest of bows.

'He pisses over Brahms from a mountain, don't you think?' Hendrich whispered to me at one point.

I had no idea. I just knew it was good to be back inside the world of feeling.

I realised, even at the time, that the visit to Music Hall was all part of the sales technique. Hendrich's way of getting me inside. Not only would he find my daughter, I would have a good life in the process. I didn't yet understand what I was really being sold, but by the time that became clear I had already bought in. I had been sold, in reality, since he first mentioned Marion. But now I was starting to believe Hendrich's hype. That the Albatross Society was a way not just to find my daughter, but also myself.

The next day, in Hendrich's apartment, as we finished our champagne breakfast, the conversation happened. The one I always think of.

'The first rule is that you don't fall in love,' he said, wiping a waffle crumb off the table with his finger before lighting a cigar. 'There are other rules too, but that is the main one. No falling in love. No staying in love. No daydreaming of love. If you stick to this you will just about be okay.'

I stared through the curving smoke of his cigar. 'I doubt I will ever love again.'

'Good. You are, of course, allowed to love food and music and champagne and rare sunny afternoons in October. You can love the sight of waterfalls and the smell of old books, but the love of people is off limits. Do you hear me? Don't attach yourself to people, and try to feel as little as you possibly can for those you do meet. Because otherwise you will slowly lose your mind . . .' He paused for a while. 'Eight years, that's the rule. That's the most an alba can stay anywhere before things get really tricky. That's the Eight-Year Rule. You have a nice life for eight years. Then I send you on a task. Then you have a new life. With no ghosts.'

I believed him. How could I not? Hadn't I lost myself after Rose? Wasn't I still, in a sense, waiting to find myself again? *A nice life.* Maybe it was possible. With a structure. With something to belong to. With a purpose.

'Do you know your Greek myths, Tom?'

'A little.'

'Well, I am like Daedalus. You know, the creator of the labyrinth that held the minotaur safe. I've had to build a labyrinth to protect all of us. This society. But the trouble with Daedalus is that for all his wisdom people didn't always listen to him. His own son, Icarus, didn't listen. You know *that* story, don't you?'

'Yes. He and Icarus try to escape from the Greek island—'

'Crete.'

'Crete. Yes. But their wings are made of wax and feathers. And his father . . .'

'Daedalus.'

'His father tells him not to fly too close to the sun or to the sea, or his wings will catch fire or get soaked.'

'And of course both things happen. He goes too close to the sun. The wax melts. He falls in the sea. Now, you are not too high. But you have lived too low. It's a balance. I am here to help you get the balance right. How do you see yourself, Tom?'

'Not as Icarus.'

'Then who?'

'That's a big question.'

'It's a most important question.'

'I don't know.'

'Are you someone who watches life, or someone who participates?'

'Both, I suppose. Watching, participating.'

He nodded. 'What are you capable of?'

'What?'

'Where have you been?'

'I've been around the world.'

'No, I mean, where have you been *morally*? What have you done? How many lines have you crossed?'

'Why are you asking me that?'

'Because, within the structure of the rules, you need to be free.'

I was uneasy. I should have trusted that feeling, instead of just sipping champagne. 'What do we need to be free to do?'

He smiled. 'We live long lives, Tom. We live long lives. Long and secret lives. We do whatever's necessary.' The smile became a laugh. He had good teeth, considering how many centuries he'd had them. 'Now, today, hot dogs.'

London, now

We live long lives, Tom . . .

There is a tree in California, a Great Basin bristlecone pine that was found, after an intensive ring count, to be five thousand and sixty-five years old.

Even to me, that pine seems old. In recent years, whenever I have despaired of my condition and needed to feel a bit more mortal and ordinary, I think of that tree in California. It has been alive since the Pharaohs. It has been alive since the founding of Troy. Since the start of the Bronze Age. Since the start of yoga. Since *mammoths*.

And it has stayed there, calmly in its spot, growing slowly, producing leaves, losing leaves, producing more, as those mammoths became extinct, as Homer wrote *The Odyssey*, as Cleopatra reigned, as Jesus was nailed to a cross, as Siddhārtha Gautama left his palace to weep for his suffering subjects, as the Roman Empire declined and fell, as Carthage was captured, as water buffalo were domesticated in China, as the Incas built cities, as I leaned over the well with Rose, as America fought with itself, as world wars happened, as Facebook was invented, as millions of humans and other animals lived and fought and procreated and went, bewildered, to their fast graves, the tree had always been the tree.

That was the familiar lesson of time. Everything changes and nothing changes.

I stand like a vertical headache in front of twenty-eight fourteen-year-olds, slumping back on chairs, playing with pens, surreptitiously checking their phones. It is a tough crowd, but I've had tougher over the years. This is certainly easier than playing to the drunken sailors, thieves and drifters of the Minerva Inn in Plymouth, for instance.

Everything changes and nothing changes.

'The East End is a multicultural area because it has always been a multicultural area,' I say, as an opener to the lesson focusing on Pre-Twentieth-Century Immigration. 'No one was ever a native of Britain. People arrived here. The Romans, the Celts, the Normans, the Saxons. Britain was always a place made of other places. And even what we think of as "modern" immigration goes quite a long way back. Well over three hundred years ago, you had Indians who came here after being recruited on ships run by the East India Company. Then came Germans and Russian Jews and Africans. But it is true that, while immigration has always been a part of English society, for a long time visibly different immigrants were treated as exotic oddities . . . For instance, in the eighteenth century a man called Omai arrived here from the Pacific Islands. He arrived back on Cook's second voyage . . .' I pause. I remember sitting on the deck of the boat with him, Omai, my old friend, showing him my daughter's coin and teaching him the word *money*. 'And when Omai came here he was seen as so unique that every celebrity of the day, from the king down, went to meet him and have dinner with him . . .' I remember his face, flickering in the shadow of a flame. 'He even had his portrait painted by the most famous artist of the time, Sir Joshua Reynolds. He was a celebrity, for a time. Omai . . .'

Omai.

I hadn't said his name out loud for a long time. Not since I had spoken to Hendrich about him, in 1891. But I often thought about him. About what happened to him. Thinking of him now, though, seems to add to my headache. Everything spins a little.

'He was . . .'

A girl on the front row, Danielle, chewing gum, frowns at me. 'Are you all right, sir?'

Cue laughter. Danielle turns around. Soaks it up.

Steady thyself.

I try to smile at the class. 'Fine. I'm fine . . . This part of London in particular has always been defined by immigration. For instance, over there' – I point out of the window, westwards – 'back in the fifteen hundreds and sixteen hundreds you had the French. They were the first immigrants in great numbers of the modern age. Not all of them stayed in London. A lot went to Canterbury. Others went into rural areas. Kent . . .' I pause. Breathe. '. . . Suffolk. But many based themselves in Spitalfields, and a real community built up. They started the silk industry here. Many of them were silk weavers. Many were former aristocrats who were suddenly having to make a new life for themselves in very different circumstances to the life they knew at home.'

There is a boy sitting on one of the middle tables. Anton. A quiet boy with a brooding and serious look about him. He raises his hand.

'Yes, Anton?'

'Why did they come here? I mean, if they had it so good at home?'

'Well, they were Protestants. Huguenots, they were called, though they didn't call themselves that. They followed the teachings of Jean Cauvin – John Calvin. And at that time it was a dangerous thing to be a Protestant in France, just as it was to be a Catholic in England. So many of them . . .'

I close my eyes, trying to blink away a memory. The pain in my head becomes too much.

They sense my weakness. I hear their laughter flare up again.

'So many of them had to . . . had to escape.'

I open my eyes. Anton isn't laughing. He gives me a small smile of support. But I am pretty sure he, like the rest of the class, thinks I am not quite *there.*

I feel my heart beat a frenzied jazz rhythm as the room starts to tilt.

'Just one minute,' I say.

'Sir?' Anton seems concerned.

'I'm fine. I'm fine. I just . . . I'll be back in a minute.'

I walk out of the room, down the corridor. Past one classroom. Past another. I see Camille through a window. She is standing in front of a whiteboard full of verb formations.

She looks so calm and in control of the class. She sees me and smiles and I smile back, despite my panic.

I go into the bathroom.

I stare at my face in the mirror.

I know my own face too well to actually *see* it. Familiarity could make you a stranger to yourself.

'Who am I? Who am I? Who am I?'

I splash my cheeks with water. I breathe slowly.

'My name is Tom Hazard. Tom Hazard. My name is Tom Hazard.'

The name itself contains too much. It contains everyone who has ever called me it and everyone I have ever hid it from. It contains my mother and Rose and Hendrich and Marion. But it isn't an anchor. Because an anchor fixes you in one place. And I am still not fixed. Could I just keep sailing through life for ever feeling like this? A boat has to stop eventually. It has to reach a port, a harbour, a destination, known or unknown. It has to get *somewhere*, and stop there, or what is the point of the boat? I have been so many different people, played so many different roles in my life. I am not a person. I am a crowd in one body.

I was people I hated and people I admired. I was exciting and boring and happy and infinitely sad. I was both on the right and wrong side of history.

I had, in short, lost myself.

'It's okay,' I tell my reflection. I think of Omai. I wish I knew where he was. I wish I hadn't just let him go without trying to keep in touch. It is lonely, this world, without a friend.

The slow breaths get my heart rate down. I dry my face on a paper towel.

I walk out of the toilets and back down the corridor and make an effort to keep looking ahead, to not look into Camille's classroom as I make my way back to my own. To act like a normal non-shitty teacher with only, say, forty years of memories inside him.

I head back into the classroom.

'Sorry about that,' I say, trying to smile. Trying to be light. Trying to say something amusing. 'I took a lot of drugs when I was younger. I get the occasional flashback.'

They laugh.

'So don't do drugs. It can lead to a life of mental torment and history teaching in later life. Right, okay, on with the lesson . . .'

I see Camille again that day. Afternoon break. We are in the staff room. She is talking to another language teacher, Joachim, who is Austrian, and teaches German, and whose nose makes a whistling sound when he breathes. She breaks off and comes over while I sit on my own drinking a cup of tea.

'Hello, Tom.'

'Hi,' I say. The smallest available word accompanied by the smallest of available smiles.

'Were you okay earlier? You looked a bit . . .' She searches for the word. 'Intense.'

'I just had a headache. I get headaches.'

'Me too.'

Her eyes narrow. I worry that she is trying to work out where she knows me from. Which is probably why I say, 'I've still got it . . . the headache. That's why I'm just sitting on my own.'

She looks a bit hurt and awkward. She nods. 'Oh, right. Well, I hope it gets better. They have ibuprofen in the First Aid cupboard.'

If you knew the truth about me your life would be in mortal danger.

'I'll be fine, thanks.'

I stop looking at her, and wait for her to go away. Which she does. I feel her anger. And I feel guilty. Actually, no, it isn't just that. There is something else. A kind of homesickness, a longing for something – a feeling – I haven't known for a very long time. And when she goes and sits down on the other side of the staff room, she doesn't smile, or look at me, and I feel like something is over before it has a chance to begin.

Later that night I am walking Abraham back from the park via Fairfield Road. I don't normally go this way. I have avoided it since arriving back in London.

The reason I have been avoiding it is because this is where I first met Rose. My ventures to Chapel Street and Well Street had been too painful. But I need to get over her. I need to get over everything. I need 'closure' as people say these days. Though you can never close the past. The most you can do with it is accept it. And that is the point I want to reach.

I am on Fairfield Road, outside the illuminated despair of the bus station, putting my hand in a plastic bag to pick up Abraham's shit, then placing it in the bin. The history of London could be charted by the steady and consistent decline of visible faeces in public streets.

'You know, Abraham, you shouldn't really do this on the street. That is why we go to the park. You know, that green place, with the grass?'

Abraham feigns ignorance as we carry on walking.

I look around. Trying to work out where it is that I first saw her. It is beyond impossible. There is nothing recognisable. As with

Chapel Street and Well Lane, not a single building that is there now was there then. I see, through a window, a row of people running on treadmills. They are all staring up at what I assume is a row of TV screens above their heads. Some of them are plugged into headphones. One is checking her iPhone as she runs.

Places don't matter to people any more. Places aren't the point. People are only ever half present where they are these days. They always have at least one foot in the great digital nowhere.

I try to work out where the geese stalls used to be, and where she had been standing with her fruit basket.

And then I find it.

I stand still a moment, with Abraham tugging on the lead as traffic whooshes by, oblivious. The headache ups a notch and I feel dizzy enough to need to stand back against a brick wall.

'Just a minute, boy,' I tell Abraham. 'Just a minute.'

And the memories break through like water bursting a dam. My head pulses with a pain even stronger than I'd had in the class earlier, and for a moment, in a lull between the sound of cars, I feel it, I feel the living history of the road, the residue of my own pain lingering in the air, and I feel as weak as I did in 1599, when I was still heading west, delirious and ready to be saved.

PART THREE
Rose

Bow, near London, 1599

I had been walking near continuously for three days. My feet were red and blistered and throbbing with pain. My eyes felt dry and heavy from the short doses of sleep I had managed to steal beside forest paths and on grass verges by the highway. Though, in reality, I had hardly slept at all. My back was sore from carrying the lute. I was hungrier than I had ever been, having had nothing in the last three days but berries and mushrooms and a small end of bread thrown to me by a pitying squire who passed me on his horse.

But all of that was fine.

Indeed, all of that was a welcome distraction from the intensity of my mind. The intensity seemed to have spilled out of me, infecting the grass and the trees and every brook and stream. Every time I closed my eyes I thought of my mother on that last day, high in the air, her hair blowing in the wind towards me. And her cries still echoed in my ears.

I had been a ghost of myself for three days. I'd gone back to Edwardstone a free man, but I couldn't stay there. They were murderers. Every single one of them. I went back to the cottage and picked up mother's lute and searched for some money but there was none. Then I left. I just ran. I couldn't be in Edwardstone. I never wanted to see the likes of Bess Small or Walter Earnshaw again, just as I never wanted to walk by the Giffords' cottage. I wanted to run away from this feeling of terror and loss inside me, of infinite loneliness, but of course there was no running away from *that*.

But now I was getting close to London. I had been told by a man with a lisp in the village of Hackney that if I was heading in to London I would pass by the Green Goose Fair, at Fairfield Road in Bow, and there would be food there, and 'various madness'. And now here I was. Fairfield Road. And there was the start of the madness: a cow, standing square in the road, eyeballing me. As if trying to communicate something that was too easily lost in the chasm between animals and people.

As I carried on walking, beyond the cow, there were houses on either side of me. And unlike in other villages, the houses just kept going on and on, in a straight line, on either side of the road. There was hardly any space between them. This was London, I realised. And I saw crowds and crowds of people ahead of me, filling the street.

I remembered how much my mother hated crowds, and felt her fear inside me, like a ghost emotion.

And then, as I got closer I noticed the noise. The competing shouts and cries of traders. The drunken laughter of the ale-sozzled. The grunts and moos and hisses of assorted animals.

Pipes. Singing. Mayhem.

I had never seen anything like it. It was chaos. The scene was made more intense by my delirium.

There were so many people. So many strangers. Laughter flapped out of people like bats from a cave.

An old red-cheeked woman sighing like a carthorse as she carried two panniers dangling from a wooden brace and loaded with fish and oysters.

Two boys fighting near an impromptu pen of pigs.

A pie stall.

A bread stand.

Radishes.

Lace.

A girl, no more than ten, carrying a basket full of cherries.

Roast goose stalls on both sides of the road.

A lettuce lying in a puddle.

An amused man passing me and pointing to a drunkard struggling to get back on his feet. 'Two of the bell and mark him, boy,
whip-cat tippled already.'

Rabbits.

Two live geese, hissing and widening their wings at each other.

More pigs. More cows. More drunks. Many more drunks.

A well-dressed blind woman being led around by a scruffy-
looking orphan girl.

Lame beggars.

A woman, coming in close to a random stranger, grabbing
between his legs and whispering a drunken offer.

The rowdy bustle around the ale stalls.

A giant 'from the Nether Lands' – cried a man, hawking the
novelty – and a dwarf 'from the West Country', side by side, to
maximise the money-making effect.

A man swallowing a sword.

A fiddler. A piper. A flautist, eyeing me with suspicion, with
dexterous fingers playing 'Three Ravens'.

And the smells: roasting meat, ale, cheese, lavender, fresh shit.

The dizziness was back, but I kept on staggering forward.

My hunger, presented with the scent of so much food, was now
actually a kind of pain. I walked over towards one of the goose
stalls. I stood there, inhaling the roast meat.

'How much is the goose?'

'Three shillings, lad.'

I didn't have three shillings. The truth was: I didn't have any
money at all.

I staggered backwards. Stood on a man's foot.

'Mind yourself, boy!'

Boy, boy, boy.

'Yes, I am a boy,' I mumbled, even though eighteen was positively
middle-aged at that time.

And that is when things began to spin.

I was generally quite strong. One of the many quirks of my biology was that I was never really ill. I'd never had a cold, or the flu. I'd never vomited in my entire life. I'd never even had a bout of diarrhoea, which, in 1599, was an incredibly, suspiciously rare thing to be able to say. Yet right then I was feeling dreadful. There had been rain earlier, but now the sun was out and the sky was a hard blue. The same oblivious blue it had been above the River Lark. The heat added to the intensity of everything, which was intense enough to begin with.

'Maman,' I muttered, delirious. 'Maman.'

I felt like I could die. And, in that moment, I was perfectly fine with that.

But then I saw her.

She was standing holding a basket of fruit, frowning at me. She was about my age, but looked it. She had long dark hair and eyes that shone like pebbles in a stream.

I walked towards her, staring in wonder at the plums and damsons in the basket.

I felt a strange sensation, like I wasn't in my own body.

'Can I have a plum?' I asked her.

She held open her palm. I thought of Manning's hand and the outstretched fingers that kept my mother under the water.

'I don't . . . I . . . I . . . the . . . I . . .'

I saw the stray cow I had seen earlier, walking through the crowd. I closed my eyes and my mother fell through the sky with the weight of timber. I opened them and the fruit seller was frowning at me, cross or confused or a little of both.

I wobbled a little, as the street sped in circles.

'Steady thyself,' said the fruit seller.

Those were her first words to me.

Steady thyself.

But I couldn't steady myself.

I could see why my mother needed walls to lean onto after Father died. Grief tilts you.

Things went very light and then very dark.

The next thing I knew – a moment, or five minutes later – was that I was lying flat on my front, half my face in a muddy puddle, surrounded by plums and damsons. Most of them were in the mud too. Some were getting crushed underfoot by passers-by. One was being eaten by a dog.

I slowly got to my feet.

A crowd of boys were laughing and mocking me.

The girl was scrabbling around on her knees trying to salvage any plums she could.

'I'm sorry,' I said.

I picked up a muddy plum and walked away.

'Ho! Hey! Ho! You!' She grabbed my shoulder. Her nostrils were flaring with rage. 'Look what you have done!'

I thought I was going to faint again, and decided to keep moving, so I didn't do any more damage.

'Stop walking! You can't just walk away!'

I bit into the muddied plum. She grabbed it out of my hand, fast as a bird, and threw it on the ground.

'That basket was a week's money. A good week. Now I have to pay Mr Sharpe for fruit I never sold.'

'Mr Sharpe?'

'So, you can pay me now.'

'I have no money.'

She was red-faced with humiliation and anger. She looked confused about the money situation. Maybe it was because, despite the dirt on my clothes and compared to most of the crowd around us, I was quite well dressed. My mother had always made sure that, even though our circumstances had drastically changed since moving to England, we looked as noble as we could afford. Which was, with hindsight, one of the many reasons we had struggled to fit in among the raggedy villagers of Edwardstone. Not the main reason, obviously.

'That,' she said, pointing to the lute on my back.

'What?'

'Give me that. That can be your payment.'

'No.'

She picked up a rock. 'Well, I shall break it then, the way you broke my basket.'

I raised my hands. 'No! No.'

She must have seen something in my face that made her think twice. 'You have no food but you are worried about a lute.'

'It was my mother's.'

Her face softened, went from anger back to confusion. 'Where is your mother?'

'She died three days ago.'

She folded her arms. Yes. She looked around eighteen or nineteen years of age. I can tell you that she wore an ordinary white dress, a 'kirtle' as folk used to call it, and a simple red neckerchief, worn at an angle, with the knot tied at the left side of her neck. I can tell you that she had very clean skin – a rarity among this crowd – and had two moles on her right cheek, one smaller than the other, like a moon in a planet's orbit, and a small constellation of freckles over her nose. Her dark hair was half inside a little white cloth cap, half free and wild.

She had the kind of face that had spent most of its time frowning, but there was also a glint of mischief to her that played around with the corners of her mouth, as if a smile was always in the process of wanting to emerge but being tightly regulated by some disapproving authority inside her mind. I can tell you she was tall too. A quarter head taller than me at that time, if shorter than me when I became, physically, a 'grown up'.

'Died?'

'Yes.'

She nodded. Death was nothing remarkable. 'So who do you have?'

'I have myself.'

'And where do you live?'

'Nowhere now.'

'You have no home?'

I shook my head and felt the shame of it.

'Do you play?' She pointed to the lute on my back.

'I do.'

'Then,' she said resolutely, 'you will come and live with us.'

'I couldn't do that.'

A young girl came and stood next to her, with an identical but unbroken basket. It was the cherry seller I had seen further along the street. She looked about ten or eleven. Sisters, clearly. The same dark hair and fierce stare. A drunk tried to grab a cherry, but she had quick reflexes and turned her basket away from him, and made daggers with her eyes.

'This is not charity,' said the older girl. 'You will come and live with us until you have paid what you owe. For the fruit and the basket. And you can pay for your lodging too.'

The younger girl stared at me with eyes as direct as arrows.

'This is Grace,' the older girl explained. 'And I am Rose Claybrook.'

'Hello there, Grace.'

'He sounds peculiar, and smells like a horse's arse,' Grace said, unimpressed. Then, to me, 'Where did you spring from?'

'Suffolk,' I croaked. And very nearly added: *and France.* But I sensed I wouldn't have to. Suffolk would be foreign enough.

I felt dizzy again.

Rose came to hold me up.

'Suffolk? You *walked* from Suffolk? We will take you home. Grace, help me hold him. And give him some cherries. It's a long walk in this state.'

'Thank you,' I whispered, as soft as the air, concentrating hard on placing one foot in front of the other, as though learning to walk again. 'Thank you.'

And that is how my second life began.

London, now

Maybe I had been leaning against the wall too long in the gentle rain. Maybe you couldn't be still any more in a relentlessly frantic city, without the city seeking some kind of soft unconscious revenge.

I hadn't seen them approach. I had been lost, thinking about Rose, feeling the intense story of the road. But I hear Abraham growl and I look up and they are there.

Five of them. Boys, or men, or something in between. They have stopped to look at me, as if curious, as if I am a sculpture in a museum. One of them, tall and gym-shouldered, comes close, in my face. Another boy, behind him, says, 'Ah, don't be a psycho, man, 's' late. Let's go.'

But the large one isn't going anywhere. He pulls a knife. The blade shines yellow under the streetlight. He expects to see fear in my eyes, but he doesn't. You get to the point, after everything has happened to you, that nothing can surprise you.

Abraham growls and bares teeth.

'Set your dog on me and he gets it too . . . Phone and wallet. Then we go.'

'You don't want to do this.'

The boy – he *is* a boy, I now realise, despite his height – shakes his head. 'Quiet. Phone, wallet. Phone, wallet. Now. We got things to do.' He looks around. The wet whisper of a car sloshes by in the rain. Keeps moving. It is then I recognise one of the boys. The youngest one. His face is half hidden, inside his hood. He has scared wide eyes. He is hopping from foot to foot, eyes darting, uttering words of panic under his breath, taking out his phone, pocketing it, taking it out again. It is the boy I had seen in class today. Anton.

'Leave him,' he says, his voice muffled, backing away, and my heart breaks for him. 'C'mon, let's go.'

Time, I realise, is a weapon these days. Nothing weakens people like having to wait. In the street. With a knife in their hand.

'It's small,' I say, referencing the knife.

'What?'

'Everything gets smaller over time. Computers, phones, apples, knives, souls.'

'Stop talking, man, now or for ever.'

'Apples used to be *giant*. You should've seen them. They were like green pumpkins.'

'Fucking shut up, you dead cunt.'

'Have you ever killed someone?'

'Fuck, man. Phone and wallet. Or I slice your throat.'

'I have,' I told him truthfully. 'It's horrible. You don't want that feeling. It's as though you become dead yourself. Like their death inhabits you. It sends you insane. And you carry it, you carry them, inside you, for ever . . .'

'Stop talking.'

My eyes lock with his. I press the invisible force of centuries into him.

Abraham growls again. A growl that becomes a bark.

'He's basically a wolf. Very protective. If you stab me you just better make sure I don't let go of the lead.'

The knife trembles a little, with the boy's fear. Maybe it is this. This shame of his own fragility that makes him lower his arm.

'Fuck this, man,' he says. He walks away, backwards, then fast, with the other boys following. Anton steals a glance back at me and I smile and confuse him more. I understand. The way you can get caught up in things, find yourself floating, heading towards trouble you can hardly avoid.

Hackney, near London, 1599

They didn't live in Bow. They lived further out, in a small narrow house on Well Lane, in the village of Hackney. There were a lot of strawberry fields and fruit orchards in Hackney at that time. Compared to much of the areas in and around London, Hackney smelled quite inoffensive, and the air healthy to inhale, though it was very different to the countryside I had known in Suffolk. For one thing, there had been a theatre there. It had been dismantled a few months before I arrived, but Rose told me it had been wonderful and that Richard Burbage himself had performed there and Lord Brown the bear.

I don't know if it was the result of having a theatre but Hackney seemed to be a more open-minded kind of village than Edwardstone. There was no palpable fear of the outsider. Well, except for a lady called Old Mrs Adams who spat at people she walked past and often shouted 'Shit-arse' or 'You walking Hell turd' at them, but people laughed it off. And that didn't really feel like fear of the outsider so much as general hatred for everyone, which was at least a non-discriminatory attitude.

'She spat on my apples once and Grace went for her like a wild cat,' Rose said, the first time I was Hell-turded, which was on my first walk to their cottage.

Their cottage was a timber and plaster affair, near a small stone wall that had its own overly ambitious name – the Great Stone Wall – and was a pebble's throw from a modest stretch of water known as the Great Horsepond. The horses in question could mainly be found in a barn called – I kid you not – the Great Barn.

There was another barn behind that – called, alas, Oat Barn – and beyond there were the fruit orchards, with trees crammed close together for acres and acres. Further along was the stone circle of the well itself, tucked amid beech trees. To a twenty-first-century gaze it would all look quite rustic but to mine, then, the various walled partitions of the land and the close proximity of the trees in the orchard made it seem a very modern kind of place.

Rose and Grace had a deal with one of the local fruit farmers, whereby they would pick and sell the fruit of the season – plums and damsons and cherries, but also apples and greengages and gooseberries – and split the money they made unevenly in the favour of the farmer, Mr Sharpe, 'a tight-fisted miser', who had cultivated the fruit.

The cottage had more windows than I had seen in a house for a long time. It was nothing at all to what I had known in France, but it was a more advanced kind of lodging to the one I'd known in Edwardstone.

'So,' Rose asked me. She had a forthright look about her. A grown-up, take-no-nonsense look. 'What is your name?'

'Tom,' I said. Which was the truth. But then I worried about the truth of me, and how it was dangerous. So I lied about my surname, for the first of many times: 'Tom *Smith*.'

'And so, how old are you, Tom Smith?'

I had to be careful here. The truth – eighteen – probably wouldn't have been believed. And if it had been believed then it would have been dangerous for her to know. And yet I simply could not tell her the age she most likely assumed, thirteen or fourteen.

'How old are you?'

She laughed at me. 'I asked you first.'

'I have sixteen years.'

She didn't bat an eye at that. I suppose I was lucky in that when the condition took hold I was already tall, thick-necked and broad-shouldered. 'Your eyes look older,' is all she said. Which I found a marvellous comfort, as everyone in Edwardstone had been convinced I was set in stone in my early teens.

'And I have eighteen,' she said. 'And Grace has ten.'

This was fine. This talk. It was fine. But I didn't want to reveal any more. I couldn't. I was a dangerous secret. It was better for them not to know about me.

They gave me a meal of bread and parsnip pottage and cherries.

Rose's smile was like warm air. 'You should have been here yesterday. We had pigeon pie. Grace is a master pigeon-catcher.'

Grace mimed catching a pigeon and twisting its neck.

A moment passed. Then, inevitably, another question.

'Why did you come here?' Rose asked.

'You invited me.'

'Not *here*. Why were you heading to London? On your own? What are you fleeing from?'

'Suffolk. If you had ever been there you wouldn't even question it. It is full of pig-headed superstitious hateful people. We were from France, you see. We never fitted in there.'

'We?'

'I mean, when my mother was still alive.'

'What happened to her?'

I stared at Rose. 'There are some things I would rather not talk of.'

Grace noticed my hand, the one holding the soup spoon. 'He is shaking.'

'He is also across the table,' Rose said. 'You can speak as if he is here.' Then her eyes were upon me again. 'I didn't mean to upset you.'

'If the price of this food and a night of comfort is to talk of painful things then I would rather sleep outside in a ditch.'

Rose's eyes flashed with anger. 'You will find Hackney has some excellent ditches.'

I put down my spoon and stood up.

'Do they never jest in Suffolk?'

'I told you I am from France. And I am in no mood for jesting.'

'You are a sour thing, aren't you? Curdled like milk.'

Grace made a show of sniffing the air like a dog. 'He even smells sour.'

Rose was stern with me. 'Sit down, Tom. You have nowhere to go. And besides, you must stay here until you have paid us what you owe.'

I was a mess. I was confused. There was too much intensity inside me, after three weary days of walking and grieving. I wasn't angry with these sisters, I was grateful to them, but that gratitude was swallowed up inside the pain of closing my eyes and seeing Manning's hands.

'You are not the only one with sorrows in this world. Don't hoard them like they are precious. There is always plenty of them to go around.'

'I'm sorry,' I said.

Rose nodded. 'That is all right. You are tired. And other things. You will sleep in the boys' room.'

'The boys' room?'

She explained it was called the boys' room because there had been two brothers – Nat and Rowland – but they were both dead. Nat had died of typhoid when he was twelve, and poor baby Rowland had died of a mystery cough before his first birthday. This led on to an explanation of how their parents were dead too: their mother had died of 'childbed fever' (a common thing back in the day), a month after giving birth to Rowland, which explained the baby's frailty, and their father had died of smallpox. The girls seemed quite matter-of-fact about it all. Though apparently Grace often woke in the night, having nightmares about little Rowland.

'See,' Rose said, sprinkling salt on my shame. 'Plenty of sorrows to go around.'

She took me into the room. There was a little square window about the size of a portable television from 1980. (When I lived in a hotel in São Paulo in 1980 I watched a lot of TV. It made me think of the small square Hackney window.) The room was spare and modest but the bed had blankets and even though the mattress was stuffed with straw I was so tired that the queen's four poster itself wouldn't have seemed any comfier.

I fell on the bed, and she pulled my shoes off and she looked at me, and the motherly sternness she had displayed before melted away and she said softly, as if to my soul itself, 'It will be fine, Tom. Rest now.'

But the next thing I knew it was the dead of night and I was sitting up in bed awake from the sound of my own scream with a fat full moon outside the window and my whole body was shaking and I could hardly breathe. Terror was flooding into me from every side.

Rose was now there, holding my arm. Grace, behind her, yawned sleep away at the doorway.

'It is all right, Tom.'

'It will never be,' I said, half delirious.

'Dreams are not to be believed. Especially the bad ones.'

I didn't tell her the dream was a memory. I had to try instead to deny the reality of what I knew and dream up a new one, as Tom Smith. She sent Grace back to bed and stayed there beside me. She leaned towards me and kissed me on the lips. It was just a peck, but a peck on the lips was not just a peck.

'What was that for?' I asked.

I could just about see her smile in the moonlight. It wasn't a flirtatious smile. It was a plain, matter-of-fact one. 'For you to have something else to occupy your mind.'

'I am not sure I have ever met someone like you,' I said.

'That is good. What point would my life have, if there was a duplicate?'

There was a tear in her eye.

'What's the matter?'

'This was the bed Nat slept in. It's strange. The space where he was being filled again. That's all. He was there, and now he isn't there.'

I saw she was hurt, and for a moment I felt selfish in my own grief. 'I can sleep somewhere else. I could sleep on the floor.'

She shook her head and smiled. 'No, no.'

Breakfast was rye bread and a small cup of ale. Grace had some ale too. It was the one drink people could afford that they knew wouldn't kill them. Unlike water, of course, which was basically Russian roulette.

'This is my house,' Rose explained, 'and the lease has passed to me now my parents have died. So, so long as you live here, you must live by my rules. And the first rule is that you will pay us what you owe, and after that you can pay us two shillings a week as long as you stay here. And help us fetch the water.'

As long as you stay here.

It was quite a nice prospect, having somewhere I could stay indefinitely. And the cottage was a sufficient home. Dry and clean and well aired and smelling of lavender. A bunch of lavender, I now noted, stuck out of a simple vase. There was a fireplace for when the weather became cool. The cottage was a little larger than the one in Edwardstone, with separate rooms, but the same level of care was taken to keep everything as clean and tidy and well scented as possible.

And yet, the offer of indefinitely staying there – if that is what it was – made me feel sad.

I had the sense, even then, that there could be nothing permanent in my life from now on.

You see, at this point, I didn't know things were going to change. I had no understanding of my condition. It had no name. And I wouldn't have known even if it had. I just assumed that was it. I was going to stay looking this age for ever. Which you might think would be quite joyful but, no, not really. My condition had already caused the death of my mother. I knew I wouldn't be able to tell Rose or her sister about it, without putting them at similar risk. And back then, things changed fast, especially if you were young. Faces changed almost with the seasons.

'Thank you,' I told her.

'It will be good for Grace, having you here. She misses her brothers greatly, we both do. But if you cause any mischief – if you bring us into any disrepute – and if you refuse to pay' – she held the moment like a cherry still to be swallowed – 'you will be out on your arse.'

'In a ditch?'

'Covered in shit,' said little Grace, having finished her ale.

'Sorry, Tom. Grace is her name, not a description.'

'Shit is a fine word,' I said diplomatically. 'It is quick to its point.'

'There are no ladies in this house,' Rose said.

'And I am no lord.' Now wasn't the time to tell them that I was, however, technically a member of the French aristocracy.

Rose sighed. I can remember her sighs. They were rarely sad sighs. They always had a sense of *this is the way things are and how they are going to be and that is perfectly fine* about them. 'Good. Well, today is a new day.'

I liked these two. They were a comfort amid the silent howl of grief.

I wanted to stay. But I didn't want them to be in danger. They couldn't be curious about me. That was the main thing.

'My mother was thrown from a horse,' I said, from out of nowhere. 'That's how she died.'

'That's sad,' said Grace.

'Yes,' said Rose. 'Very sad.'

'That is what I dream of sometimes.'

129

She nodded. She may still have had questions but she kept them inside.

'You should probably rest today. Restore your humours. So, while we go to the orchard you can stay in the cottage. And tomorrow you can go and play your lute and bring us money.'

'No, no, I will pay my debt. I will earn some money today. You are right, I will go into the street and I will play.'

'Any street?' asked Grace, amused.

'A busy one.'

Rose shook her head. 'You need to be in London. South of the city walls.'

She pointed. She showed me the way.

'A boy playing the lute! They will rain pennies on you.'

'Do you think so?'

'Look, the sun is out. There will be good crowds. It might give you new things to dream about.'

And the sun shone through the window and lit her face and strands of her brown hair turned gold, and for the first time in four days my soul – or what I used to consider my soul – for the smallest sliver of a moment felt something other than insufferable torment.

And her little sister picked up her basket and opened the door and the day streamed in, a slanted rectangle of light working its alchemy on the wooden floor.

'So then,' I said, as if I was going to say something more. And Rose caught my gaze and smiled and nodded as if I just had.

London, now

It is three in the morning.

I really should be in bed. There are only four hours left before I have to be up for work, for school.

Yet, realistically, there is no way I am getting to sleep. I switch off the Discovery Channel documentary about Ming, the five-hundred-and-seven-year-old clam, which I was watching on the computer.

I am sitting here staring at the screen. It probably isn't very good for my headache to be doing this. But I am resigned to it now. It is the curse of the alba. A kind of altitude sickness, but of time, not height. The competing memories, the jumble of time, the stress of it all, made these headaches an inevitability.

And then, of course, being threatened at knife point hadn't helped. And seeing Anton among the boys had unsettled me.

I go on the BBC and *Guardian* websites. I read a couple of news articles about fracturing US and Chinese relations. Everyone in the comments section is predicting the apocalypse. This is the chief comfort of being four hundred and thirty-nine years old. You understand quite completely that the main lesson of history is: humans don't learn from history. The twenty-first century could still turn out to be a bad cover version of the twentieth, but what could we do? People's minds across the world were filling with utopias that could never overlap. It was a recipe for disaster, but, alas, a familiar one. Empathy was waning, as it often had. Peace was made of porcelain, as it always was.

After reading the news, I go on Twitter. I don't have an account but I find it interesting – all the different voices, the squabbles, the arrogance of certainty, the ignorance, the occasional, but wonderful, compassion, and watching the evolution of language head towards a new kind of hieroglyphics.

I then do what I always do, and type the names 'Marion Hazard' and 'Marion Claybrook' into Google, but there is nothing new. If she is alive, she isn't using either name.

Then I head over to Facebook.

I see a post from Camille.

'Life is confusing.'

That is all it says. It has six likes. I feel guilty about how rude I was to her. I wonder, as I often do, if it is ever going to be possible to have anything resembling a normal life. Looking at Camille made me want that. There was an intensity to her that I could sense and relate to. I can imagine sitting next to her on a bench, watching Abraham. Just sitting there, in the comfortable silence of a couple. I haven't wanted such a thing for centuries.

I shouldn't do anything, really. But I find myself pressing 'like' on her update, and even adding 'C'est vrai' as a comment. The moment I comment and see the words there with my name beside them I think I should delete them.

But I don't. I leave them. And I go to bed, a bed Abraham is already asleep on. He is whimpering in his sleep.

For years now I had convinced myself that the sadness of the memories weighed more and lasted longer than the moments of happiness themselves. So I had, through some crude emotional mathematics, decided it was better not to seek out love or companionship or even friendship. To be a little island in the alba archipelago, detached from humanity's continent, instead. Hendrich was right, I believed. It was best not to fall in love.

But recently, now, I was starting to feel that you couldn't do mathematics with emotions. In protecting yourself from hurt you could create a new, subtler type of pain. It is a dilemma. And not one I am going to solve tonight.

Life is confusing.

That is all we really know, I think, and the thought keeps repeating like a musical motif as I slowly fall into sleep.

London, 1599

Bankside, in those days, was made up of liberties. A liberty was a designated area outside the city walls where normal laws didn't apply. In fact, no laws applied. Anything went. Any kind of trade could be plied. Any entertainment was allowed, however disreputable. Prostitution. Bear-baiting. Street performance. *Theatre.* You name it. It was there.

It was an area, essentially, of freedom. And the first thing I discovered about freedom was that it smelled of shit. Of course, compared to now, everywhere in or out of London smelled of shit. But Bankside, in particular, was the shittiest. That was because of the tanneries dotted about the place. There were five tanneries all in close proximity, just after you crossed the bridge. And the reason they stank, I would later learn, was because tanners steeped the leather in faeces.

As I walked on, the smell fused into others. The animal fat and bones from the makers of glue and soap. And the stale sweat of the crowd. It was a whole new world of stench.

I walked past the bear garden – called the Paris Garden for some reason I never knew – and saw a giant black-furred bear in chains. It looked like the saddest creature I had ever seen. Wounded and unkempt and resigned to his fate, sitting on the ground. The bear was a celebrity. A major draw of Bankside. 'Sackerson' they called him. And there would be many times I would see or hear him in action over the coming weeks and months, pink-eyed, clawing dogs from his throat, his mouth frothing with rage, as the crowd roared in cruel and fevered excitement. It was the only time the bear ever seemed alive, when it was fighting off death. And I would often think of that bear, and that pointless will to survive, through whatever kind of cruelty and pain life chose to throw in his direction.

Anyway, on that first day, I had followed Rose's directions but I did not necessarily feel like I had come to the right place. It was far enough away from the noise of the soapmakers, though not as far as I would have liked from a shit-smelling tannery. There were some people milling around. There was a woman in green, with a blackened tooth and coarsely powdered face, staring at me with some curiosity as she leaned against the wall of a stone building with a painted sign depicting a cardinal's hat. This, as I already suspected, was one of the many brothels in the area. The busiest, it turned out, with a flurry of trade at any time of day. There was also an inn. The Queen's Tavern. It was one of the more pristine buildings in the area, although its clientele turned out to be at the filthier end of the scale.

There was an open space in front of this pub and the brothel, a rectangle of grass where people hung about, and that was the spot where I decided to stand.

I took a deep breath.

And then I started to play.

There was no shame in music. There was no shame even in *playing* music. Even Queen Elizabeth herself could strum the odd instrument or two. But playing music in public – in both France, and here in England – was something you didn't do if you were from a noble background. Certainly you didn't do it on the street. For the son of a French count and countess to be there, playing music in the least salubrious part of Bankside, would have been something of a disgrace.

And yet, I played.

I played some French chansons my mother had taught me and people walked by and raised the occasional eyebrow. But throughout

135

the day my confidence grew and I switched to English songs and ballads and I quickly acquired an audience. Once or twice, someone in the audience even threw a penny. I had seen from the other performers that the thing to do was to take around a hat at regular intervals – much as buskers still do today – but I had no hat, so I went around after every couple of songs with my left shoe, hopping around, which the crowd seemed to enjoy as much as the music. The audience was a strange and intimidating mix of watermen and hawkers and drunks and prostitutes and theatre-goers. Half heading from the tenements to the south and half – the half more prone to losing pennies – from across the bridge. It may have been because of the gawping crowd that I found I played best when I closed my eyes. At the end of the first day, I had made enough to pay for the basket of fruit. By the end of the week, I had paid for a new basket.

'Don't get ahead of yourself, Tom Smith,' said Rose, stifling her smile, eating the hot rabbit pie I had bought on my way home. 'You still have your lodgings to pay for.'

'Can we have a meat pie every day?' asked Grace, her face deco-rated in pastry crumbs. 'It's a lot better than stew and shitting parsnips.'

'Parsnips do not shit, Grace.'

'And better for you than parsnips too,' I told her, recounting the wisdom of the day. 'You'd never catch the queen or a nobleman eating a parsnip.'

Rose rolled her eyes. 'We are not noblemen, though, that is the thing.'

To them I was just Tom Smith from Suffolk and that was how it would have to stay. And besides, I knew I would never be a count. I would never live in a fine house again. There would be no manservants for me. My parents were dead. France was a hostile world to me. I was a street performer in London. Any airs above that station would only lead to trouble.

I had duly paid my first two weeks' lodgings by the following Tuesday. And from that moment on, I was an equal in the cottage, and part of the family. I felt, in short, like I belonged, and I tried my best to ignore the future and the problems that might come. While singing a madrigal to a large pre-theatre crowd or watching Rose's cheeks bloom with colour, mid-laugh, I could imagine that I was happy.

Grace wanted to learn how to play the lute so one night I began giving her lessons. Her hand hung over the strings like a spider dangling from a roof. I repositioned it, so her fingers were parallel with the length of the instrument.

She wanted to learn how to play 'Greensleeves' and 'The Sweet and Merry Month of May', two of her favourites. I was a bit worried about teaching her 'Greensleeves'. As with much of the popular music throughout history, 'Greensleeves' was a wildly inappropriate tune for a child to know. I wasn't that worldly wise at that time but I was wise enough to know that Lady Greensleeves was the standard insult du jour for promiscuous women. Her sleeves were green because of all that outdoor sex she was supposedly having. But still, Grace was adamant, and I didn't want to burst her innocence in the name of protecting it, and so I obliged her with lessons. She was quite hard to teach, wanting to run before she could walk, but we persevered with each other. We played outside on midsummer's eve and I turned to see Rose watching us from the window, smiling.

One evening, around the beginning of autumn, Rose came into my room. She was tired. She seemed different. A bit muted, a bit lost.

'What's the matter?'

'A million little things. No matter.'

There was something I felt she wanted to tell me but didn't.

She sat on the bed and asked if I could teach her to play the lute. She said if I taught her how to play she would lower the rent by five pence. I said yes. Not so much because of the rent, but because I welcomed the excuse to sit next to her a while.

She had another little mole, like the two on her cheek, between her thumb and forefinger. Her hands were stained a little from the leftover cherries she'd been eating. I imagined holding her hand. What a childish thought! Maybe my brain was still as young as my face looked.

'It is a beautiful lute. I have never seen one like it. All the decoration,' she said.

'My mother received it from . . . a friend. And you see this here?' – I pointed to the ornately crafted sound-hole, under the strings – 'It's called the rose.'

'It is nothing but air.'

I laughed. 'It is the most important part.'

I got her to play two strings, back and forth, plucking at a quickening pace, along with my heart. I touched her arm. I closed my eyes, and felt fearful of how much I felt for her.

'Music is about time,' I told her. 'It is about controlling time.'

When she stopped playing, she looked thoughtful for a moment and said something like, 'I sometimes want to stop time. I sometimes want, in a happy moment, for a church bell never to ring again. I want not to ever have to go to the market again. I want for the starlings to stop flying in the sky . . . But we are all at the mercy of time. We are all the strings, aren't we?'

She definitely said that last bit: *We are all the strings.*

Rose was too good for picking fruit. Rose was a philosopher, really. She was the wisest person I ever knew. (And I would soon know Shakespeare, so that's saying a lot.) She talked to me as if I was her age and I loved her for that. When I was with her, everything faded away and I felt calm. She was a counterbalance. She gave me peace just by looking at her, which might explain why I looked at her for too long, and with too much intensity in my eyes. The way people never look at people any more. I wanted her in every sense. To want is to lack. That is what it means. There was an emptiness, a void, made vast and wide when my mother had drowned, which I thought was never-ending, but when I looked at Rose I started to feel solid again, as if there was something to hold on to. Steady.

'I want you to stay, Tom.'

'Stay?'

'Yes. Stay. Here.'

'Oh.'

'I don't want you to have to leave. Grace likes having you here. And I do too. Very much so. You are a comfort to us both. The place has felt too empty, and now it does not.'

'Well, I like being here.'

'Good.'

'But one day I may have to leave.'

'And why would that be?'

I wanted to tell her, right then. I wanted to say that I was different and strange and peculiar. That I would not grow old like other people grow old. I wanted to tell her that my mother had not been bucked off a horse and that she had drowned on the ducking stool, accused of murder by witchcraft. I wanted to tell her about William Manning. I wanted to tell her how hard it was to feel responsible for losing the person you had loved the most. To tell her the frustration of being a mystery, even to yourself. That there was some flaw in the balance of my humours. I wanted to tell her that my first name was Estienne and that my last name was Hazard, not Smith. I wanted to tell her that she had been the one true comfort I had known since Mother died. All these wants rose up, but had nowhere to go.

'I can't say.'

'You are a mystery to be solved.'

A moment of stillness.

Birdsong.

'Have you ever been kissed, Tom?' I thought of that first night, when she had given me a small peck on my lips. 'A proper kiss, Tom?' Rose clarified, as if reading my mind.

My silence was the embarrassing answer.

'A kiss,' she said, 'is like music. It stops time . . . I had a romance once,' she said simply. 'One summer. He worked in the orchard. We kissed and did merry things together but I never really felt for him. If you feel for someone, just one single kiss can stop the sparrows, they say. Do you think that can happen?'

And she placed the lute beside her on the bed and kissed me and I closed my eyes and the rest of the world faded. There was nothing else. Nothing but her. She was the stars and the heavens and the oceans. There was nothing but that single fragment of time, and this bud of love we had planted inside it. And then, at some point after it started, the kiss ended, and I stroked her hair, and the church bells rang in the distance and everything in the world was in alignment.

London, now

I am standing in front of the year nine class. Again. I am tired. Going to bed after three is not what teachers should do. Raindrops shine like jewels on the windows. Continuing from the disastrous previous lesson on immigration, I am starting to discuss the social history of late Tudor, specifically Elizabethan, England.

'What do you know about Elizabethan England?' I ask, while thinking, *Maybe this time I should have chosen, say, Sardinia. Or to be among lemon groves in Mallorca. Or by a beach in Indonesia. Or on a palm-filled island beside turquoise waters in the Maldives.* 'Who lived there?'

A girl puts her hand up. 'People who're dead now.'

'Thanks, Lauren.'

'Anyone else?'

'People with no Snapchat.'

'True, Nina.'

'Sir Francis Someone.'

I nod. 'Drake and Bacon. Take your pick. But who now do we think of as the person who defined that era in England?'

For decades and decades and decades I have bemoaned people who say they feel old, but I now realise it is perfectly possible for anyone to feel old. All they need to do is become a teacher.

And then my eyes rest on the one person I am surprised to see here.

'Anton? Do you know anyone from Elizabethan times?'

Anton looks at me timidly. He is scared. Guilty. 'Shakespeare,' he says, almost like an apology.

'Yes! It was the age of Shakespeare. Now, what do you know about Shakespeare, Anton?'

Lauren obliged. 'He's dead, sir.'

'I'm detecting a theme, Lauren.'

'Happy to help, sir.'

'*Romeo and Juliet*,' says Anton, his voice quiet, hoping he is making things all right. 'And *Henry the Fourth Part One.* We're studying it in English.'

I hold his gaze, enough for him to look down at his desk in shame.

'What do you think he was like? How do you think he lived?'

Anton doesn't answer.

'The thing I want to get across, though, is that Shakespeare was a person. I mean, he lived. He was a man. He was an actual man. Not just a writer, but a businessman, a networker, a producer. A man who walked real streets in real rain and drank ale and ate real oysters. A man who wore an earring and smoked and breathed and slept and went to the toilet. A man with hands and feet and bad breath.'

'But,' says Lauren, coiling her hair around a finger, 'how do you know what his breath smelled like, sir?'

And I think for a moment how nice it would be if they could know. But of course I just smile and say something about a lack of toothpaste and get on with the lesson.

London, 1599

I had been playing the lute in Southwark all summer and into autumn. I often worked late, till after they closed the city gates, and had to walk the long way home, which could take over an hour.

Now, the weather had turned and the crowds were thinning out. I went around all the inns, asking for work, but they didn't have any room for me. Being an inn musician was seen as a far better thing to be than a random street performer. I was part of a dying and undesirable breed, I realised. The trouble was, though, that there was a band of musicians – Pembroke's Men – who had the market pretty much sewn up.

And having heard I was after a job, one of them – a giant bearded fiddler known locally as 'Wolstan the Tree' on account of his size and, possibly, the fact that his wild hair looked a bit like foliage in a storm – came up to me outside the Cardinal's Hat just as it was getting dark.

He grabbed me by the neck and slammed me hard against a wall.

'Leave him be,' said Elsa, a friendly flame-haired prostitute I always spoke to on the way home.

'Shut up, wench.' Then he turned to me. His teeth were rotten, just a random row of brown pebbles. It was hard to tell if the smell of shit was coming from him or the tanners next door. 'You ain't playin' music in any inn this side of Bishopsgate, lad. Especially not round Bankside. Not alive, you ain't. This is ours. Ain't no place for lamb-faced boys like you.'

I spat in his face.

He grabbed the neck of the lute.

'Get off that!'

'I'm going to break this first, and then your fingers.'

'Give it me back, you thieving—'

Elsa was over at him now. 'Ho, Wolstan! Give it him back!'

He swung the lute high behind him, ready to swing it and smash it against the wall.

Then came a voice, a grand, deep theatrical kind of voice.

'Stop there, Wolstan.'

Wolstan turned to see the three men who had just appeared on the path behind him.

'Oh my,' said Elsa, suddenly excited – or, very possibly, feigning it – as she smoothed the creases in her dress with strokes as slow as cat licks. The whole area was theatre. On or off the stage. 'It's Richard the Third himself.'

Of course, it wasn't Richard the Third. It was Richard Burbage, who even I knew was the most famous actor in London. He was quite formidable-looking at that time. He was not an Errol Flynn or a Tyrone Power or a Paul Newman or a Ryan Gosling. If he was on Tinder he'd be lucky to get a single swipe right. His hair was thin and mousy and his face as lumpy and misshapen as Rembrandt's, but he had something else, something Elizabethans recognised in a way people in the twenty-first century no longer do: an *aura*. Something strong and metaphysical, a soul sense, a presence, a power.

'A splendid evening to you, Mr Burbage, sir,' said the Tree, lowering the lute.

'But not, it would appear, to everyone,' said Burbage.

I noticed the other two men. One was as round as a barrel, and with an impressive beard, neater than Wolstan's. He was sneering so dramatically I guessed he was another actor. He seemed quite drunk.

'You frothing stream of bull's piss, give the boy his lute back.'

The other man was slim and quite handsome, albeit with a small mouth and long hair combed back ill-advisedly. His eyes were soft and cow-like. Like the other two, he was dressed in a padded, laced and buttoned doublet; in his case gold-coloured, I think, though it was hard to tell in the fading light. A well-paid bohemian, complete with gold hooped earring. These were clearly actors, and well-paid ones. I knew they must have been members of the Lord Chamberlain's Men, along with Burbage.

'Fie . . . Look here. Look at this. Hell is empty and all the devils are here on Bankside,' said the handsome one, in a resigned but bitter kind of way.

Elsa noticed this man. 'Shakespeare himself.'

Shakespeare – for it was he – smiled the smallest of smiles.

Elsa turned to the man next to Shakespeare, who was as large as a barrel. 'And I know who you are too. You're the other Will. Will Kemp.'

Kemp nodded, and patted his stomach with pride. 'I am he.'

'Give me my lute,' I told Wolstan one more time, and this time he knew the night was against him. He placed the lute in my hands and sloped off.

Elsa gave a mocking wave, waggling her little finger. 'A pox on you, maggot-cock!'

The three actors laughed. 'Come on, let's head to the Queen's for a quart,' said Kemp.

Shakespeare frowned at his friend as if he were a headache. 'You ale-soused old apple.'

Elsa was whispering into Richard Burbage's ear as he was helping himself to a feel of her.

Shakespeare came over to me. 'Wolstan is a beast.'

'Yes, Mr Shakespeare.'

He smelled of ale and tobacco and cloves. 'It is a shame to see the Tree being himself . . . So, lad, do you play well?'

I was still a little shook up. 'Well?'

'At the lute.'

'I suppose, sir.'

He leaned in closer. 'How old are you?'

'Sixteen, sir,' I said, keeping my age consistent with what Rose thought.

'You look two years less than that. At least. But also two years more. Your face is a riddle.'

'I have sixteen years, sir.'

'No matter, no matter . . .' He wobbled slightly and rested his hand on my chest, as if for support. He was as drunk as the others, I realised. But he straightened himself up.

'We, the shareholders of the Lord Chamberlain's Men, are currently looking for musicians. I have written a new play, *As You Like It*, and it requires music. There are a lot of songs. And we need a *lute*. You see, we had a lutist but the pox has taken him.'

I stared at Shakespeare. His eyes contained two golden fires, reflecting a nearby burning torch.

Kemp, tugging Burbage away from Elsa's attentions, was keen to speed things up, so said to me brusquely: 'Tomorrow, the Globe, by eleven of the clock.'

Shakespeare ignored him. 'Play now,' he said, nodding at the lute.

'Now?'

'While the iron is hot.'

Elsa started singing a bawdy song I didn't know.

'The poor lad is still shaken,' said Kemp, feigning sympathy. 'Onwards.'

'No,' said Shakespeare. 'Let the boy play.'

'I don't know what I shall play.'

'Play from the heart. Pretend we are not here. To thine own self be true.'

He hushed Elsa.

Eight eyes watched me.

146

So I closed mine and played a tune I had recently been playing, and thought of Rose as I did so.

> *All the day the sun that lends me shine*
> *By frowns do cause me pine*
> *And feeds me with delay;*
> *Her smiles, my springs that makes my joys to grow,*
> *Her frowns the Winters of my woe.*

When I stopped singing I looked at the four faces staring silently at me.

'Ale!' shouted Kemp. 'Lord, give me ale!'

'The boy's good,' said Burbage, 'if you ignore the song.'

'And the singing,' said Elsa.

'You play well,' said Shakespeare. 'Be at the Globe Theatre tomorrow. Eleven o'clock. Twelve shillings a week.'

'Thank you, Mr Shakespeare.'

'Twelve shillings a *week*?'

Rose couldn't believe it. It was morning. We were out fetching water before work. Rose had to stop and place the bucket of water down. I placed mine down too. The water – for cleaning, not drinking – was from the well at the end of the lane, nearly a mile north of Oat Barn and the orchards, so we needed the rest. The morning sky blushed an ominous pink.

'Yes. Twelve shillings a week.'

'Working for Mr Shakespeare?'

'The Lord Chamberlain's Men. Yes.'

'Tom, that is joy.'

She hugged me. Like a sister. More than a sister.

And then a cloud of sadness fell across her face as she picked up her bucket again.

'What?'

147

'I expect we won't be seeing much more of you then.'

'I will walk home each evening just the same. Around the walls or through.'

'That was not my meaning.'

'So, what is your meaning?'

'Your life will be too colourful for a dull market girl.'

'You are not dull, Rose.'

'A blade of grass is not dull until you see a flower.'

'It is. A blade of grass is always dull. You are not a blade of grass.'

'And you are not a stayer, Tom. You ran from France. And you ran from Suffolk. You will run from here. You do not settle. Since we kissed even your eyes fear settling on mine.'

'Rose, if ever I flee it will not be because of you.'

'So when you flee why will it be, Tom? Why will it be?'

And that I couldn't answer.

The water was heavy but we were nearly home. We had reached the stables now, and saw a row of horses, like lords in a gallery watching a play they had already seen, staring at us. Rose fell silent. I felt guilty for the lie I had told about my mother's death. I needed to tell her the truth about me. At some point, I would surely have to.

Just as we were reaching the cottage, we saw two women in the street. One of the women was Old Mrs Adams. She was shouting at another. Hell-turding away.

Rose knew the other woman from Whitechapel Market. Mary Peters.

A quiet woman, with a sad look about her. She was probably forty. Which, back then, was an age you could not take for granted you would reach. She wore widow's black all the time.

Old Mrs Adams was leaning in, spitting mad words at her, but Mary turned to stare her down with such a silent fury the old lady backed away like a cat suddenly scared of its prey.

Then Mary kept on walking down Well Lane towards us.

She didn't seem the least bit disturbed by her encounter with Old Mrs Adams. Rose, I noted, seemed to tighten a little at the sight of Mary.

'Good morrow, Mary.'

Mary smiled briefly. She looked at me. 'Is this your Tom?'

Your Tom.

It felt embarrassingly good. To know Rose had spoken of me. To feel as if I belonged to her. It made me feel solid, real, as if the space I occupied was meant to be occupied by me.

'Yes. Yes, it is.' Rose blushed a little. Faint pink, like the morning clouds.

Mary nodded. Took it in. 'He's not there today. You and Grace will be pleased to hear this.'

'Really?' Rose seemed relieved.

'He has a fever. Let's hope it is the pox, eh?'

I was confused. 'Who are we talking about?'

Mary shrank back a little, as if she had said something she shouldn't have.

'Just Mr Willow,' Rose said. 'The warden from the market.'

Mary was walking away. 'I shall see you there later.'

'You shall.'

As we carried on towards the cottage I asked Rose about Mr Willow.

'Oh, don't worry. He is a little strict, that's all.'

And that was all she said. The next thing I knew she was talking about Mary. Rose said that she had come to the area a few years ago and was a very private person. She wouldn't be drawn into talking about her past so there wasn't much to tell.

'She is a kind woman. But she is a mystery. Much as you are. But I will solve you. Tell me something I do not know. A small thing. A crumb.'

I could buy all the gold on the Strand and I would still rather be living in a small cottage on Well Lane if it meant living with you, I didn't say.

'I saw a boatman fall in the Thames just yesterday, right below Nonesuch House, with all the crowds there watching, and all I thought was how I wished you were there to see it too.'

'My sense of amusement isn't as cruel as yours.'

'He lived, I believe.'

She gave a suspicious and cynical kind of look. I gave her something else.

'I like the way you look after Grace. The way you know yourself. The way you have made a life, a good one, with a good home, when you have lost so much. You find beauty where there is none. You are the light that glimmers in a puddle.'

'A puddle?' she laughed. 'I am sorry. Go on . . . I am starved of compliments. Feed me more.'

'I like the way you think. I like the way you don't just go through life unaware of its nature.'

'I am not a pale theatre lady. I am a fruit picker. I am plain.'

'You are the least plain thing I know.'

Her hand was on me. 'My clothes are just rags with dreams.'

'You may be better without them, then.'

'Dreams?'

'No.'

I was standing close to her now. And I held her gaze. There was no running away. I had no idea I had been looking for her, but now I had found her, I had no idea what would happen. I felt like I was spinning fast and out of control, like the seed of a sycamore, travelling on a changing wind.

'Go,' she said. 'Save our pleasure. You will be late.'

We kissed and I closed my eyes and inhaled lavender and her, and I felt so terrified and so in love that I realised they – the terror, the love – were one and the same thing.

150

London, now

I remember how it feels, that dizzy spinning fusion of love and terror. I remember, as the bell rings. I remember the orchard scent of her hair, and still miss her so much it can burn.

Steady thyself.

I open my eyes, and see Anton sloping out of the room.

'Anton,' I say, 'a minute.'

He looks scared. He has looked like that for the whole lesson. He is in the process of putting an earphone in his ear.

'Do you like music?'

He seems confused by the question. He'd been expecting another one. Everything about him was playing it cool except his eyes. 'Yeah. Yes, sir.'

'Do you play?'

He nods. 'Yeah, piano, a bit. My mum taught me when I was younger.'

'You have to be careful with that. It can screw you up. Messes with your brain chemistry. The emotion.'

He looks at me quizzically.

I move on. 'Does your mum know about your friends?'

He shrugs sheepishly.

'Because you could do better.'

He knows he can't sulk, but he almost does. Pouts a little. 'Si isn't my friend. He's just the older brother of someone I know.'

'Someone? A school someone? Someone from here?'

He shakes his head. 'Used to be.'

'Used to be?'

'He got expelled.'

I nod. It made sense.

There is a pause. His face clenches, building up to something. 'Did you mean what you said last night? About killing someone.'

'Oh yes. Yes, I did. In a desert. Arizona. Quite a long time ago. I don't advise it.'

He laughs, doesn't quite know if it is a joke. (It isn't.) 'Did you ever get caught?'

'No, not in the way you mean. No, I didn't. But as you get older, Anton, you realise that you never get away with things. The human mind has its own. . . prisons. You don't have a choice over everything in life.'

'Yeah. I've worked that one out, sir.'

'You can't choose where you are born, you can't decide who won't leave you, you can't choose much. A life has unchangeable tides the same as history does. But there is still room inside it for choice. For decisions.'

'I suppose.'

'It's true. You make the wrong decision in the present and it haunts you, just as the Treaty of Versailles in nineteen nineteen sowed the ground for Hitler to take power in nineteen thirty-three, so every present moment is paying for a future one. Just one wrong turn can get you very lost. What you do in the present stays with you. It comes back. You don't get away with anything.'

'Seems that way.'

'People talk about a moral compass and I think that is it. We always know the right and wrong for ourselves, the north and south. You have to trust it, Anton. People can tell you all kinds of wrong directions, lead you around any corner. You can't trust any of that. You can't even trust me. What do they say in car adverts? About the navigation system? *Comes as standard.* Everything you need to know about right and wrong is already there. It comes as standard. It's like music. You just have to listen.'

152

He nods. I have no idea if any of this has gone in, or if he is just bored or frightened and wants to get out of the room as quickly as he can.

'Okay, sir. Good speech.'

'Okay.'

Strange saying this to a mayfly. As if I care. Hendrich has always told me there is nothing more dangerous than caring for an ordinary mortal human, because it 'compromises our priorities'. But maybe Hendrich's priorities are no longer my priorities, and maybe they need to be compromised. Maybe I just need to feel vaguely human again. It has been a while. It has been four hundred years.

I decide to lighten the tone. 'Do you like school, Anton?'

He shrugs. 'Sometimes. Sometimes it seems . . . irrelevant.'

'Irrelevant?'

'Yeah. Trigonometry and Shakespeare and shit.'

'Oh yes. Shakespeare. *Henry the Fourth.*'

'*Part One.*'

'Yes, you said. So you don't like it?'

He shrugs. 'We went to see it. School trip. Was pretty boring.'

'You don't like theatre?'

'Nah. It's for old posh people, innit?'

'It didn't used to be like that. It used to be for everyone. It used to be the maddest place in London. You'd get everyone there. You'd get the posh old people, sure, up on the balconies, dressed to be seen, but then you'd get everyone else. You could get in for a penny, which even then wasn't so much. A loaf of bread, that's all. There used to be fights too, sometimes knife fights. People used to throw stuff at the actors if they didn't like what they saw. Oyster shells. Apples. All kinds of stuff. And Shakespeare used to be on the stage too. William Shakespeare. That dead man from the posters. There. On stage. It's not that long ago, not really. History is right here, Anton. It's breathing down our necks.'

He smiles a little. This is the point of being a teacher. A glimmer of hope where you thought it didn't exist. 'You almost sound like you were there.'

'I was,' I say.

'What, sir?'

I smile this time. It is tantalising, to be this close to revealing your own truth, like holding a bird you are about to set free.

'I knew Shakespeare.'

And then he laughs like he *knows* I am joking.

'All right, yeah, Mr Hazard.'

'See you tomorrow.' Tomorrow. I have always hated that word. And yet, somehow, it doesn't grate too much. 'Tomorrow. Yeah.'

London, 1599

I sat in the gallery high above the stage next to an old, snooty, cadaverous man named Christopher, who played the virginal. I say 'old'. He was probably no more than fifty, but he was the oldest of any man working for the Lord Chamberlain's Men. We were visible to much of the audience, should they have cared to look up in our direction, but we were in shadow, and I felt safely anonymous. Christopher rarely said a word to me, either before or after the performance.

I remember one conversation with him.

'You are not from London, are you?' he asked me with disdain.

It was a peculiar disdain, really. Then, as now, much of London was from elsewhere. That was the whole point of London. And, given that there were far more deaths about than births, it was the only way London kept going, and growing.

'No,' I said. 'I am from France. My mother sought refuge here. From the king's forces.'

'The Catholics?'

'Yes.'

'And where is your mother now?'

'She passed.'

Not a flicker of sympathy. Or curiosity. Just a long studious look. 'You play like a Frenchman. You have foreign fingers.'

I stared at my hands. 'Do I?'

'Yes. You stroke the strings rather than pluck them. It makes a strange noise.'

'Well, it is a strange noise that Mr Shakespeare likes.'

'You play well for your age, I suppose. It is a novelty. But you shan't stay young for ever. No one does. Except that boy out east.'

And there it was.

The moment I realised, even in a place as large as London, I still had to be on my guard.

'They killed his mother. She was a witch.'

My heart started beating uncontrollably. It took every ounce of effort to fake a semblance of calm.

'Well, if she drowned, that proved her innocence.'

He looked with suspicion. 'I never said *drowned*.'

'I assumed it was the ducking stool, if it was for witchcraft.'

His eyes narrowed shrewdly. 'You seem most excited about this. Look, your French fingers tremble. To be honest, I don't have the details. It was Hal who told me.'

Hal, the mild-mannered flautist, sitting on the bench in front of ours, didn't really want to be dragged into the conversation. They had known each other for quite a while, and worked on other productions together.

'The son didn't age.' Hal, pale and mousy and small-mouthed, relayed. 'She had cast a charm and killed a man to give her boy eternal life.'

I had no idea what to say.

Christopher was still scrutinising me. And then we heard footsteps on the galley.

'Is this an open conversation?'

It was Shakespeare himself. Standing there, opening an oyster shell, then sucking the mollusc out, careful not to make any mess on the quilted taffeta of his costume. As he savoured the taste his eyes stayed on Christopher.

'Yes,' said Christopher, 'of course.'

'Well, I trust you are making young Tom feel at home.'

'Oh yes, *young* Tom is just fine.'

Shakespeare let the oyster shell drop to the floor. He gave a quick smile. 'Good.'

He pointed at me. 'We need to move you forward, to the next bench. To hear the lute.'

I could see Christopher simmering. It was quite a delicious moment. I stood up and walked to my new position, as Hal budged along. I sat down. The inside of an oyster shell shone up at me from the dusty wood, like a watching eye.

'Thank you, sir,' I said to my employer.

Shakespeare shook his head, impassive. 'I assure you it isn't charity. Now, all of you, play your finest. Sir Walter is in attendance.'

The thing about the front bench was that it meant I had a good view. And the audience was always a show in itself. On a sunny afternoon thousands of people crammed into the place. Far more than you'd fit in the average theatre nowadays, even the Globe. There were often brawls and raucousness among the penny groundlings in the pit and the tuppenny benchers further back. If you had the three pennies needed for a bench *and* a cushion it seemed, somehow, that you thought yourself *above* such things, though I noticed that the bad behaviour returned again when you cast your eye up to the upper classes in the balconies.

In other words, you would get all types. Thieves. Troublemakers. Prostitutes. Pale-faced ladies with artificially blackened teeth to simulate the mark of luxury that was sugar-induced decay (a fact I always remember in our modern age of bottle tans and teeth whitening procedures).

There were many songs to enliven the crowd. I particularly enjoyed 'Under the Greenwood Tree', sung by a jolly blond actor I have forgotten the name of, who played the faithful Lord Amiens, one of the loyal men willing to go into exile in the French forest with the heroine Rosalind's father, Duke Senior.

Who loves to lie with me,
And turn his merry note
Unto the sweet bird's throat,
Come hither, come hither, come hither:
Here shall he see no enemy
But winter and rough weather.

In my mind, the French Forest of Ardennes became la Forêt de Pons that I had known as a child, where Maman and I would sometimes go. We would sit by a large sycamore tree, and she would sing to me there, as I watched falling sycamore seeds. A world far away from the stench and squalor of Bankside, or the smell of beer and shellfish and urine coming from the pit below. Yet the play stirred many other things in me. There were people being exiled, changing their identities, falling in love.

It was a comedy, but I found it quite troubling.

I think it was the character of Jaques that was the problem. He does absolutely nothing. I saw the play eighty-four times and I still can't remember what he did. He just walked around, amid all the bright young optimists, being cynical and miserable. He was played by Shakespeare himself, and every time he spoke, the words got into my bones, as if warning me of my own future:

All the world's a stage,
And all the men and women merely players;
They have their exits and their entrances,
And one man in his time plays many parts . . .

Shakespeare was a strange actor. He was very quiet – I don't mean in volume, I mean in mannerisms and presence. Such the opposite of a Burbage or a Kemp. There was something very un-Shakespearean about Shakespeare, especially when he was sober. A quietness, on stage and off it, as though he was absorbing the world rather than projecting it.

One Thursday I came home and found Grace crying and Rose hugging her. It turned out that Mr Willow had given their space to a woman who gave him sexual favours. He had tried it on with Rose too. And had strong words for both her and Grace.

'It will be all right. We can still work there. Just not in the spot we had.'

I felt such rage. A burning anger devoured me. The next day, before heading to Southwark, I went to the market and I found Mr Willow, and, in my juvenile stupidity, ended up hitting him and shoving him into the spice stall. He fell in an orange cloud of exotic New World aromas.

Grace and Rose were now banned from the market completely. And it was only the knowledge that we knew about his desire for sexual favours that prevented him from taking further action against us.

Rose cursed my hot-headedness, even as she fired back her own in my direction.

It was our first argument. I remember the fury more than the words. I remember her worry about what she would tell Mr Sharpe.

'We can't just *pick* fruit, Tom. We have to *sell* it. Where will we sell it?'

'I will mend this. I broke this. I will mend it, Rose. I promise.'

So I spoke to Shakespeare about the chance of Rose and Grace working as fruit sellers in the theatre. I saw him, after a performance, walking through the crowds on the green, in front of the Queen's Tavern. He was heading into the alehouse, on his own, ignoring a man who recognised him as he disappeared in through the door.

I followed him. I had been in the Queen's before. My young face was no problem there. I found Shakespeare, jar in hand, in a quiet corner.

I was wondering how – and *if* – I should approach him when his hand raised and beckoned me over.

'Young Tom! Take a pew.'

I went over and sat on the bench opposite him, with a small oak table between us. Two men further along the table were studiously engaged in a game of draughts.

'Hello, Mr Shakespeare.'

A barmaid nearby was clearing up abandoned jars, and Shakespeare called over.

'An ale for my friend here.'

She nodded, then Shakespeare reconsidered. 'But you are from France, aren't you? You probably like beer.'

'No, sir. I prefer ale.'

'Your wisdom calms me, Tom. They serve the greatest and sweetest ale in all of London in here.'

He sipped on his, closing his eyes. 'Ale doesn't live well,' he said. 'A week from today this will taste as sour as a knight's breeches. Beer lasts for ever. All the hops, they say, causes its immortality. Ale is a more worthy lesson on life. You wait too long, and you will be saying farewell before you say good day. My father was once an ale taster. I have an education in it.'

The ale came. It was indeed sweet. Shakespeare filled and lit a pipe. Like most theatre types with access to money he was a fan of tobacco. ('The indian herb works wonders for my ailments.') He told me it also helped with his writing.

'Are you writing a new play?' I wondered aloud. 'Am I keeping you from your writing?'

He nodded. 'I am, and, no, you are not.'

'Ah,' I said. (There was no one like Will Shakespeare to make you feel tongue-tied.) 'Good. And good.'

'It shall be called *Julius Caesar*.'

'So it is about the life of Julius Caesar?'

'No.'

'Oh.'

He sucked long on his pipe. 'I hate writing,' he said, through the spiralling smoke. 'That is the truth of it.'

'But you are very good at it.'

'So? My talent is not worth a pot of ale. It signifies nothing. Nought. To be good at writing is to be good at pulling out your own hair. What use is a talent that pains you? It is a gift that smells to heaven and it smells of fox shit. You should rather be a whore in the Cardinal's Hat than be a writer. My quill is my curse.'

I had, I sensed, caught him on a bad day.

'I write because then I can make a play happen and then I and my shareholders can make money. And money is no bad thing. Money stops a man from going mad.' He stared sadly a while. 'I saw my father suffer when I was a boy, not so younger in years than you are now. He was a good man. He could never read but knew many a trade. Ale taster, a glover, then traded wool. And other things. He did well. We dined happily. Fowl every supper. He lost all his money. Loaned it with not a shilling in return once too often. And with a wife and seven children to keep it sent him into an antic disposition for a long time. He would shake and rock and fear the shadow of a mouse. That is why I write. I am just for ever running from madness.' He sighed, glancing over at the draughts board a moment, as one of the men laid their piece down. 'Now, you. What about you? Was your father mad too?'

'I don't know, sir. He died when I was young. He was killed at war. In France.'

'The Catholics?'

'The Catholics.'

'So you came to England?'

I obviously didn't want to be talking about myself, but Shakespeare seemed to want to do exactly that, and if I was going to ask him for a favour, then I had no choice but to oblige.

'We did, yes. Myself and my mother. To Suffolk.'

'And did you not like the country air, Tom?'

'It was not the air that was the problem.'

'The people?'

'There were all manner of things.'

He sipped, he smoked, he studied. 'You possess a young face and a wise tongue. People hate that. They know it could fool them.'

I was worried, felt for a moment like he was testing me. Remembered the conversation with Christopher and Hal.

'Do you know of the Queen's Men?' he asked.

'The troupe of players?'

'That is them. Yes. Well, this man joined them. Henry Hemmings. He had been in some other player companies before, and when people turned suspicious that he was not at time's mercy, he moved to a new company. It gives reason, I would suppose. But by the time he reached the Queen's Men the whispers were flying like sparrows. One of the actors recognised him, from north of ten years before, and a fight broke out. The most vicious fight anyone watching had ever witnessed. At the town of Thame, in the county of Oxfordshire. By the end, two more of the troupe were at him, like dogs at a rabbit.' He rested his pipe carefully on the table, the smoke twisting a thin line directly to the ceiling.

'Were you there?' I asked.

He shook his head. 'I never knew him. Yet I have to thank him.'

'For?'

He smiled, a life-weary smile. 'His death. He died and the Queen's Men had lost one of their key players. So when they came to Stratford I saw their predicament and my opportunity. I asked to join them. I drank with them. We spoke a little on general matters. We spoke of Plutarch and Robin Hood. And then chance blessed me. I became a Queen's Man. And that led me to London.'

'I see.'

He sighed. 'Yet it was in truth an ominous beginning. Though I had no part in his death, the shadow of Hemmings passes over me quite often. And I often feel as though I am, even now, in a place that is not mine. That it happened unjustly. They were a violent and amoral rag-tag band of brothers. Killers. Twelve Wolstan the Trees. And Henry Hemmings had committed no crime, except being different. He had a face that didn't age. That was my beginning – the rotten acorn of it all.'

He looked quite fragile for a moment, then scratched at his beard, and picked up his pipe again. Inhaled and closed his eyes. Blew the smoke over his left shoulder as I sipped my ale.

'The acorn wasn't rotten,' I said.

'Ah, yet the tree is twisted. But there is no moral to this tale, except with mirth and laughter let wrinkles come.' I didn't know for sure if he thought of me as another Henry Hemmings. Nor did I know for sure if Henry Hemmings actually had been like me, or if he was someone who was blessed and cursed with a more youthful disposition than average. I didn't know if Shakespeare knew the story of what had happened in Edwardstone, and whether, possibly, my Suffolk connection had made a link in his mind. Yet I sensed a kind of warning, a friendly one, in his words. 'So, why did you want to see me?'

I took a breath.

'I know two sisters, Grace and Rose, and they need work. They need it urgently . . . They could sell apples.'

'I have no say over the pippin-hawks.'

He shook his head. Seemed irritated that I would burden his great mind with such an irksome triviality.

'Please, talk to me of something else, or leave me.'

I thought of Rose's worried face. 'I am sorry, sir. I owe these girls a great debt. They took me into their home at a time when I had no one. Please, sir.'

Shakespeare sighed. I felt like I was baiting a bear, and feared what he was going to say next. 'And who is Rose? You spoke her name soft when you said it.'

'She is my love.'

'Oh dear. A serious love?'

He pointed over at Elsa and another worker from the Cardinal's Hat, who often touted for trade in the tavern. Elsa was holding a gentleman's groin under a table, her thumb caressing the bulge. 'Look at the man she hangs on. Is that the kind of love you feel?'

'No. Well, yes. But the other kind too.'

Shakespeare nodded. His eye glimmered with a tear. Maybe it was the smoke. 'I will have a word. You can tell these girls they can sell their apples.'

And so they did.

And all was sweet and light, though every time I heard Jaques' soliloquy I worried. I, more than most, was an actor in life. I was playing a part. What would my next role be, and when would I have to take it? How would I be able to leave this one behind, and when it would mean leaving Rose?

The night I told Rose that she and Grace could work at the Globe because 'Mr Shakespeare made it so' was a happy one, and I had bought a pack of cards on the way home. We sat all night laughing and singing and playing triumph and eating pies from Old Street and drinking more ale than usual.

Conversation turned to how Grace was looking more like a woman, and then Grace said to me, not in a rude way but in the straight-as-an-arrow truthful way that was the essence of Grace, 'I will pass you by soon.'

And she laughed, because she had drank too much ale. She was used to drinking it, just not four jugs of it in a row.

But Rose didn't laugh. 'It is true. You haven't aged a day.'

'It is because I am happy,' I said weakly. 'I have no worries to line my face.'

Though of course the reality was that I had a sea of them, but it would be decades before a single line appeared.

I used to watch Rose, between the musical interludes, and she used to observe me too, in the gallery. What was it about those silent exchanges in a crowded place? There was a magic to them, like a secret shared.

The crowds, however, seemed to be getting rowdier as the season went on. On opening night – with the queen and her court in attendance – there hadn't been a single scuffle. Towards the season's end, there was always, at any time, some skirmish going on amid the groundlings in the pit. Once, for instance, a man sliced another man's ear off with an oyster shell over one of the prostitutes who was always there. I worried about the girls being down there while I was safely up in the rarefied air of the gallery but generally they were all right, and enjoyed selling four times as much fruit as they would have sold at Whitechapel Market.

But then, one afternoon, under a sky full of stone-grey rain clouds: trouble.

I was midway through the tune of 'What Shall He Have That Killed the Deer?' – which by now, as with all the songs in the play, I could pretty much pluck my way through in my sleep – when I noticed something. Someone – a mean-looking saggy-lipped man from the benches – had stolen a pippin from Grace and was biting into it as she asked him for the penny it cost. He tried to bat her away like a fly, but Grace was Grace so she stood her ground. She was shouting words I couldn't hear, but knowing Grace I could guess them. As she was standing in the way of another man, she was now getting into broader bother. This man – a grizzled brown-toothed brute in ale-soaked clothes – pushed Grace to the floor, sending her apples flying to the ground amid the sand and the nut and oyster shells, triggering a memory of all those scattered plums on Fairfield Road. Then it was a free for all, as several people jostled to grab the apples.

Grace got to her feet, and the first man, the apple thief, then grabbed her and made a gargoyle of his face, shoving his tongue in her ear.

I had, by this point, stopped playing.

Hal, next to me, tapped my foot while still playing his flute, as the actors continued singing below. I heard Christopher sighing his disapproval behind me. So I began to start playing again, but then spied Rose, leaving her basket and rushing back through the pit, concerned for her sister. She reached Grace, who was still having trouble with the ear-licker, when the apple-thief's companion made a grab at her, pulling up her skirt and reaching his hand beneath it.

She slapped him, he yanked at her hair, I felt her distress as if it was my own, just as Grace was elbowing her harasser hard in the face, bloodying his nose. I didn't know what happened next because I was climbing over the oakwood rail of the balcony, holding my lute like a club, and – to the sound of a thousand gasps – jumping down onto the stage.

I landed on top of Will Kemp, then shouldered past a shocked Shakespeare himself, as I lunged forward and leapt off the stage to reach Rose and Grace.

I ran around the side of the pit and pushed my way through as nuts and ale and apples were thrown in my direction from the angry crowd. The play went on behind me, as the play always did, but I doubt if even those in the fivepenny seats could hear a word that was being said, such was the commotion now in the pit and around the benches. Even in the balconies people were roaring and jeering and raining their theatre food down on me.

Rose was fine now – she had broken free of her lecherous assailant – and was trying to help Grace, who was still in trouble, being held in a headlock with a thick arm squeezed hard around her neck.

Between Rose and myself we managed to get Grace free.

I grabbed the sisters' hands and urged them, 'We have to go.'

But there was potentially an even bigger problem now.

One of the men from the expensive seats was now standing in our path as we tried to get out of the theatre. I hadn't spotted him, and I doubt he had spotted me, before I had leapt out of the gallery.

He stood tall and strong and solid, better dressed than I had seen him last, with his thinning hair flattened in stripes across his head, clasping those thick butcher's hands in front of him.

'So,' said Manning, looking down at me with his one good eye. 'I see it is true. You made it to London . . . How long is it since I saw you last? It seems only yesterday. You haven't changed in the slightest. But then, you don't, do you?'

I see it is true.

I would never know for sure if Christopher had spread his suspicions about me beyond the musicians' gallery. Nor would I ever know if the men who manhandled Rose and Grace were in on the whole thing.

'I see you have made some friends.'

'No,' I said, as if a word could cancel a reality. He surveyed a confused Grace and Rose.

'No?'

'They are not my friends,' I said, determined he knew as little about the sisters as possible, or their connection to me. 'I have never seen them before this day.'

I gestured with my eyes for Rose to leave, but she wouldn't.

'Ah, and still he lies. Well, be aware of this, girls, for he is not what he seems. He is an unnatural malevolence, incarnate. A witch's boy.'

'My mother died an innocent woman. She died because of you.'

'Her last charm for all God knows. Perhaps she changed form. Perhaps she stands among us now.'

He stared at Rose, then Grace, as if trying to read an abstruse text. I couldn't stay another moment. The nightmare was coming true. A mere knowledge of me was a danger to anyone. My very existence a curse. The crowd around us was becoming still, but watching Manning more than the stage. I recognised a face staring at me. I didn't know his name but I knew he was a knife grinder. I had seen him on the bridge of a morning, plying his trade.

He was a pale weak-looking skinny man, no more than twenty, who always wore a belt of shining knives.

I contemplated grabbing one of them, but that would only have assured me a one-way ticket to Tyburn and a noose around my neck.

But I knew it was too late. The risk of Manning knowing I knew the girls was less than the risk of my leaving and them staying with him.

So I implored Rose, 'We *must* leave.'

'. . . *I will kill thee a hundred and fifty ways. Therefore tremble and depart . . .*'

But then even the actors fell quiet as Manning grabbed a handful of Grace's hair.

'This one!' Manning shouted. 'How many years has she?'

Grace was kicking at him.

'Has she twenty? Has she thirty? She might have sixty years to her. She looks like a child but we know of other deceptions, don't we?'

Grace punched him hard in the groin.

'Get off me, you eel, you piss-cunt!'

But it seemed no good. The crowd was with Manning and against us. We would be contained here. Manning would get some kind of hearing. Accusations of witchcraft and devilry would follow. I had endangered Rose and Grace. The only thing that could have saved us, right at that moment, was the one thing that did.

'Pray, get thy hands off that young girl.'

It was Shakespeare himself, front of stage and out of character. Manning held on. 'I am William Manning, I am the—'

'I care not,' said Shakespeare. 'These players care not. This Globe cares not. Unhand her and free her and her friends afore we end this play.'

This was enough. The threat of no more of the performance was enough. Even then it was clear that the masses wanted something far more than justice. They wanted entertainment. And Shakespeare knew that as well as anyone.

The whole theatre was now jeering at William Manning. Oyster shells were flung at his reddening face. A nerve bulged blue in his forehead. His hand let go of Grace. We clutched onto her as we made our way towards the side of the building, our feet crunching the detritus in the sand. I turned to the stage, wondering if Shakespeare had returned. He caught my glance, then when he spoke to the enlivened crowd to tell them the rest of the performance was dedicated to an actor to whom he owed a debt – 'a man by the name of Henry Hemmings' – I knew it was a message, a code, and one intended for me.

And so it was that I knew we could never return to the Globe, or Bankside, ever again.

Hackney, outside London, 1599

Gossip.

Gossip lived. It wasn't just a currency, it had a *life*.

Stories buzzed and hummed and circulated like gadflies in the air, hovering amid the stench of sewage and the clatter of carts.

For instance, when Mary Peters suddenly went missing, every household to the east of the walls seemed to know about it. Rose, incidentally, had been so upset about that she hardly spoke for a day. And now, due to what Rose called 'the heat of my tempers', the story of the lutist who jumped onto the stage at the Globe would surely be talked about in every inn in London.

'But you and Grace were in trouble!'

'We can handle ourselves. We always have. And now we shall have to go back to Whitechapel . . .'

The conversation turned, and headed where I knew it would. She wanted to know who the man was. Manning.

'I don't know.'

'That is a lie.'

'I can't tell you who he is.'

'He said your mother was a witch. What was his meaning?'

'He must have been confused. He must have mistaken me for somebody else.'

Her green eyes glared at me, alive with quiet fury. 'Do you take me for a fool, Tom Smith?'

And it was that. The saying of the name that was only half mine, that made me feel I had to tell her *something*.

'Forgive me, Rose. It was a mistake. I should never have come here. I should have earned the money I owed and left. I should never have let my feelings for you grow, and I should never let you feel anything for me.'

'What are you saying, Tom? Your talk is a puzzle.'

'Yes. Yes, it is. And I am a puzzle too. And you won't solve it. I can't even solve it myself.'

I had stood up from the stool and was pacing around in frantic circles. Grace was now asleep in her room, so I kept my voice low but urgent.

'You need to find someone else. Look at me. Look at me, Rose! I am too young for you.'

'Two years, Tom. That is not such a difference.'

'The difference will grow.'

She looked confused. 'How can it? What can you mean, Tom? How can a difference grow? You are not making sense.'

'I am no use to you now. I can't go back to Southwark.'

'Use? *Use*? You have my heart, Tom.'

I exhaled heavily. I wanted to sigh away reality. I wanted the tear that was in her eye never to fall. I wanted her to hate me. I wanted not to love her. 'Well, you gave it to the wrong person.'

'Tell me about your mother, Tom . . . the truth.'

Her eyes wouldn't let me lie.

'The reason they killed her is me.'

'What?'

'There is something most strange about me, Rose.'

'What is it?'

'I am not growing older.'

'What?'

'Look at me. Time passes, but not on my face. I am in love with you. I am. I truly am. And what use is that? I am like a boy trying to climb a tree but the branches keep getting higher and higher.'

She was so dumbfounded by what I was saying she could only utter, 'I am not a tree.'

'You will look fifty years old and I will still look like this. It is best you leave me. It is best I go. It is best I—'

And she kissed me, then, simply because she wanted me to stop talking.

And she could only half believe it. For days, she thought I was insane. But, as the weeks and months passed by, she realised it was true.

It was something she couldn't comprehend, yet there it was. There it was.

My truth.

London, now

I have no idea if anything I have said to Anton has got through. I have only been alive for four hundred and thirty-nine years, which is of course nowhere near long enough to understand the minimal facial expressions of the average teenage boy.

So, it is pretty late, twenty past twelve, when I finally make it into the staff room for lunch break. I sit there inhaling the scent of instant coffee and processed ham. My headache is bad today. Also, I have tinnitus. I get that too, sometimes. Have had it on and off since the near-deafening artillery fire I heard in the Spanish Civil War.

I no longer go to the supermarket at lunch. Instead I make my own sandwich in the morning. But I'm not even hungry, so I just sit there, eyes closed.

When I open them I see Isham, the geography teacher, busy working out which sachet of herbal tea to put in his mug.

I also see Camille.

She is on the other side of the room and is peeling open her carton of salad. She has apple juice too, and a book, which she is using as a kind of makeshift little tray.

Daphne, taking a clementine from the communal fruit bowl, gives me a smile that might be a smirk. 'How are you, Tom? How are things going?'

'Good,' I say. 'I feel good.'

She nods, knowing it is a lie. 'It will get better. The first ten years here are always the hardest.' She laughs, and heads out of the staff room to her office.

I feel bad about Camille. I had been rude to her the last time we had spoken. I notice now that she is taking something out of her pocket. A pill. She swallows it down with the help of some apple juice.

I should just stay in my seat.

That is what Hendrich would want me to do. I mean, it is now – from an Albatross Society point of view – perfect. Camille will probably never speak to me again.

Yet, here I am, crossing the room.

'I just want to say sorry,' I tell her.

'What for?' she says, which is good of her.

I sit down, so I can speak to her at a lower volume, and less suspiciously. Another teacher, a maths teacher called Stephanie, is frowning at us as she eats a plum.

'I didn't mean to be so weird. So rude.'

'Well, some people can't help it. Some people are just like that.'

'Well, I didn't mean to be.'

'What we are and what we mean are different things. It's fine. The world makes it very hard not to be a prick.'

She just says it casually, gently. I have never been so insulted so delicately.

I try to explain without explaining. 'I'm just . . . I have a lot of stuff going on, and I have one of those faces. Generic. I get a lot of people thinking I'm a friend of a friend. Or some actor they've seen on TV.'

She nods, unconvinced. 'That's probably it, then. Let's say it's that.'

I then notice the book beneath Camille's salad. It is a novel. I wonder if it is the novel she had been reading that day I saw her in the park. A Penguin Classic. *Tender Is the Night* by F. Scott Fitzgerald, with a photograph of the author on the front cover.

She must have seen me staring. 'Oh, have you read it? What do you think?'

I find it hard to talk. The memories jam my mind, like too many open windows on a computer, or too much water in a boat.

My headache rises.

'I . . . I . . . don't know . . .' Each word feels like an oar in the water. 'Boats against the current,' I say aloud.

'Boats against the current? *Gatsby*?'

I hold my breath and I am now in a staff room in London and a bar in Paris all at once, torn between centuries, between place and time, now and then, water and air.

Paris, 1928

I was on my own, walking the long walk home from the grand hotel where I had been doing my shift, playing the piano for the rich Americans and Europeans who were enjoying tea or cocktails. I felt alone. I needed to be around people, to mask the loneliness inside myself. So I headed into the thronging buzz of Harry's Bar, as I did on occasion. Almost everyone in there was from somewhere else, which was always the kind of crowd I liked.

I fought my way to the bar and found a place next to a glamorous couple with matching centre partings.

The man looked at me, and maybe sensed my loneliness.

'Try the Bloody Mary,' he said.

'What's that?'

'It's *the thing*. A cocktail. Zee loves it, don't you, sweetheart?'

The woman looked at me with sad, heavy eyes. She was either drunk or ready for sleep or both. They both looked pretty drunk, now that I thought about it. She nodded. 'It is a great ally in the war.'

'Which war is that?' I wondered aloud.

'The war against boredom. It is a very real war. It is a war in which the enemy is all around us.'

I ordered the Bloody Mary. I was surprised to see it involved tomato juice. The man eyeballed the woman sternly. It was hard to tell if it was fake stern or the real deal. 'I have to say I feel mildly insulted when you talk like that, Zee.'

'Oh, not you, Scott . . . you haven't been too dull. This has been one of your better evenings.'

It was then he held out his hand. 'Scott Fitzgerald. And this is Zelda.'

The great thing about being deep into your fourth century was that you rarely got star struck, but even so it was quite something to accidentally happen upon the author of the book that was beside your bed.

'I've just finished reading your book, *The Great Gatsby*. And I read *This Side of Paradise* when it came out.'

He suddenly seemed sober. 'What did you make of it? Of *Gatsby*? Everyone prefers *Paradise*. Everyone. My publishers struggle on with the poor thing, out of pity mainly.'

Zelda made a face as if she was about to be sick. 'That *dust jacket*. Ernest is so seldom right about anything but he was right about that. It is a war against eyes.'

'Not everything is a war, sweetheart.'

'Of course it is, Scott.'

They looked like they were about to squabble, so I interjected: 'Well, I thought it was exceptional. The book, I mean.'

Zelda nodded. She looked like a child, I realised. They both did. They looked like children dressing up in grown-up clothes. There was such a fragile *innocence* to them.

'I try to tell him it is good,' she said. 'You can tell him and tell him and tell him but it is just raindrops against the roof.'

Scott seemed relieved I liked it, though. 'Well, that makes you a better person than the guy at the *Herald Tribune*. Now, there's your drink . . .' He handed me the Bloody Mary.

'They invented it here, you know,' said Zelda.

I sipped the strange drink. 'Did they really?'

And then Scott interrupted and said, 'Tell us, what do you do?'

'I play piano. At Ciro's.'

'As in the Paris Ciro's?' he asked. 'Rue Daunou? How wonderful. You win already.'

Zelda took a long mouthful of some kind of gin cocktail. 'What are you scared of?'

Scott smiled apologetically. 'It's her drunk question. Every time.'

'Scared of?'

'Everyone is scared of something. I'm scared of bedtime. And housekeeping. And all the things you have housemaids for. Scott is scared of reviews. And Hemingway. And loneliness.'

'I am not scared of Hemingway.'

I tried to think. I wanted, for once, to give an honest answer. 'I'm scared of time.'

Zelda smiled, leaning her head in a kind of glazed sympathy, or resignation. 'You mean growing old?'

'No, I mean—'

'Scotty and I don't plan to grow old, do we?'

'The plan is,' Scott added, with exaggerated seriousness, 'to hop from one childhood to the next.'

I sighed, hoping this would make me appear thoughtful and serious and in possession of a great Golden Age intelligence. 'The trouble is, if you live long enough, you end up running out of childhoods eventually.'

Zelda offered me a cigarette, which I accepted (I was smoking now – everyone was smoking now), and then placed one in Scott's mouth, and another in her own. A kind of wild despair flared suddenly in her eyes as she struck the match. 'Grow up or crack up,' she said, after the first inhale. 'The divine choices we have . . .'

'If only we could find a way to stop time,' said her husband. 'That's what we need to work on. You know, for when a moment of happiness floats along. We could swing our net and catch it like a butterfly, and have that moment for ever.'

Zelda was now looking across the crowded bar. 'The trouble is they stick pins in butterflies. And then they are dead . . .' She seemed to be looking for someone. 'Sherwood's gone. But, oh, look! It's Gertrude and Alice.'

178

And within moments they had disappeared through the packed room with their cocktails and, though they made it perfectly clear I could join them, I stayed there with nothing but vodka and tomato juice for company, staying in the safe shadows of history.

London, now

It is strange how close the past is, even when you imagine it to be so far away. Strange how it can just jump out of a sentence and hit you. Strange how every object or word can house a ghost.

The past is not one separate place. It is many, many places, and they are always ready to rise into the present. One minute it is the 1590s, the next it is the 1920s. And it is all related. It is all the accumulation of time. It builds up and builds up and can catch you violently off guard at any moment. The past resides inside the present, repeating, hiccupping, reminding you of all the *stuff that no longer is.* It bleeds out from road signs and plaques on park benches and songs and surnames and faces and the covers of books. Sometimes just the sight of a tree or a sunset can smack you with the power of every tree or sunset you have ever seen and there is no way to protect yourself. There is no possible way of living in a world without books or trees or sunsets. There just isn't.

'Are you okay?' Camille asks me, her hand resting on the cover of her book, so only the word 'tender' is visible.

'Yes. I'm still getting these headaches, though.'

'Have you been to the doctor?'

'No. But I will.' Going to the doctor, of course, is the last thing I am going to do.

I look at her. She has the kind of face that makes you want to speak, to tell things to. It is a dangerous face.

'Maybe you need some more sleep,' she says.

I wonder what she means, and she can see me wondering, because then she says: 'I saw on Facebook that you liked my post at three in the morning. That's an interesting time for you to be awake on a school night.'

'Oh.'

There is a sliver of mischief in her smile. 'Is it a habit of yours? Spying on women's Facebook pages in the middle of the night?'

I feel ashamed.

'It . . . wh . . . came up on my feed.'

'I'm only joking with you, Tom. You need to lighten up a little bit.'

If only she could understand the weight of things. The gravity of time. 'I'm sorry,' I say, 'for the heaviness.'

'It's all right. Life is like that sometimes.'

Maybe she *does* understand. 'I'm just a bit awkward around people.'

'I get it. L'enfer, c'est les autres.'

'Sartre?'

'Oui. Dix points. Sartre. Mr Comedy himself.'

I force a smile and don't say anything because the only thing I have in my head is that the sight of her face comforts me and scares me all at once. So instead I ask her something. It is a question I have often asked over the years. The question is: 'Do you know anyone called Marion?'

She frowns. I really confuse her.

'A French Marion or an English one?'

'English,' I say. 'Or either.'

She thinks. 'I went to school with a Marion. Marion Rey. She told me about periods. My parents were prudes. They never told me. And it is quite a thing not to be told about, you know, this blood coming out of you.'

She says this at a normal volume. There are still other people in the room. Stephanie is still frowning at us, holding the stone of her plum between her fingers. Isham is on his mobile phone, two seats away. I like her lack of shame.

181

I know I should engage in chit-chat. I know all the signs that chit-chat is required are there. But I ignore the signs.

'Any other Marions?'

'No, I'm sorry.'

'That's all right. I'm sorry. That is all I really wanted to say.'

She smiles and looks at me, and finds something in my gaze that troubles her. I feel she is trying to think where she knows me from again.

'Life is always mysterious,' she says. 'But some mysteries are bigger than others.'

And then there is a little silence, and I force another smile and I walk away.

PART FOUR
The Pianist

Bisbee, Arizona, 1926

It was August. I was in the living room of a small timber house on the edge of town, on assignment for Hendrich. Every eight years there was an assignment. That was the deal. You did the assignment and then you moved on to the next place and Hendrich helped you change your identity and kept you safe. The only time you were ever in danger was during the assignment itself. Though I had been lucky. I had done three assignments before this one and they had all been successful. In other words: I had managed to locate the albas in question and convince them to join the society. No violence had been necessary. No real test of character. But here, in Bisbee, everything changed. Here, I was about to find out who I was. And the lengths I would go to, to find Marion.

Even though it was now evening and the dark was quickly dissolving the red mountains outside the window, the heat was intense. It was like the burning air outside but concentrated, like someone had decided to squeeze all of the desert heat into that timber house.

Sweat dripped off my nose and onto the nine of diamonds.

'Y'aint used to heat much, are ya? Where you been hiding? Alaska? You been gold digging up in Yukon?' That was the skinny toothless one who asked that. The one with two fingers missing on his left hand. The one who went by the name of Louis. He took another slug of whisky and swallowed it down without a flinch.

'Been hiding all over,' I said. 'I have to.'

Then the other one – Joe – the one who'd just surprised me with a royal flush, the larger, cleverer one, started to laugh

185

ominously. 'This is all very interessin' an' all, and we always appreciate suppin' moonshine with strangers. 'Specially ones wi' some green in their pockets. But y'aint from Cochise County. Can always tell. Just from your clothes. See, everyone round here has a taint to 'em. From the dust. From the mines. You don't see no cotton that white 'round Bisbee. And look at your hands. Clean as snow.'

I looked down at my hands. I was very used to the sight of them, these days, from all the music I had been playing. I had taught myself piano. That is what I had done with the last eight years.

'Hands are hands,' I said pathetically.

We had been playing poker for over an hour. I had already lost a hundred and twenty dollars. I drank some more of the whisky. It felt like fire. Now was the time, I realised. Now I had to say what I had come here to say.

'I know who you two are.'

'Oh?' said Joe.

A clock ticked. Outside, far away, something howled. A dog or a coyote.

I cleared my throat. 'You are like me.'

'Sure doubt that.' Joe again, with a laugh as dry as the desert.

'Joe Thompson, that's your name, is it?'

'What you diggin' at, mister?'

'Not Billy Stiles? Not William Larkin?'

Louis then sat up tall. His face hardened. 'Who are you?'

'I have been many people. Just like you. Now, what should I call you? Louis? Or Jess Dunlop? Or John Patterson? Or maybe Three-fingered Jack? And that's just the start, no?'

Four eyes and two guns were now staring hard at me. Never seen anyone so quick on the draw as those two. It was them all right.

They pointed at the pistol I was carrying. 'Place it on the table, nice and slow . . .'

I did so. 'I'm not here for trouble. I'm here to keep you safe. I know who you are. I know at least some of the people you have been. I know you haven't always been working in a copper mine. I know about the train you robbed at Fairbank. I know about the Southern Pacific Express you took for more than most can ever dream of. I know neither of you need to be mining for copper.' Joe was clenching his jaw so hard I thought he was going to lose teeth, but I kept going. 'I know the two of you were meant to have been shot twenty-six years ago in Tombstone.' I dug in my pocket and pulled out the pictures Hendrich had got hold of. 'And I know these photographs of you were taken thirty years ago, and you have hardly aged a day.'

They didn't even break away to look at the photos. They knew who they were. And they knew I knew who they were too. I had to talk.

'Listen, I'm not trying to get you into any trouble. I'm just trying to explain that it's all right. There are lots of people like you. I don't know your whole story, but you both look about the same age. I'm guessing you were born shortly after seventeen hundred. Now, I don't know if during that time you have come into contact with other people with this condition, apart from each other, but I can assure you there are many of them. Many of *us*. Thousands, possibly. And our condition is dangerous. It has been called by a doctor in England, *anageria*. When it becomes public – either because we decide to tell people, or people find us out – then we are in danger. And the people we care for are in danger. We are either locked away in a madhouse, pursued and imprisoned in the name of science, or murdered by the servants of superstition. So, as I am sure you know, your lives are at risk.'

Louis scratched his stubble. 'From this side of the gun, looks like you are the one whose life hangs in the breeze.'

Joe was frowning. 'So what are you asking us, mister?'

A deep breath. 'I'm just here with a proposition. Look, people here in Bisbee already have their suspicions about you. Word is leaking out. This is the age of photography now. Our past has evidence.' As I was hearing myself, with fear slowly creeping into my voice, I realised how much I was simply parroting Hendrich. Everything I was saying was the kind of thing Hendrich said. There was something hollow to every word. 'There's a society, like a union, working for the collective good. We are trying to get every person with this condition, this condition they call anageria, to be part of the society. It helps people. It assists them, when they need to move on and begin being someone else. That help can be money, and it can be in the form of papers and documents.'

Joe and Louis exchanged thoughts with their eyes. Louis' eyes were duller, less illuminated with intelligence. He looked danger-ously stupid, but he was the more malleable one. The one most likely to be sold. Joe was the strong one, in body and mind. Joe was the one who held his Colt without a quiver.

'How much money you talkin'?' Louis asked as an insect buzzed around his head.

'It depends on need. The society allocates budgets according to the requirements of each particular case.' God, I really was starting to sound like Hendrich.

Joe shook his head. 'Didn't you hear the man, Louis? He's tellin' us to move out of Bisbee. And that just ain't gonna work, see. We've got it good here. We have good relations with folk here. We done our roamin', and I been all over this country since I got off the boat all those years ago. And I ain't bein' told to move.'

'It will be best for you if you do. You see, the society says that after eight years—'

Joe sighed a sigh that was halfway to a growl. 'The society says? The society says? We ain't in no society and we ain't ever gonna be in no society. You understand me?'

'I'm sorry but—'

'I wanna put a hole in that head of yours.'

'Listen, the society have contacted the law officials. They know I am here. If you shoot me, you will be caught.'

They both laughed at this.

'You hear that, Louis?'

'I heard 'im all right.'

'Best we explain to Mr Peter Whicheverhisnameis why the joke is funny.'

'You can call me Tom. See, I'm like you. I've had many names.'

Joe ignored me completely and carried on with his train of thought. 'It's all right. I'll do it. See, the joke is funny cos there ain't no law that touches us 'round here. This here ain't an ordinary town. We've been helping Sheriff Downey and old P.D. out for some time now.'

P.D. Phelps Dodge. I'd been given enough information about Bisbee to know that Phelps Dodge was the major mining company in the area.

'In actual fact,' Joe went on, 'we helped them instigate the Bisbee deportation. You know about that, right?'

I knew something about it. I knew that, in 1919, hundreds of striking miners had been roughly kidnapped and deported out of town.

'So comin' here and talkin' about propositions and your little union ain't gonna sway us too much. The last union men we dealt with we kicked all the way to New Mexico, and we did it with the sheriff's seal of approval . . . Now, you really do look hot and bothered. Let's go for a little walk and cool your blood a little . . .'

It was dark now. Desert-dark.

The air was turning chill, but I was sweating and sore and aching and my whisky-sour mouth was as dry as the grave I had been digging for over an hour.

Bullets weren't infections. They weren't the plague or one of the other hundred or so illnesses albas were able to resist. As with

189

ultimate old age, there was no immunity from a bullet. And I didn't want to die. I had to stay alive for Marion. Hendrich had convinced me we were getting closer to finding her.

At least one of them had had their revolver fixed on me the whole time I'd been digging. This situation didn't change as they beckoned me out of the hole. And all the time their two dark Saddlebred horses stayed nibbling and whispering at each other.

'Now,' said Joe, as I hauled myself out, making sure I kept hold of the shovel as I did so. I leaned on it, as a kind of resting aid. 'We ain't buryin' your money with ya. Empty those pockets and place all you have on the ground.'

I knew this was the moment. The only one I would get. I gave a curious glance towards the horses, causing the men to do the same. By the time Joe's cold hard eyes were back upon me, the shovel was swinging fast towards his face. He fell back, semi-conscious, losing his hold of the gun, which landed with a thud in the dust.

'Kill 'im,' slurred Joe.

Louis, the one I'd gambled on being a little more cowardly, a little slower on the trigger, fired a shot as I was scrambling for Joe's gun. The noise echoed around the desert as I felt the pain in my back, near my right shoulder. But I had Joe's gun and one good arm, and I turned and shot Louis in the neck and he fired again but only hit the night that time. Then I shot Joe a couple of times too and there was blood slick black in the dark, and somehow inside my pain I managed to kick and roll them into the grave I had dug and put the earth back on them. I slapped the rump of one of the horses, causing it to gallop away, before I hauled myself on the other one.

The pain was beyond anything I had known, but somehow I made it away and I kept going and I kept going and I kept going across the desert and over dry hills and mountains and past a large quarry that seemed to my delirious mind like the blackness of death itself calling me towards it like the River Styx. I resisted and the horse kept walking through that night until I reached Tucson as the morning sun slowly bled its light into the sky and I found the Arizona Inn where Agnes poured alcohol on my wound and I bit into a wet towel to mask my screams as she tweezered the bullet out of my flesh.

Los Angeles, 1926

My bullet wound was healing, but there was still pain in my shoulder. I was at the Garden Court Apartments and Hotel, on Hollywood Boulevard, in the restaurant they had there. All marble and columns and grandeur. A mesmerising-looking woman with dark painted lips and a ghostly pale face sat at a table not too far away, talking to two fawning men in business suits. It was Lillian Gish, the movie star. I recognised her from *Orphans of the Storm*, a film set during the French Revolution.

For a moment or two, I was entranced.

I had come to love the cinema during my time in Albuquerque, where I had been stationed for the last eight years. The way you could just sit on your own in the dark and forget who you were, just let yourself feel what the film was telling you to feel for an hour or so.

'They have them all in here,' Hendrich was explaining discreetly as he set about his halibut in shrimp sauce. 'Gloria Swanson, Fairbanks, Fatty Arbuckle, Valentino. Just last week Chaplin was at this very table. In your seat. He just had the soup. That was his entire meal. Just soup.'

Hendrich grinned. I had never hated that grin until now. 'What's the matter, Tom? Is it the beef? It can be a little overdone.'

'The beef is fine.'

'Oh, so it's about what happened in Arizona?'

I almost laughed at this. 'What else would it be about? I had to *kill* two men.'

'Quiet now. I doubt Miss Gish wants to hear such things. Discretion, Tom, please.'

'Well, I don't see why we had to do this in the restaurant. I thought you had an apartment upstairs.'

He looked confused. 'I like the restaurant. It's always good to be around people. Don't you enjoy being around people, Tom?'

'I will tell you what I don't enjoy . . .'

He glided his hand through the air, as if inviting me through a door. 'Please do,' he said. 'Tell me what you don't enjoy. If that makes you happy.'

I leaned forward to whisper. 'I don't enjoy fleeing a murder scene on a horse with a bullet lodged in my shoulder. A *bullet*. And . . . and . . .' I was losing my flow. 'I didn't want to do that. I didn't want to kill them.'

He sighed philosophically. 'What was it Dr Johnson said? *He who makes a beast of himself gets rid of the pain of being a man.* Do you know what I think? I think you are finding yourself. You were lost. You didn't even know who or what you were. You had no purpose. You were living in poverty. You were moping around, burning yourself to feel something. Now look. You have a purpose.' He waited a beat or two. 'This shrimp sauce is really divine.'

The waiter came over and poured some more wine. We concentrated on our food until he disappeared again. A piano started to play. Some of the diners leaned over the backs of their seats to have a look at the pianist for a moment or two.

'I'm just saying I didn't like it. Those men were never going to join the society. You should have known that. I should have been told that, Hendrich.'

'Please, try to call me Cecil. They know me as Cecil here. My story is that I made my money in San Francisco. Property development. I helped rebuild the city. After the quake. Don't I look like a Cecil? Call me Cecil. They'll think I'm Cecil B. DeMille, I can make them a star. It might get me some action . . .'

He drifted off into more thought. 'I love this town. They are all coming here now. All these young farm girls from South Dakota or

Oklahoma or Europe. This city has always been the same apparently. In the Ice Age animals used to come and get stuck in the tar pits that looked like shimmering lakes and the smell of the meat would bring other animals there to be trapped in that thick black tar. Anyway, I'm a safe kind of predator. They think I'm past it at seventy-eight. Seventy-eight! Imagine that. At seventy-eight I was fucking my way around Flanders. I was incorrigible. The amount of marriage proposals I made. I was the Valentino of the Lowlands . . .'

I took a big gulp of wine. 'I can't do this, Hendrich, I can't do it.'

'Cecil, *please.*'

'I am sorry I went to Dr Hutchinson. Seriously, I am. But I want my old life back. I just want to be me again.'

'I am afraid that is, as they say, impossible. Time moves forwards. We have the luxury of time but we still can't reverse it. We can't stop it. We are one-way traffic, just the same as all these mayflies. You can't simply cut away from the society any more than you can be unborn. You do understand that, don't you, Tom? And what about your daughter, Tom? We are going to find her. We will.'

'But you haven't.'

'Yet, Tom, we haven't *yet.* I sense she is out there, Tom. I know she is out there. She is *there*, Tom.'

I said nothing. I was angry, yes, but as was so often the case with anger, it was really just fear projecting outwards. The society was nothing – it had no physical presence in the real world, there was no stone plaque outside a grand building announcing its existence. It was just Hendrich and the people who had faith in him. And yet . . . Hendrich was enough. His *aptitude.* Indeed, maybe it was that aptitude that caused him to reel me in again with just the right words. Maybe it wasn't just words, either. Maybe he actually *could* sense she was out there.

But then a thought. 'If your aptitude is so good, then why didn't you know? Why didn't you know they could have killed me?'

'They didn't kill you. If they had killed you then, yes, I would have made a terrible mistake. But the fact is that you are a survivor, and I knew that, and it has been proven. Obviously, we are all survivors. But you . . . I don't know. There is something special about you. You have a desire to live. Most people who get to your age feel like everything is behind them. But when I look at you I see a thirst for the future, a yearning for it. For your daughter, yes, but for something else too. The great unknown.'

'But what kind of life is it? Having to change who you are every eight years?'

'You had to change who you were before. What is the difference?'

'The difference is that I could decide. It was *my* life.'

He shook his head, and smiled solemnly. 'No. You were in retreat. You were hiding from life. You were hiding, if I dare say, from yourself.'

'But that's what the society is for, isn't it? To hide?'

'No, Tom, no. You misunderstand everything. Look at us. In the centre of the most famous restaurant in a sunlit city everyone wants to visit. We are not hiding. We are not tucked away in St Albans pulling metal out of a forge. The aim of the society is to provide a structure, a *system*, which enables us to enhance our lives. You do the occasional favour, a spot of recruitment, and you get to live a good life. And this is how you thank me.'

'I have just spent eight years on a farm in Albuquerque with nothing but three cows and some cacti for company. It seems the society works better for some than it does for others.'

Hendrich shook his head. 'I have a letter for you, from Reginald Fisher. You remember? The man you recruited in Chicago?'

He handed me the letter and I read it. It was a long letter. The one line that stood out was this one, near the end. *I would have betrayed God to finish myself if you had never come and seen me, but I feel so happy now, knowing I am not a freakish specimen of humanity, but part of a family.*

'All right, Arizona was a mistake. But not everything has been. Lives are lost in wars but it doesn't mean they shouldn't ever be fought. You had a piano, Tom. Did you play it?'

'Five hours a day.'

'So how many instruments can you play now?'

'Around thirty.'

'That's impressive.'

'Not really. Most of them no one wants to hear any more. It's hard to play Gershwin on a lute.'

'Yes.' Hendrich ate the last of his fish. Then he stared at me earnestly. 'You are a murderer, Tom. Without the society's protection you would be in a very vulnerable place right now. You need us. But I don't want you to stay out of sheer necessity, Tom . . . I hear you, I hear you. I do. And I will never forget the people whose lives you have saved by bringing them into the society. So, from now on I am going to be a little more considerate of your needs. I am going to allocate a few more resources to finding Marion. We've got some new people. Someone in London. Someone in New York. One in Scotland. Another in Vienna. I'll get them working on it. And, of course, I will fund those needs. I am going to listen. I am going to help you as much as I can. I want you to thrive, Tom. I want you to find not just Marion but the future you are waiting for . . .'

A group of four men entered the room and were escorted to a table. One of them had the most recognisable face on the planet. It was Charlie Chaplin. He spotted Lillian Gish and went over and spoke to her, his calm expression punctuated by the occasional quick nervous smile. She laughed gracefully. I had breathed the same air as Shakespeare, and now I was breathing the same air as Chaplin. How could I be ungrateful?

'We are the invisible threads of history,' Hendrich told me, as if reading my mind. Chaplin saw us looking and tipped an invisible bowler hat in our direction.

'See. Told you. He loves this place. Must be the soup. Now, what do you want to do with your life?'

I considered the attention Chaplin was getting, and couldn't think of a greater nightmare. Then, as I continued to contemplate the question I stared at the pianist, in his white dinner jacket, closing his eyes and drifting away, note by note, bar by bar, unnoticed except by me.

'*That*,' I said, nodding in the pianist's direction. 'That is what I want to do.'

London, now

'But why couldn't the League of Nations stop Mussolini from entering Abyssinia?'

Aamina is in the front row. Serious, frowning, alert, holding a pencil, she is wearing a T-shirt that says 'Proud Snowflake'.

I am giving a lesson on the causes of the Second World War, trying to go back from 1939 through the 1930s, talking about Italy taking over Abyssinia, now Ethiopia, in 1935, as well as Hitler's rise in 1933, the Spanish Civil War and the Great Depression.

'Well, they tried, but in a really half-hearted way. Economic sanctions, but nothing that was majorly enforced. But the thing is, at the time, a lot of people didn't realise what they were dealing with. You see, when you look at events in history there is a two-way perspective. Forwards and back. But at the time everything is one way. No one knew where fascism was heading.'

The lesson is going okay and my headache isn't too bad – I think having made peace with Camille helped – but maybe because of this I slip into a kind of autopilot. I am not really thinking about what I am saying.

'The news about Abyssinia felt like a real turning point, though. It made people realise *something* was happening. Not just with Germany but Italy too. With the world order. I remember reading a newspaper on the day Mussolini declared victory and I . . .'

Fuck.

I stop.

Realise what I have said.

Aamina, sharp as her pencil, also notices. 'You said that as if you were there,' she says.

A couple of other pupils nod in agreement.

'No. I wasn't there, but I felt I was. That's the thing with history. You inhabit it. It's another present . . .'

Aamina makes an amused face.

I continue. I cover my tracks, I think. It is a pretty minor mistake to make and yet it is the kind of mistake I never used to make.

During the break I see Camille chatting to someone, out in the corridor. Leaning against some pupil artwork inspired by Rio's favelas, which looks very bright and Fauvist and late nineteenth century.

She is talking to Martin. The hopeless music teacher. Martin is wearing black jeans and a black T-shirt. He has a beard and longer hair than the average male teacher. I have no idea what they are talking about, but he is making Camille laugh. I feel a strange unease. And then I walk past and Martin sees me first and smirks at me, as if I amuse him. 'Hi, Tim. You look a bit lost. Did they give you a map?'

'Tom,' I say.

'You what, mate?'

'My name's Tom. It isn't Tim. It's Tom.'

'All right, mate. Easy mistake.'

Camille is smiling at me. 'How was your lesson?' she asks, her eyes on me like a detective. A smiling detective but still a detective.

'Fine,' I say.

'Listen, Tom, every Thursday a few of us go to the Coach and Horses for a couple of drinks. We meet at seven. Me, Martin, Isham, Sarah . . . You should come along. Tell him, Martin.'

Martin shrugs. 'It's a free world. Yeah, knock yourself out.'

Of course, there is only one answer I should give. *No.* But I glance at Camille and find myself saying, 'Yeah, okay. Coach and Horses, seven. Sounds good.'

199

An interlude about the piano

I moved from place to place and from time to time like an arrow immune to gravity.

Things did improve for a little while.

My shoulder healed.

I went back to London. Hendrich set me up as a hotel pianist in London. Life was good. I drank cocktails and flirted with elegant women in beaded dresses and then went out into the night to dance to jazz with playboys and flapper girls. It was the perfect time for me, where friendships and relationships were expected to be intense and burn out in fast gin-soaked debauchery. The *Roaring* Twenties. That's what they say now, isn't it? And they did kind of roar, compared to the times before. Of course, previous London decades had been noisy – the bellowing 1630s, for instance, or the laughing 1750s – but this was different. For the first time ever, there was always a sound, somewhere in London, that wasn't quite natural. The noise of car engines, of cinema scores, of radio broadcasts, the sound of humans overreaching themselves.

It was the age of noise, and so suddenly playing music had a new importance. It made you a master of the world. Amid the accidental cacophony of modern life to be able to play music, to make *sense* out of noise, could briefly make you a kind of god. A creator. An orderer. A comfort giver.

I enjoyed the role I was in, during this time. Daniel Honeywell, born in London, but who had been tinkling the ivories for upper-class tourists and émigrés on ocean liners since the Great War.

Slowly, though, a melancholy set in. At the time I thought it was another episode of personal melancholy, the futility of loving a woman who had died so long ago. But I think it was also a product of being in tune with the times.

I wanted to do something. I was fed up of simply doing things to help myself. I wanted to do something for humanity. I was a human after all and my empathy was for other human beings, not just those with the curse – or the gift – of hyperlongevity. 'Time guilt', that's what Agnes called it, when I chatted with her about it. She came to see me in London, towards the end of my eight years. She had been living in Montmartre. She had lots of stories. She was still fun.

'I feel a sense of dread,' I told her, her feet resting on my stomach, as we smoked cigarettes in bed in my Mayfair apartment. 'I keep having nightmares.'

'Have you been reading Mr Freud?'

'No.'

'Well, don't. It will make you feel worse. Apparently we are not in control of ourselves. We are ruled by the unconscious parts of our psyche. The only truth we can hope to find about ourselves is in our dreams. He says that most people don't want to be free. Because freedom involves responsibility, and most people are frightened of responsibility.'

'I think that Freud has clearly never had to change his identity every eight years for ever.'

Then we went on what Agnes called an 'adventure' – a mission that Hendrich had given us via telegraph. It was one we were going to go on together. We *drove* in a *car* up to Yorkshire. In the bleak countryside at a grim gothic mental asylum called the High Royds Hospital, a woman had been locked up for telling people the truth of her condition. We kidnapped her from the grounds. Agnes held the chloroform handkerchief over the faces of three members of staff, and then had to do the same to poor Flora Brown, who was understandably frightened by the appearance of two strangers with their faces wrapped in scarves.

Anyway, we carried her out of there and escaped quite easily, and, for whatever reason – the hospital's embarrassment? the total lack of care for their patients? the failure of the local authorities to check records? – the incident was never reported in the press. If it had been, we'd have been safe, Hendrich would have seen to that, but it wasn't, and I have always found that terribly sad.

Anyway, Flora was young. She was only eighty years old. She looked seventeen or eighteen. She was a bewildered stuttering damaged thing when we found her, but the society saved her; it really did, the way it saved many others. She had honestly thought she was mad, and to discover her own sanity made her weep with relief. She left for Australia with Agnes and started a new life. Then she moved to America and started another one. But the point was: the society was doing good. It had saved people. Flora Brown. Reginald Fisher. And many, many more. And maybe myself, too. I realised Hendrich was right. There was a meaning and purpose to all this. I might not always have believed in him, but – most of the time – I believed in the *work*.

I didn't want to go back to London. I told Hendrich by telegraph that I had arranged it with my employers Ciro's to work in their sister restaurant, in a hotel in Paris. So, I went to live in Montmartre, in the apartment where Agnes had been living. I was her 'brother'. There was a brief moment we overlapped. I mention this because we had a very interesting conversation. She told me that, as you get older, somewhere around the mid-millennium mark, albas develop a deep insight.

'What kind of insight?'

'It's incredible. Like a third eye. The feeling for time becomes so profound that inside a single moment you can see everything. You can see the past and the future. It is as though everything stops and, for just that moment, you know how everything is going to be.'

'And is that good? It sounds horrifying.'

'It's not good or horrifying. It just *is*. It's just an incredibly powerful feeling, neither good or bad, where everything becomes clear.'

The conversation stayed with me, long after she left. I craved such clarity at a time when I could hardly understand my present, let alone my future.

I eventually moved to Montparnasse and wrote a lot of poetry. I once wrote a poem in the cemetery there, leaning against Baudelaire's headstone, and I played the piano every night and made the most superficial acquaintances with poets and painters and artists that often only lasted a night.

I anchored myself in music. As well as Ciro's, I sometimes worked at a jazz club called Les Années Folles. I had been playing the piano near-continuously for three decades now and it had become natural to me. Piano could carry a lot. Sadness, happiness, idiotic joy, regret, grief. Sometimes all at the same time.

I gained a routine. I would start my day with a Gauloise then I would head to Le Dôme Café on the Boulevard du Montparnasse and have a pastry (it was usually around midday by the time I was out of the apartment). I sometimes had a coffee. More often I had cognac. Alcohol became more than just alcohol. It felt like freedom. Drinking wine and cognac was almost a moral duty. And I drank and drank and drank, until I almost convinced myself I was happy.

But there was a sense of something tipping out of balance. The times seemed out of joint. There was too much decadence. Too much intensity. Too much change. Too much happiness juxtaposed with too much misery. Too much wealth next to too much poverty. The world was becoming faster and louder, and the social systems were becoming as chaotic and fragmented as jazz scores. So there was a craving, in some places, for simplicity, for order, for scape-goats and for bully-boy leaders, for nations to become like religions or cults. It happened every now and then.

It seemed, in the 1930s, that the whole course of humanity was at stake. As it very often does today. Too many people wanted to find an easy answer to complicated questions. It was a dangerous time to be human. To feel or to think or to care. So, after Paris I stopped playing the piano. And I didn't play it again. The piano had been taking it out of me. I often wondered if I'd ever play it again. And I don't know if I ever would have, if I hadn't been sitting next to Camille when the opportunity arose.

London, now

'I like the old stuff,' Martin is saying, nodding at his own wisdom, before taking a sip of his lager. 'Hendrix mainly, but also Dylan, The Doors, the Stones. You know, stuff before we were born. Before everything was commercialised.'

I don't like Martin. The great thing about being in your four hundreds is that you can get the measure of someone pretty quickly. And every era is clogged with Martins, and they are all dickheads. I can remember a Martin called Richard who used to stand right near the stage at the Minerva Inn in Plymouth in the 1760s, shaking his head at every tune I played, whispering to the poor prostitute on his knee about my terrible taste in music, or shouting out the name of a Broadside ballad better than the one I was playing.

Anyway, so here we all are, seated around a table in the Coach and Horses. The table is small, a dark wood, the colour and feel of the back of a lute, and barely contains the assortment of drinks and crisps and peanuts which we huddle around. The atmosphere of the pub is quiet and civilised, although maybe that is because I now have the riotous stinking brawl-pit of the Minerva Inn in my mind.

'Oh, me too,' says Isham. 'But then all geography teachers like old rock.'

Everyone eye-rolls Isham's attempt at a joke, even Isham.

'But also a bit of eighties hip-hop,' Martin has to add. 'De La Soul, A Tribe Called Quest, PE, NWA, KRS-One . . .'

'Anything modern?' Camille asks him.

He takes a quick micro-glance at her chest, then up to her eyes. 'Not really. No one you'd have heard of.'

'That is possibly true. After all, I am from France. We don't have music there. Literally none.' Her gentle sarcasm is lost, or maybe he didn't hear her, but I like it.

'Okay,' Martin says. 'What are you into?'

'My tastes are quite eclectic, I suppose. Beyoncé. Leonard Cohen. Johnny Cash. Bowie. Bit of Jacques Brel. But *Thriller* is my favourite album of all time. And "Billie Jean" is the best pop song ever written.'

'"Billie Jean"?' I say. 'It's a great song.'

Martin turns to me. 'What about you, then? You into music?'

'A little.'

His eyes widen, waiting for me to clarify.

'Do you play anything, music wise?' Camille asks me, frowning, as if there is more to the question than it seems.

I shrug. It would be easy to lie, but it falls out of me. 'Bit of guitar, little bit of piano . . .'

'Piano?' Camille's eyes widen.

Sarah, the sports teacher, in a capacious Welsh rugby shirt, points over to the corner of the room. 'They've got a piano in here, you know. They let people play.'

I stare at the piano. I had been trying so hard to act like an ordinary mayfly that I hadn't even noticed it when I'd walked in.

'Oh yes, you can give it a tinkle,' says the barman, a lanky twenty-something with a weak wispy beard, who is clearing our glasses away.

I begin to panic, the way anyone might panic when being offered a drug they had fought to give up. 'No, I'm fine.'

Martin, sensing my awkwardness in front of Camille, pushes it a little further. 'No, go on, Tom. I had a go last Thursday. Have a go.'

Camille looks at me sympathetically. 'It isn't compulsory. It's not an initiation ritual. He doesn't have to if he doesn't want to.'

'Well,' I find myself saying, 'it's been a while.'

I don't want her to pity me, so maybe it is for that reason that I stand up and walk over to the scratched and well-worn upright piano, passing the only other customers in the place – three grey-haired friends staring in the timeless mute sorrow of old men at their half-drunk pints of bitter.

I sit down on the stool and the room falls quiet with expectation. Well, quiet, except for a little snorted giggle from Martin.

I stare down at the keys. I haven't played the piano since Paris. Not properly. That was the best part of a century ago. There was something about the piano, compared to the guitar. It demanded more of you. It cost too much emotion.

I have no idea what to play.

I push up my sleeves.

I close my eyes.

Nothing.

I play the first thing that comes to mind.

'Greensleeves'.

I am in a pub in East London and playing 'Greensleeves' on a piano. Martin's laughter flaps into my head but I keep going. 'Greensleeves' blurs into 'Under the Greenwood Tree', which makes me pine for Marion, and so I move on to a bit of Liszt's *Liebestraum No. 3*. And by the time that I reach Gershwin's 'The Man I Love' Martin isn't laughing and I am on my own inside the music. I feel exactly how I used to feel, playing in Paris at Ciro's. I remember, in short, what the piano can do.

But then other memories rise up, and my head pounds as my mind goes into a kind of cramp of emotion.

When I eventually stop I turn to look at the group. Mouths are open. Camille leads a little round of applause. Even the three old men and bar staff join in.

Martin mumbles the word 'Greensleeves'. Isham tells me: 'That was epic!' Sarah tells Martin: 'You might be out of a job!' Martin tells Sarah to fuck off.

I sit on my stool next to Camille.

'When you played I really had that feeling again. Like I'd seen you playing before. It was like déjà vu or something.'

I just shrug. 'Well, they say déjà vu is a real thing.'

'A symptom of schizophrenia,' says Martin.

'But truly,' Camille says, her hand touching the back of mine, then retreating before anyone sees. 'That was amazing – si merveilleux.'

And I feel a brief but intense surge of desire. I haven't truly lusted after another human being for centuries, but when I look at Camille, when I hear her kind, strong voice, when I see the delicate creases around her eyes, when I feel the skin of her hand against the skin of mine, when I look at her mouth, my mind switches to what it would be like to be with her, to lose my way with her, to whisper longings into her ear, to devour and be devoured. To wake up in the same bed and talk and laugh and be in comfortable silence with her. To give her breakfast. Toast. Blackcurrant jam. Pink grapefruit juice. Maybe some watermelon. Sliced. On a plate. She would smile, and I see it in my mind, the smile, and I would dare to feel happy with another human being.

This is what playing the piano does.

This is the danger of it.

It makes you human.

'Tom?' she says, breaking my reverie. 'Would you like another drink?'

'No thanks,' I say, embarrassed, as though I am a book left open with every secret written on the page for all to see. 'I think I've probably had enough.'

Isham gets his phone out. 'Anyone want to see the scan?' he asks. 'It's 3D.'

'Ooh,' says Camille, 'me!'

Isham and his wife are expecting a baby. We lean in around the moving ultrasound image. I can remember when the concept of

209

ultrasound was first spoke of in the 1950s. It still, even now, feels like the future. Though it is a strange kind of future that makes you see a potential human as the delicate primitive clay-like being it is. Like watching a half-made sculpture seeking definition.

I notice, for a second, that Camille is staring at the scar on my arm. I pull down my sleeves, self-conscious.

'We don't know the sex yet. Zoë wants it to be a surprise.'

He has a tear glistening in his eye.

'I'd say it's a boy,' says Martin, and he points to the screen.

'That is not a penis,' Isham says.

Martin shrugs. 'It's a penis.'

I stare down at the screen, and I remember what it felt like when Rose told me she was pregnant. I wonder what Rose would have made of sonograms. And whether she'd have wanted to find out the gender. And I sit back in my chair and don't say much after that. A guilt takes over me. The guilt of desiring someone who isn't Rose.

So ridiculous.

And I drift away again, forgetting my headache, forgetting this is the Coach and Horses, and imagining it is the Boar's Head in Eastcheap, and that I could step outside into the night and walk back through the dark narrow streets to reach Rose and Marion and a version of me I had abandoned for centuries.

London, 1607–1616

In 1607 I was twenty-six years old.

I obviously didn't *look* twenty-six but I was looking a fraction older than I had done back when I'd worked on Bankside. When I had first become aware of my difference I thought that was it, I thought my physical being was frozen in time, but then, slowly, very slowly, things happened. For instance, *hair*. My crotch, chest, underarms and face were growing more hairs than they had done before. My voice, which had broken when I was twelve, became deeper still. My shoulders broadened a little. My arms found it easier to carry washing water back from the well. I gained greater control over my erections. And my face, according to Rose, became more like the face of a man. I was becoming so much more like a man that Rose suggested we get married, and we did so, in a small parentless wedding, with Grace as our witness.

Grace was now married too. She had become happily betrothed to her precise opposite – a shy, God-fearing, flush-cheeked shoemaker's apprentice called Walter – at the age of seventeen and she now lived with him in a tiny cottage in Stepney.

After we married, Rose and I moved too. The reason for this was quite simple. The longer we stayed in one place, the more dangerous it became. Rose's idea was to head further out, to one of the villages, but I knew of the potentially perilous consequences of this, so I suggested we do the opposite. I suggested we go and live inside the walls, go where we could disappear into the safety of crowds, and so we moved to Eastcheap, and life was good for a while.

Yes, there was rot and rats and misery all around us, but we had each other. The problem was, of course, that, although I was ageing, I wasn't ageing at the same speed as Rose. She was now twenty-seven years old, and looked it. While I was, gradually, starting to look young enough to be her son.

I said to people I was eighteen, which I could just about get away with, at least at the Boar's Head Inn, where I had started to play most nights of the week, but by the time Rose came to me and told me she wasn't bleeding, and that she thought she was pregnant, I had already felt like I was endangering her. Anyway, it was true. And I had no idea if the news was wonderful or devastating. She was pregnant. We had hardly enough money to feed ourselves, and now there was going to be a third mouth to feed.

Of course, there were other worries too. I worried something would happen to Rose. After all, I had heard of so many women dying during childbirth that it seemed a wholly ordinary occurrence. So I kept the windows closed against the cold. And I prayed for God to protect her.

And, for once in my life, nothing terrible happened.

What happened was this. We had a daughter. We called her Marion.

I would hold her in my arms while she was still wrapped in swaddling bonds, and I used to sing to her in French to calm her when she cried, and it generally seemed to work.

I loved her, instantly. Of course, most parents love their children instantly. But I mention it here because I still find it a remarkable thing. Where was that love before? Where did you acquire it from? The way it is suddenly there, total and complete, as sudden as grief, but in reverse, is one of the wonders about being human.

She was small, though. Obviously babies, as a rule, are small and delicate but back in those days the delicacy came with an extra edge.

'Will she last, Tom?' Rose used to say, when Marion was asleep and we watched her, seeking the comfort of her every breath. 'God won't take her, will He?'

'No. She's as healthy as a goose,' I used to say.

Rose obsessed over memories of Nat and Rowland, her dead brothers. Any time Marion coughed – or even made any kind of noise that could be loosely interpreted as one – Rose would become ashen and declare, 'That's how it began with Rowland!'

At night she would watch the stars, not quite knowing what she was watching them for, but knowing that our fates – and the fate of Marion – were written on them.

All of this anxiety took its toll on Rose, who became very quiet and withdrawn in the following months. She looked pale and tired, and kept blaming herself for being a terrible mother, which she wasn't at all. I wonder now if it was a form of postnatal depression. She was always up before it was light. And became more religious than she had ever been, saying prayers even as she held Marion. She lost her appetite, eating barely more than a few mouthfuls of pottage a day. She never worked now, or sold fruit at the market, as Marion had taken over her days, and I think she missed the company and liveliness of the time, so I encouraged Grace to come and see her, which she did from time to time, bringing baby clothes or calming ointments from the apothecary, along with her earthy humour.

We had lovely neighbours, Ezekiel and Holwice, who'd had nine children of their own, five of whom were still alive, and so Holwice – although in her fifties, worked now as a wool-walker at the watermill – had lots of childcare advice. It was the usual kind of stuff. Open the windows to ward away bad spirits. No bathing. A dab of breast milk and rosewater solution on the baby's forehead to aid sleep.

But Rose thought all manner of things could endanger little Marion (and she was, always, *little*, which added to Rose's concern). She would get cross with herself, or me, for instance, if either of us scratched our head.

'It is a dirty habit, Tom. It could make her sick!'

'I am sure it won't.'

'You must stop it, Tom. You must stop it. And you mustn't belch around her.'

'I didn't know I did belch around her.'

'And you must wipe your mouth after drinking ale. And be quiet when you come home at night. You always wake her.'

'I am sorry.'

Other times, when Marion was asleep, Rose would just burst out crying for no apparent reason, and ask me to hold her, which I did. Often, when I came back from a night playing music, I would hear her tears as I entered the door.

Anyway, I don't know why I dwell on this. This was only a matter of months. And Rose returned back to her old self by the end of summer. I suppose I am relaying it because it added to my guilt. I knew, deep down, that I was part of the strain on things. Rose had, of the two of us, been the strong one, the organiser and initiator, the one who always knew what was best to do for the both of us. And it was her strength that had, obviously, enabled Rose to marry me, knowing all that she knew.

But, out of sorts, her doubts rose up. Even if Marion survived infancy, and childhood, what then? What would happen when she looked older than her father? The questions, we both knew, would breed like rabbits.

I had a new worry too. While Rose stayed concerned that Marion would die, or otherwise overtake me, I worried with an equal intensity that she wouldn't. What I mean is, I worried she would be like me. I worried she would be abnormal. That she would reach the age of thirteen and then stop getting any older. I worried that Marion would face the same problems – or even worse ones – for I knew (of course I knew) that women were the ones who had to die at the bottom of rivers to prove their innocence.

I couldn't sleep at night, however much ale I had drunk (and the quantity was increasing at a daily rate). I kept thinking of Manning, still alive, probably still in London. Though we never encountered him, I often had the *sense* of him. I sometimes imagined I could feel his closeness, as if his malevolent essence was contained in shadows or cesspits or the single hand of a church clock.

Superstition was rising everywhere. People like, occasionally, to see human life as a generally smooth upwardly sloping line towards enlightenment and knowledge and tolerance, but I have to say that has never been my experience. It isn't in this century and it wasn't in that one. The arrival of King James onto the throne let superstition off the lead. King James, who not only wrote *Daemonologie* but also asked puritanical translators to refashion the Bible, was a boost for intolerance.

The lesson of history is that ignorance and superstition are things that can rise up, inside almost anyone, at any moment. And what starts as a doubt in a mind can swiftly become an act in the world.

And so our fears grew. One night in the Boar's Head, a fight started when a group of men turned on one of their members and accused him of devil worship. Another night I got speaking to a butcher who refused to take any pork from a certain farmer, on account that he believed all his pigs were 'dark spirits' and their meat could corrupt the soul. He gave no evidence for this but he believed it with a passion, and it caused me to remember the case of a pig in Suffolk that had once stood trial and had been burned at the stake on account of being a demon.

We never went to the Globe to see *Macbeth*, for obvious reasons, but it was no coincidence that this tale of politics and supernatural malevolence was the most popular and talked-about piece of entertainment at the time. I wonder, now, if Shakespeare would have been so kind to me. And if, in this new environment, he believed the death of Henry Hemmings had been justified. But I also had more specific worries.

There was a man at the end of our street, a smartly dressed man who read aloud emphatically enunciated dialogues from *Daemonologie*, alongside extracts from the King's Bible. Also, by the time Marion was four, even our once kindly neighbours, Ezekiel and Holwice, were beginning to give me funny looks. I don't know if this was because they had noticed I wasn't ageing, or if it was more that the age difference between Rose and me was starting to look a little wide. She seemed a good decade older than me.

And even though we never saw Manning again, I would hear his name. Once, in the street, a woman I had never seen before came up to me and stuck her finger in my chest.

'Mr Manning told me about you. He told everyone about you . . . They say you have a child. They should have smothered her at birth, to be safe.'

Another time, while Rose was out alone with Marion she was spat at, for living with the 'enchanter'.

Marion, now a girl, was aware of such things. She was an intelligent, sensitive child, and seemed to carry a sadness around with her a lot of the time. She cried after that incident. And she would fall very quiet if she heard us talk, however quietly, about our worries.

Slowly, and for her sake, we began to change the way we lived. We deliberately made sure we were never out together. We tried to stop questions when they arose. And we managed it.

Marion, being a girl, and not being nobility, did not go to school. Yet we still thought it important for her to read, to be able to broaden her mind and give her places in her thoughts to hide inside. Reading was a rare skill, in those days, but was one I possessed. And, as I had grown up with a mother who could read (albeit in French) I saw nothing strange in the idea of a girl reading.

She was, it turned out, an extremely gifted and curious reader. We possessed only two books but she adored them. She could read Edmund Spenser's *The Faerie Queene* by the age of six, and by the

216

age of eight could quote Michel de Montaigne – I had an English translation of his essays that I had acquired years before at Southwark's Wednesday market. The book was damaged – the pages unfixed from the spine – and I'd bought it for two pennies. She would see, for instance, her mother touch my hand and say, 'If there is such a thing as good marriage, it is because it resembles friendship rather than love.' Or, on questioning why she looked so sad, she would remark, 'My life has been full of terrible misfortunes, most of which never happened.'

'That's Montaigne, isn't it?'

And she would give the tiniest nod. 'I quote others only in order the better to express myself,' she'd say, which was itself, I sensed, another quote.

Then one day she read something else.

You see, she sometimes went outside on her own in the morning to play. And one day she came in, while I was learning a new lute song – 'I Saw My Lady Weepe' by John Dowland – and she looked a little like someone had slapped her in the face.

'What is it, sweetheart?'

She seemed out of breath. It took her a moment. She was frowning at me, with an intensity and seriousness that seemed beyond her age. 'Are you Satan, Father?'

I laughed. 'Only in the mornings.'

She wasn't in joking mood, so I quickly added, 'No, Marion. What would make you ask such a thing?'

And then she showed me.

Someone had scraped the words 'Satan Resides Here' on our door. It was a horrifying thing to see, but more horrifying to know Marion had seen it too.

And when Rose saw it she knew, absolutely, what needed to be done.

'We need to leave London.'

'But where would we go?'

217

That seemed, to Rose, to be a secondary question. She was resolute. 'We need to start again.'

'To do what?'

She pointed at the lute leaning beside the door.

'People's ears like music in other places.'

I stared at the lute. At the darkness of the small holes amid the twisting decoration of the wood. I imagined, ridiculously, a world inside there. Deep in the shell of the lute. Where some miniature version of ourselves could live, safe and invisible and unharmed.

London, now

I had brought my lute in for year nine. I am holding it, leaning against my desk.

'This was hand-crafted way over four hundred years ago in France. The design is a little more intricate than English lutes of that period.'

'So that's what guitars used to look like in the olden days?' wonders Danielle.

'Lutes aren't technically guitars. They're obviously close cousins but a lute has a lighter kind of sound. Look at the shape of it. Like a teardrop. And look at the depth. Look at the back. It's called a shell. The strings are made of sheep's intestines. They give it a very precise perfect sound.'

Danielle makes a disgusted face.

'This was *the* instrument once upon a time. This was the keyboard and electric guitar in one. Even the queen had one. But playing music in public was a bit vulgar so that was generally left to the lower orders.'

I play a few notes. The first bars of 'Flow My Tears'. They seem unimpressed.

'That was a big tune, back in the day.'

'Was that from the eighties?' wonders Marcus, the boy with the gold watch and the complicated hairstyle who sits next to Anton.

'No, a little earlier.'

But that made me remember something.

I start to play a chord – E minor – and keep going at it in short stabs before switching to A minor.

'I know this song,' says Danielle. 'My mum loves this.'

Anton is smiling and nodding his head. And then I start singing the words to the song, to 'Billie Jean', in a slightly ridiculous falsetto.

The class is laughing now. Some of them are singing along.

And then, because of the commotion, Camille and her class of year sevens, on their way outside for one of her French lessons on the playing field, stop to watch me. Camille opens the door to hear.

She is clapping in time from behind the glass. She smiles and closes her eyes and sings the chorus.

And then her eyes open and are on me and I feel happily terrified or fearfully happy, and now even Daphne is out in the corridor so I stop playing. And the kids release a collective moan. And Daphne says, 'Don't stop for me. There's always time for a lute rendition of Michael Jackson at Oakfield. Love that song.'

'Me too,' says Camille.

But of course I already know that.

Canterbury, 1616–1617

Canterbury had been where many French Huguenots, people like myself and my mother, had settled. The Duke of Rochefort had indeed recommended that my mother move to either London or Canterbury, telling her that Canterbury – a 'godly place' – was very welcoming to outsiders seeking refuge. My mother had ignored that advice, seeking the quiet of Suffolk instead, and mistaking, fatally, quietness with security. But the advice had stayed with me.

So we moved to Canterbury.

We managed to find a warm, comfortable cottage, paying less in rent than we ever had in London. We were impressed by the cathedral and the clean air, but other things were a struggle. Not least, work.

No one paid for musicians in the inns and alehouses there, and there was no theatre work either. I resorted to playing in the street, which was only busy on days when crowds were gathering at the gallows in the market square.

Then, when the money became too tight (after all of two weeks) Rose and Marion, now nine, gained work selling flowers. Marion was such a miraculous musical Montaigne-quoting girl. I often spoke to her in French and she picked up the language, though Rose was a little bit uncertain about this, as if all this education was going to be another thing that would separate her from the masses and mark her difference.

Marion would sometimes walk around the room in circles, in her own world, humming songs softly, or making clicking sounds with her mouth to amuse herself. She often seemed somewhere else entirely and would stare longingly out of the window. Sometimes some invisible worry would crease her forehead that she would never tell me about. She reminded me a lot of her grandmother. The sensitivity and intelligence and musicality. The mystery. She preferred playing the pipe (a tin pipe bought for tuppence at the market) to the lute. She liked music 'made of breath not formed from fingers'.

She would play the pipe in the street. She would walk along playing it. I remember, most of all, a wonderful Saturday morning – with the sun brightening the world – when Marion and I headed into town to the cobbler's to get Rose's shoes mended. While I was talking to the cobbler Marion stood outside and played 'Under the Greenwood Tree' on the pipe.

A few moments later, she ran in and held up a shining clean silver penny, as bright as day. She had a broad, rare smile on her face. I had never seen her so happy.

'A lady just gave me this. I will keep this coin and it will give us luck, Father, you'll see.'

However, our luck didn't last long.

The very next day we were all out together as a family, on our way to church, when a group of teenage boys began mocking us.

They were laughing at me and Rose holding hands, and we stopped doing so, then looked at each other, ashamed of our shame.

Then our landlord, an old growling badger of a man called Mr Flint, started to ask things every time he collected the rent money.

'Are you her son, or . . .?'

'So, your girl can speak French?'

And, with grim inevitability, things descended from there. Gossip gained life here too. We began to inhabit a world of whispers and sharp looks and cold shoulders. It was easy to think that even the starlings were chirping about us. We stopped going to church, to try to hide out of view, but of course this stoked the embers of suspicion even more. And instead of scratching words on our door, they scratched overlapping circles into the tree outside our house, to ward off the evil spirits we were thought to associate with.

One day at the market a man claiming to be a witchhunter came up to Marion and told her she was the child of a witch, a witch who kept her husband young for her own pleasure. And then the man told Marion that she too, as the progeny of a witch, must be a demon.

Marion had held her head high and arguably made things worse by telling the man that 'a monster who meets a miracle would see a monster'. Which wasn't quite Montaigne, but was certainly influenced by him. But shortly after the man had gone Marion cried her eyes out and she remained mute for the rest of the day.

Rose was almost sick with fear, her voice trembling, as she told me of the incident that evening, after Marion had woken from a nightmare and fallen back asleep.

'Why can't these maggots leave us alone? I'm so worried for her. For all of us.'

She had a tear in her eye, even as her face hardened. She had made a decision. It was a terrifying one.

'We must go back to London.'

'But we fled *from* there.'

'It was a mistake. We will go. All of us . . . all of us . . . all of us.' She kept saying those words, as if she was scared of the words that would come after, though they eventually came.

The tears streamed now. I held her and she held me back and I kissed the top of her head.

'You and Marion will be for ever in danger so long as I am with you.'

'There must be a way—'

'There is no way.'

Rose smoothed her skirt and stared down at it. She closed her eyes and wiped them and inhaled courage. A cart rattled by on

223

the road outside. She looked at me and didn't say anything but the silence was its own message.

'You aren't safe with us, Tom.'

She didn't say the other half of this. That they weren't safe with me, but I knew she knew that too, and the knowledge was near enough to kill me. To be the danger I wanted to protect them from.

I said nothing. What could I say? I knew Rose could survive without me. I knew, in fact, it was more likely without me.

She was now able to look at me in the face. 'It is not for myself. I am not scared for myself. I will not be truly alive without you. I will be a ghost that breathes.'

And that was it. That was the moment all hope disappeared.

Marion knew I was going away. It hurt her. I could see it in her eyes. But, as she tended to do with things that troubled her, she kept it inside.

'You will be safe, my angel. People won't ask questions any more. No one will mark your door. No one will spit at your mother. Nothing terrible will happen. I have to go away.'

'Will you return?' she asked, almost formally, as if I was already at a distance from her. 'Will you come and live with us?'

The truth would have broken both our hearts, and so I didn't offer it. I did what you sometimes have to do as a parent. I told a lie. 'Yes, I will return.'

She frowned darkly, and then she disappeared into her room. A moment later she returned, clutching something in her fist.

'Open your hand.'

I opened it and a penny dropped onto my palm.

'My lucky coin,' she explained. 'You must keep it with you always, and, wherever you are, you must think of me.'

We decided to leave for London, unseen, at night. Coach travel from Canterbury to London was available to anyone with money, and we managed to find a coachman with good horses who could take us there for a little less than two shillings.

And later that night, Marion, the only child I have ever had, fell asleep on my shoulder in the coach. My arm was around her. Rose stared at me, her eyes glistening with tears in the dark, as I clutched the coin Marion had given me.

It was so hard, in the years after that. I thought of all the days we'd had together as a family, all jammed close like plums in a basket. I wish I could have taken those days and spread them out for ever. One afternoon with them a month for the rest of my life. I could cope if it was just one day a year, so long as there was a time with Rose and Marion *in front* of me. But the trouble with life was that it had to be lived *consecutively*.

I fell into a nocturnal existence.

My lute and fresh face were a big hit in inns, particularly the Mermaid Tavern where fresh faces were an exotic rarity. I began to lose myself in the pleasures of alcohol and whorehouses. The city was becoming more and more crowded, and yet it just made me feel lonelier and lonelier. All those people who stubbornly were not Rose and were not Marion. I knew they lived in Shoreditch, or at least that Shoreditch had been their plan, so I sometimes went there but could never see them.

Then, one day, in one of the plague years – 1623 – I saw someone I vaguely recognised walking by the river. A woman in her thirties, holding a sleeping baby boy in her arms. (Walking by the river was a popular pastime whenever the plague struck, as the river air was seen as plague-free, bizarrely, given all the corpses that ended up there.) It took me a moment to realise it was Grace, though of course it took her no time at all to recognise me.

She looked sad and lost; the fierce life force of the girl I had once known seemed now blunted.

She stared at me for a while. 'You still look the same, and look at me, an old woman!'

'You are not an old woman, Grace.' And she wasn't. Not in age.

Not in skin. Yet, still, the sadness and weight in her voice made me feel like it was a lie. And then I heard a reason for this.

'How is she?' I asked, voicing a question I'd had inside my head, through every single moment I had been without her.

'Rose has it,' she told me.

'Has what?'

Grace didn't have to say. I knew from her face. I felt a horrible coldness sink into me, clearing everything away.

'She wants me nowhere near her for fear I catch it too. She will only speak to me from behind her door.'

'I need to see her.'

'She will not let you.'

'Has she spoken of me?'

'She misses you. It was all she was saying. That she should have never sent you away. That everything bad that happened has happened because she sent you away. She has never stopped thinking of you. She has never stopped loving you, Tom . . .'

I felt the prick of tears behind my eyes. I stared at her sleeping son. 'Where does she live now? Where is Marion? I would love to know about Marion.'

Grace looked a little sheepish, clearly not knowing if she should say. She only answered my first question.

'Rose doesn't want—'

'I won't catch it. I can't. I would have caught it by now. I never catch anything.'

Grace thought, gently rocking her baby in the cool afternoon air. 'All right, I will tell you . . .'

London, now

It is parents' evening. I am sitting behind a table, having just taken my third ibuprofen of the hour, lost in a flashback. Thinking of that last conversation with Rose. That last time I saw her. No. Not thinking of it, actually living it, again, as I sit here in a hall with parents, all with smartphones in their pockets or hands. I am hearing her whisper, from when she lay in a bed less than five hundred metres from this hall.

There is a darkness that fringes everything. It is a most horrid ecstasy . . .

She had been talking of a hallucination, but the more those words echoed, the more it seemed like a statement on life.

'It's all right, Rose,' I whisper to myself, like a madman, right there in the twenty-first century. 'It's all right . . .'

And then the other echo.

The one that reverberated day and night.

She was like you. You must try to find her. You must try to look after her . . .

'I'm sorry, Rose. I'm sorry . . .'

Another voice breaks through. A voice from right now. A voice from across the table.

'Are you all right, Mr Hazard?'

It is Anton Campbell's mother, Claire. She is staring at me, confused.

'Yes, yes, I'm fine. I was just . . . I'm sorry, I was just thinking of something . . . Anyway, you were about to tell me something. Please, go ahead.'

'I want to thank you,' she says.

'Thank me?'

'I have never seen Anton more engaged with his schoolwork than he is with history. He's even been getting books out from the library. All kinds of things. It's so good to see. He says you really make it come alive.'

It is tempting, of course, to tell her that her son's friend had threatened to stab me, but I don't. I actually feel a bit proud.

I can't really remember feeling pride. I hadn't felt like this since I helped Marion to read Montaigne and play 'Under the Greenwood Tree' on the pipe. Hendrich always said I should be proud of the work I do for the society, but I had only felt good on occasion, such as when I'd gone up to Yorkshire to help rescue Flora. Generally, though, the work for the society had been a bit tense, and at worst soul-destroying. This, though, is different. This feels good in a solid, sustainable kind of way.

'I'd been so worried about him . . . You know, he was drifting a little. A boy. Fourteen. He was very lost in himself. Hanging out with the wrong crowd. Getting in a little late . . .'

'Oh, really?'

'Wouldn't talk to me much . . . But now he's really getting back on track. So thank you. Thank you.'

'Well, he's a very bright young man. His essays on the Second World War and the British Empire's role in the slave trade were really good. He's on track for As.'

'He wants to go to university. And do history. Which, you know, these days . . . it's going to be expensive. But I want him to go. Which is why I am working every hour God sends. And God sends some *crazy* hours. But he's determined. He wants to go.'

I feel a swell of pride. *This.* This right here is why I wanted to become a teacher. To know that it is possible to change the world for the better, in however small a way.

'That is a brilliant . . .' I look over at one of the tables across the sports hall. Camille is between parents. I notice her take off her glasses and rub her eyes. She doesn't look very well. She is staring down at the papers on her little table, trying to focus.

I bring my mind back to Mrs Campbell. Or try to. My mind is haunting me with images: Rose's dead face, Marion with her book, a house being devoured by flames.

When the city had burned, in 1666, I took part in the firefighting efforts and contemplated walking suicidally into one of the burning shops that, before the blaze, lined either side of London Bridge.

'Yes,' I say, trying to reassure Mrs Campbell that I am listening. 'Yes, I bet.'

Then, suddenly, and with no warning, Camille falls off her chair. Her ribs hit the side of the table on her way down to the floor. Then her legs start to spasm violently. She is having some kind of fit, right there on the floor of the sports hall in the middle of parents' evening.

I had been conditioned, even before I had knowledge of the Albatross Society, not to get involved in the heat of the moment. To float through life with a cool detachment. But that doesn't seem to work any more. Maybe that youngest version of my adult self was returning. The one which had jumped off a theatre gallery to protect Rose and her sister.

Before I know it I am there, right over her, as Daphne comes running. Camille's whole body is jerking now.

'Pull the table back!' I tell Daphne.

She does so. Then she asks another member of staff to call an ambulance.

I hold Camille steady.

There is a crowd. Only this is a twenty-first century crowd, so everyone's macabre fascination is tempered with at least the semblance of concern.

She stops convulsing, and comes around, her confusion delaying her embarrassment. For a minute or so, she says nothing, just concentrates on my face.

Daphne brings some water. 'Let's all give her some room,' she says to the parents and staff. 'Come on, guys and gals, let's all step back a little . . .'

'It's okay,' I tell Camille. 'You just had a seizure.'

Just. That sounds terrible.

'Where . . . where . . . I . . .?'

She looks around a little. She gets up, on her elbows, then sits up fully. She is weak. Something has been taken from her. Along with Daphne I help settle her back in her seat.

'Where am I?'

'The sports hall.' Daphne's smile is reassuring. 'You're at work. At the school. It's all right, lovely, it's just a . . . You've had some kind of a seizure . . .'

'School,' she says sleepily, to herself.

'An ambulance is coming.' This is one of the parents, putting their iPhone away.

'I'm okay,' she says. She doesn't seem in the slightest bit self-conscious. Just tired and confused.

She stares up at me, frowning, not understanding who I am, or maybe understanding too much.

'You're okay,' I tell her.

Her eyes are fixed on me. 'I do know you.'

I smile at her, then, with more awkwardness, at Daphne. And I gently tell her, 'Of course you do. We work together.' I then, perhaps foolishly, underline my point for the crowd. 'The new history teacher.'

She is leaning back. She sips the water. She shakes her head.

'Ciro's.'

The name hits my heart like a hammer. Hendrich's words, that day years ago in a hurricane-ravaged Central Park, come back to me. *The past is never gone. It just hides.*

'I—'

'You played piano. When I saw you the other day, at the pub . . . I . . .'

230

Two thoughts: I am dreaming. It is possible. I have dreamed of Camille before.

Or: maybe she is old too. Old, old, old. As in, ancient. An alba. Maybe somehow the photos I have seen on Facebook of her younger self have been photoshopped. Maybe this is what I had felt for her. Maybe this was the connection. Maybe I just have a sense of our exotic sameness. Or maybe she knows some other way.

The one thing I am sure of is that I have to stop her talking. If she carries on she not only risks exposing me, but herself. I feel for her. There is no point denying that any more. The lie I had told myself for so long – that I could exist without caring for anyone new – was just that. A lie. I have no idea why Camille was the one to make me realise this, but I can no longer deny I care for her. And, in caring for her, I feel an overwhelming need to protect her. After all, Hendrich has had people permanently silenced for less than a mutter in a school hall. If she knows about albas, and is talking about it in public, she is automatically risking more than my identity. She's risking her life.

'Just relax. We'll . . . nous allons parler plus tard . . . I'll explain everything. But quiet, now. I can't tell you here. Please understand.'

She looks sleepy with the effort of sitting up. She stares at me, the confusion clearing. 'Okay. I understand.'

I lift the cup of water and help her take a sip. She smiles at Daphne and the other concerned faces. 'I'm sorry . . . I have a seizure every few months. It's my epilepsy. They make me tired for a while. I'll be fine. The tablets were meant to stop the seizures. So I probably need some new ones . . .'

She stares at me. Her eyelids seem heavy. She looks vulnerable and invincible all at once.

'You okay?' I ask her.

She gives a small nod, but looks almost as scared as I am.

Paris, 1929

It was around seven in the evening. Beside the vast empty dance floor, men in dinner jackets and women in low-necked tassel-fringed shift dresses and bobbed hair were drinking apéritifs and listening to the music I was playing.

Jazz was what Ciro's was known for. But, by 1929, the sophisticated clientele didn't just want jazz-jazz-jazz, because jazz was everywhere. So I sometimes mixed it up a little. Sometimes, if people were on the dance floor, I'd drop in an Argentine tango or some gypsy flavours, but early evening you could get away with playing anything soft and thoughtful, so I was playing some Fauré, from his melancholic period, and feeling every note.

'Prétendez que je ne suis pas ici,' the photographer had told me as I was playing.

'Non,' I whispered, remembering Hendrich's no-photographs rule. 'Pas de photos! Pas de—'

But it was too late. I had been so lost in the music he had been taking photos of me without my realising.

'Merde,' I whispered to myself, switching to Gershwin to try to better my mood.

London, now

We are in a smart gastropub in the new Globe Theatre.

I feel nervous. The reason isn't the location. It is Camille herself. The mystery is terrifying. How does she know about Ciro's? How could she? I am scared of all the answers I have thought of, and the unknown ones I haven't. I am scared for her. I am scared for me. I am twitching and looking around like an ominous bird on a windowsill. But there is also another reason I am scared. I am scared because up until now I have been surviving.

I mean, I haven't actively wanted to kill myself for a long time. The last time, precisely, was in a bunker near Tarragona in the Spanish Civil War when I placed a pistol in my mouth and prepared to blow my head off. Only by forcing myself to stare and stare at Marion's lucky penny had I managed to keep my brains on the inside of my skull. But that was 1937. That was a long time of not actively trying to die.

I have recently thought I wanted out from Hendrich but maybe, actually, this was a mistake. Yes, I am 'owned' by Hendrich but there is a comfort in that. Free will might be overrated.

'Anxiety,' Kierkegaard wrote, in the middle of the nineteenth century, 'is the dizziness of freedom.'

I had ached from the death of Rose for centuries, and that pain had faded into the neutral monotony of existing, and moving on before I had time to gather any emotional moss. I'd been able to enjoy music and food and poetry and red wine and the aesthetic pleasures of the world and that, I now realised, was perfectly fine.

Yes, there had been a void inside me, but voids were underrated.

Voids were empty of love but also pain. Emptiness was not without its advantages. You could move around in emptiness.

I try to tell myself I am just meeting her for what she is going to tell me, and that I don't have to tell her anything in return. But it is strange being here. Especially as it is *here*.

I haven't been to this specific place since the day I jumped onto the stage from the musicians' gallery. The day I landed on Will Kemp's back and saw Manning again. It had been the day of another confession, of course, to Rose. And now I can feel the faint echo of that day, amid the polite middle-class theatre chatter and clinking of cutlery around me.

The famous image of Shakespeare stares up at me from the front of the menu. I used to think it looked nothing like him – the image being all forehead and bad hair and wispy beard and lobotomised expression – but now the eyes seem to be *his* eyes. Watching me, wryly, as I continue through life. As if it amuses him, watching the man he helped to escape that day carry on in an interminable endless living tragicomedy.

The waiter is here now and Camille is smiling up at him.

She is wearing a midnight blue shirt. She looks pale, a little tired, but also beautiful.

'I would like the skate wing,' she tells the waiter, pushing her glasses a little further up her nose.

'Very good,' says the waiter, who turns to me.

'I'll have the gnocchi in kale pesto.'

He takes the menus, and their portraits of my former boss, and I turn back to look at Camille and try to relax.

'I'm sorry,' I say. 'About being a bit odd sometimes, at school.'

Camille shakes her head. 'You really have to stop saying that. Incessant apologising is never an attractive trait.'

'You're right. The thing is, I really am quite bad, you know, with *people.*'

'Ah, them. People. Yes, it's hard.'

'And I have a lot, sometimes, going on in my head.'

'Join the club.'

'There's a club?'

'No. There are too many people in clubs. But it's fine. Be how you want to be.'

'I haven't been a very public person. I have had to be careful.' I am sure, looking at her, that I have never known her. In this life of familiar patterns and people she has the wonderfully rare feature of *not reminding me of anyone.* But I have to ask. 'We never met, did we? I mean, before I saw you that day in the park. I saw you once, from Daphne's window, but we have never met *before,* have we?'

'It depends what you mean by met. But, no, in the conventional sense, no.'

'Okay.'

'Yeah.'

There is a kind of stand-off. We both have more questions but we are carrying them in holsters waiting for the other one to fire away. A single sentence could render either of us insane.

We nibble on rye bread and harpoon olives with cocktail sticks.

'How are you feeling?' I ask. The tamest enquiry, but a sincere one.

She rips some bread apart and stares at it for a moment, as if a secret is there, contained like every element in the universe, inside the leavened dough.

'Much better,' she says. 'I've had epilepsy for a long time. Used to be a lot worse.'

A long time.

'So you've had lots of seizures before?'

'Yes,' she says.

The waiter tops up our wine. I take a sip. Then another.

Camille looks at me with forceful eyes. 'Now you. You promised. I need to know your story.'

235

'I want to tell you about myself,' I tell her, still unsure of how much truth I will eventually reveal. 'But there are some things that it is better for you – for anyone – not to know.'

'Criminal things?' I feel like she is teasing me.

'No. I mean, well, there are a few of those as well. No. I am just saying if you knew about me there would be a very strong chance you would think I was insane.'

'Philip K. Dick wrote that it is sometimes an appropriate response to reality to go insane.'

'The sci-fi writer?'

'Yes. I'm a geek. I like science fiction.'

'That's good,' I say.

'You like it too?'

No. I am it, I think to myself.

'Some. *Frankenstein. Flowers for Algernon.*'

'I want you to tell me about yourself,' she says. 'Tell me, at least, what you were going to tell me. Let me know if I am mad.'

It is tempting, right then, to put an end to it by saying *you are mad.* But instead I say, 'Before I tell you about me, you have to tell me about you.' I sound firmer than I had intended.

Wide eyes. 'Do I?'

I inhale deeply. This is the moment. 'I need to know how you recognised me. I need to know why you mentioned Ciro's. Ciro's closed eighty years ago.'

'I am not that old.'

'Exactly. I didn't think so.'

A song comes on in the background. She tilts her head. 'Ah, I love this. Listen.'

I listen. A warm, sentimental melody I recognise. It's 'Coming Around Again' by Carly Simon.

'My mother used to love Carly Simon.'

'And Michael Jackson?'

'That was just me.'

She smiles, and there is a moment of awkwardness when she realises it is her turn to explain herself. And in that moment I imagine being with her. Like I had in the pub. I imagine kissing her. I have an urge to run away and to get Hendrich to book me a plane and to disappear somewhere else, somewhere I will never see her again. But it is too late.

She is ready.

'Right,' she says. 'Je vais m'expliquer.'

And she does.

She tells me she started having seizures when she was seven. Her parents safe-proofed the house. Soft carpets. Table corners blunted by glued-on napkins. Finding the right medication had taken a while. And she slowly became agoraphobic. 'I was scared of life, basically.'

When she was nineteen she'd become engaged to a handsome, funny web designer called Erik – 'with a K', his mother was Swedish. This was the Erik I'd seen online. Facebook Erik. He had died in 2011 while rock climbing.

'I was there. Not climbing, obviously. Rock climbing and seizures don't go that well. But I was there. I was with some of our friends. There was a lot of blood. I didn't see anything for months when I closed my eyes except blood. And now he was dead I thought, well . . . fuck it.'

She takes a few breaths. To talk about memories is to live them a little.

'I was always worrying I could die at any minute. And I wanted to be like him, healthy, but then – *bam* – he turned out to be mortal too. And it was too much. I had to get out of there. I had to get out, so I went travelling. I knew I couldn't live as a prisoner to my condition any more. Do you understand?'

Of course I did. 'So what happened after that? How did things turn around?'

'I travelled around South America for six months. Brazil,

Argentina, Bolivia, Columbia. Chile. I loved Chile. It was amazing. But then, eventually, my money ran out, and so I went back to France and I couldn't go back to Grenoble – just the memories, you know – so I went to Paris. I went around all the nice restaurants and hotels and I got a job at the Plaza Athénée. One of the snooty grand hotels. There was something calming about that work. You would be speaking to people all the time, all day, checking in, checking out, but there was never anything deep and meaningful to it, you know? There were never any questions about life stuff, so it suited me perfectly.'

This is it. I sense it. Anxiety tightens my chest as she continues.

'And anyway, they had these photos, this exhibition in the lobby, of Golden Age Paris, all from the twenties. And lots were of jazz clubs, and of the boulevards, and Montmartre, and they had one of what's her name . . . the jazz singer, the dancer, with the cheetah . . .'

'Josephine Baker?'

As I say the name I remember watching her through a mist of cigarette smoke dancing the Charleston at the Century Club in Paris.

She nods quickly, makes a rolling motion with her hands, as if she is nearing her conclusion. I try to steel myself.

'Yes. Josephine Baker. Anyway, the one I was facing, the one I looked at, day in, day out, was the largest one: of the pianist at a restaurant. The restaurant was called Ciro's. It had the name Ciro's in the photograph. And the photo was black and white but very good quality for the time, and the man looked so lost in the music he was playing, as he looked forward over the piano, ignoring all the people in the restaurant who were looking at him, and I became fascinated by this moment, this frozen moment . . . Because it seemed like there was something timeless about it. Something beyond time. And also, the man was handsome. He had nice hands. And a seriously brooding face. And he had this pristine white shirt on, but with his sleeves rolled up, devil may care, and there was this scar on his arm. This curved scar. And I thought it was okay to have a crush on this man because he was dead. Only he wasn't dead, was he? Because he was you.'

I hesitate. Suddenly I have no idea what to do. I remember her staring at the scar on my arm in the pub and now I know why. It all makes sense.

It is ridiculous, given that I have brought her here to tell her the truth, but I am now scared of doing so. My instinct is to lie. I am, after all, quite a good liar. Smooth and natural. I should just laugh and look disappointed, and say it is a bit of a shame, because I thought for a minute that she had really recognised me, and that now I know she is joking. Photographs could lie. Especially photographs from the 1920s.

But I don't do that. I suppose part of it is because I really don't want her to be embarrassed. Another part of me, I think, wants her to know the truth. Needs her to.

'So,' she says, into my silence.

She then makes a kind of gesture that is hard to capture. She sticks her chin out a little and does a slight nod and closes her eyes and pulls her hair back behind an ear. It is a gesture of mild defiance. I don't know what she is defying. Life? Reality? Epilepsy? It is over in two seconds but I think this is the moment in which I have to admit to myself that I am in love for the first time in four centuries.

It may seem strange, falling in love with someone because of a gesture, but sometimes you can read an entire person in a single moment. The way you can study a grain of sand and understand the universe. Love at first sight might or might not be a thing, but love in a single moment is.

'So,' I say, tentatively, testing how much she believes versus what she thinks she believes. 'You not only like science fiction, you think I could *be* science fiction. You think I could be a time traveller or something.'

She shrugs. 'Or something. I don't know. I don't know. I mean, any truth that people aren't ready to believe sounds like science fiction. The earth going around the sun. Electromagnetism. Evolution. X-rays. Aeroplanes. DNA. Stem cells. Climate change. Water on Mars. It is all science fiction until we see it happen.'

I have that urge to get out of here, out of the restaurant. It is almost as strong as the urge to want to talk to her for all eternity. But not quite.

I clench my eyes closed, as if pressing forge-hot iron against my skin.

'You can tell me. You can tell me the truth.'

'I can't.'

'I know it was you in that picture.'

'It was staged. The picture was staged. It wasn't from the twenties.'

'You're lying. Don't lie to me.'

I stand up. 'I've got to go.'

'No, you don't. Please. Please. I like you. You can't run away from everything.'

'You're wrong. You can. You can run and run and run. You can run your entire life. You can run and change and keep running.'

People stop chewing to look at me. I am making a scene. Again, here in Southwark. I sit back down in my chair.

'I have the photo,' she says. 'I have it on my phone. A photo of a photo. But it's good quality. I know that sounds weird. But if you don't tell me, I will have this question in my head for ever and I will try and find other ways to answer it.'

'That would be very unwise.'

'Sounds exactly like me. I believe that every truth should be known. Do you see? Because I've lived with epilepsy and it's a mystery. They know so fucking little about it. There is a truth and it isn't known. We should know all the truths. Especially these days. And you promised. You promised if I came here you would tell me. If you don't tell me I'll keep asking questions.'

'And if I tell you the truth and say you must not say a thing – even a hint of a thing – to anyone? What then?'

'Then I will say nothing.'

I look at her face. You can tell only so much from a face. But I trust her. I have been trained, especially for the past century or so, not to trust anyone except Hendrich, and yet I trust her. Maybe it is the wine. Or maybe I am developing aptitude.

For a terrible, bewildering moment I know her completely. I know her as if I had spent whole lifetimes with her.

'Yes, it was me. It was me.'

She stares at me for a while, as if at something slowly emerging from a mist. As if she hadn't really been so sure before, as if she had wanted to be told it was all an elaborate illusion. I enjoy this look. I enjoy her knowing.

I will worry, later, about what I have just said. The truth that has passed between us. But right now, it is nothing but a release.

Our food arrives.

I watch the waiter disappear into the noise of the restaurant.

And then I look at her and I tell her everything.

Two hours later, we are walking by the Thames.

'I am scared to believe this. I knew it was you. I knew it. But there is knowing something and *knowing* something. I feel like I may be mad.'

'You're not mad.'

There is a young man, near where the Cardinal's Hat used to be, hopping about on a BMX to the delight of a crowd.

I look at Camille and see her intense seriousness juxtaposed with the happy tourists around us and I feel guilty, as if I haven't just told her a secret, but infected her with my own emotional weight.

I had told her about Marion. And now I was taking the polythene bag holding her penny out into the light.

'I remember the day she was given it. I remember times with her more than I remember things that happened a year ago.'

'And you think she is still alive?'

'I don't know. It's hard enough being a man and living for four hundred years. And no one ever thinks we're witches or worries why we don't have children. But I have always sensed it. She was a clever girl. She could read. She could quote Montaigne when she was nine. My worry is her mind. She was always a very sensitive child. Quiet. She would pick up on things. Get upset easily. She'd brood on things. Be lost in her own world. Have nightmares.'

'Poor girl,' said Camille, but I can see she is a bit dazed from all the information.

The one thing I haven't told her about is the Albatross Society. I sense that even to talk about it is to endanger her somehow. So when she asks me if I know of any others like me, apart from Marion, I don't mention Agnes or Hendrich. But I do tell her about Omai, my old friend from Tahiti.

'I haven't seen him since he left London. He went on Cook's third voyage. Cook wanted him as translator. I never saw him again. But he didn't come back to England.'

'Captain Cook?'

'Yes.'

She grapples enough with this that I don't throw her with my stories about Shakespeare and Fitzgerald. Not just yet.

We talk some more.

She asks to see the scar again. She traces it with her finger, as if to make all this more real. I look out at the river, where Dr Hutchinson had been found, once upon a time, and I realise I need to tell her something.

'Listen,' I tell her, 'you can't tell anyone about this. I probably shouldn't have told you. It's just that you were asking lots of questions. You thought you knew me. And that thinking, that curiosity, was possibly more dangerous than knowing. So now you know, you'll have to keep quiet about it.'

'Dangerous? This isn't the age of witches. Surely you could go public about this. Get DNA tests. Proof. It might be able to help people. Help, you know, science. Fighting illnesses. You said your immune system is—'

'There is a history of bad things happening to people who know. Doctors who were about to publish evidence, and so on. They have had a habit of disappearing.'

'Disappearing? Who made them disappear?'

The truth comes with its own lies. 'I don't know. It's a shadowy kind of world.'

We talk some more, and keep walking. We walk over the Millennium Bridge and head east through the City. We are, informally, walking home. Our conversation is carrying us there.

It is an hour's walk, but the weather is mild and neither of us fancy the underground. We walk past St Paul's Cathedral, and I tell her how it used to be busier than it is today, and how the churchyard used to be the centre of the London book trade. Then we walk down a street called Ironmonger Lane and she asks me about it and I say that I used to walk down this same Ironmonger Lane on my way to Southwark, and that it used to live up to its name, with the whole road noisy and hot from the moulding of metal.

She lives further east than me. When I suggest that I should probably take Abraham for a walk and that she is welcome to come too, she accepts the invite.

We sit together on the bench where I first saw her. An empty carrier bag floats far over our heads like a cartoon ghost.

'What are the main differences, over time?'

'Everything you see. Everything you see is different. Nothing stays the same.' I point to the creature darting up a tree. 'That would have been a red squirrel once, not a grey one. And there wouldn't have been carrier bags floating about. The sound of traffic was more *clip-clopping*. People looked at pocket watches, not phones. And smells, that's the other thing. It doesn't smell as much. Everywhere stank. Raw sewage and all the waste from the factories was pumped into the Thames.'

'Lovely.'

'It used to be severe. There was the Great Stink. It was eighteen fifty-something, around then. A hot summer. The whole city reeked.'

'It's still pretty stinky, though.'

'Not even comparable. You used to live in stink. People never used to wash. People used to think baths were bad for them.'

She sniffs her armpit. 'So I'd have been just about okay, then?'

I lean in and smell her. 'Far too clean. People would have been very suspicious. You are almost twentieth-century clean.'

She laughs. It is the simplest, purest joy on earth, I realise, to make someone you care about laugh.

The sky begins to darken slightly.

'So, you really had a crush on me?'

She laughs again. 'You really sound immature, for a four-hundred-year-old.'

'Ahem, four-hundred-and-thirty-nine-year-old.'

'Sorry, a four-hundred-and-thirty-nine-year-old.'

'Asking that question made you sound five.'

'I feel five. Normally I feel my age but right now I feel five.'

'Yes, if that is what you want to hear . . .'

'I want to hear the truth.'

She sighs. Fake dramatic. Does that thing where she looks to the sky. I watch her in profile, mesmerised. 'Yes, I had a crush on you.'

I sigh too. Mine is also a bit fake dramatic. 'The past tense has never sounded so sad.'

'Okay. Okay. Have. *Have.* I have a crush on you.'

'Me too. On you, I mean. I find you fascinating.'

I am being totally sincere, but she laughs. 'Fascinating? I'm sorry.'

Her laugher fades. I want to kiss her. I don't know how to make that happen. I have been single for four centuries and have absolutely no idea of the etiquette. But I feel light, happy. Actually, I would be fine with this. This 'Ode on a Grecian Urn' moment. With a kiss forever a possibility. With her looking at me and me looking at her.

I realise I would like to solve the mystery of her just as much as she wants to solve the mystery of me and she nestles a little into me and I put my arm around her. Right there. On the park bench. Maybe that is what it takes to love someone. Finding a happy mystery you would like to unravel for ever.

We sit in silence for a while, like a couple, watching Abraham gallop around with a Springer spaniel. And I am enjoying the happy weight of her head on my shoulder, for two minutes or so. Then two things happen in quick succession. I feel a sudden pang of guilt, thinking of Rose. Of her head resting on my chest as we lay on her narrow bed in Hackney. Of course, Camille wouldn't know this is what I am thinking, except that my body might have tensed a little.

And then my phone rings.

'I'll ignore it.'

Which I do. But then it rings again and this time she says, 'You'd better see who it is,' and I look at my phone and I see a single letter on the screen. H. I realise I have to get it. I have to do exactly what I would do if I wasn't with Camille. So I answer it. And the moment, that brief moment of happiness, floats away like a bag on the wind.

I stand up from the bench, with the phone to my ear.

'Is this a bad time?', Hendrich asks.

'No. No, Hendrich. It's fine.'

'Where are you?'

'I'm walking the dog.'

'Are you on your own?'

'Yes. I'm on my own. Except for Abraham.' I say this, I hope, quietly enough for Camille not to hear, and loud enough for Hendrich not to become suspicious. I think I fail on both counts.

A pause.

'Good, well, listen . . . we have found someone.'

'Marion?'

'Alas, no. We have found your friend.'

I am confused by the word 'friend'. I look at Camille, now frowning at me, still on the bench.

'Who?'

'Your man.'

I sincerely have no idea what he is talking about. 'What man?'

'Your Polynesian. Omai. He's alive. And he's being a fool.'

'Omai?'

Even without Camille nearby, this news wouldn't make me happy. Not because I am not interested in my old friend, but because I sense there can be nothing good from Hendrich finding him. It is very unlikely he wants to be found. The happiness of just one minute ago seems totally out of reach.

'Where is he?' I ask. 'What's the story?'

'There is a surfer in Australia who looks *just* like a three-hundred-year-old portrait by Joshua Reynolds. He calls himself Sol Davis. He's becoming a little bit too known in the surfing community. This good-looking thirtysomething going on three hundred and fifty. And people are talking about how he doesn't age. People are talking about that. It's in the online comments, for fuck's sake. Someone saying, "Oh, that's the immortal guy who lives near me who's looked the same since the nineties." He's dangerous. People are getting suspicious. And apparently that's not all. Agnes' source in Berlin says they know about him. The institute. He could be in real trouble.'

The wind picks up. Camille rubs her shoulders, to mime to me she is cold. I nod and mouth the words, 'I'm coming.' But at the same time I know I must look like I am not hurrying Hendrich.

'This is—'

'You have a holiday coming up? A half-term?'

This is sounding ominous. 'Yes.'

'I can get you on a flight to Sydney. Straight through. Just a two-hour stop in Dubai. Some airport shopping. Then, Australia. Week in the sun.'

Week in the sun. He'd said the same before Sri Lanka.

'I thought you said that was it,' I say. 'I thought you said I could have this life for the full eight years. No interruptions.'

'You are sounding like a man with an anchor. You've no anchor.'

'No. Not an anchor. A dog, though. I have a dog. Abraham. He's an old dog. He won't last the eight years. But I can't just leave him.'

'You can just leave him. They have dog sitters nowadays.'

'He's a very sensitive dog. He gets nightmares and separation anxiety.'

'You sound like you've been drinking.'

I knew I couldn't endanger Camille.

'I had some wine earlier. Enjoying life's pleasures. That's the whole point, isn't it? Isn't that what you told me?'

'On your own?'

'On my own.'

Camille is standing up now. She is holding the lead. *What is she doing?* But it is too late. She is already doing it.

'Come on, boy!'

No.

'Abraham!'

The dog runs over to her.

247

Hendrich's tone becomes steel. 'Is that your anchor?'

'What?'

'The woman who called for Abraham. That's your dog's name, right?'

Hendrich has a thousand symptoms of old age. I curse that one of them isn't hearing loss.

Camille clips on Abraham's lead, then looks at me again. She is ready to go.

'Woman?'

Now Camille is listening to me.

'Who is it?'

'No one,' I say. 'She is no one at all.'

The mouth I had just been dreaming of kissing is now agape with disbelief.

'She?' she whispers, but it is one of those whispers that is more a voiceless scream.

I don't mean it, I mime.

'It's just someone I see in the park. Our dogs know each other.'

Camille is furious.

Hendrich sighs. I have no idea if he believes me or not, but he returns to his main subject. 'If it isn't you, there will still be someone seeing your old friend. A stranger. I have been recruiting quite heavily recently. This is what gives me faith I will find Marion. The point is: I have lots I could send, but they might not be able to persuade him, and then . . .' His voice trails off. 'So it is up to you. It is completely up to you.'

The myth of choice. Classic Hendrich. Either I go and talk to Omai, or Omai dies. That is essentially what he is saying. If it isn't someone from Berlin who gets to him, it will be someone else. And, even more horribly, I know he is right. Hendrich may be a manipulator, but he very often has the truth on his side.

Camille has handed me the lead and now she is walking out of the park.

'I'll phone you later. I need to think about it.'

'You have an hour.'

'An hour. Fine.'

Once off the phone, I call to Camille. 'Camille, wait. Where are you going?'

'Home.'

'Camille?'

'Who was on the phone?'

'I can't tell you that.'

'Just as you couldn't tell her who I was.'

'It wasn't a her.'

'I can't do this, Tom.'

'Camille, please.'

'Fuck off.'

'Camille?'

'I pour my heart out to you and get close to you and imagine there is something between us for you to deny we know each other. Jesus fucking Christ. I could have ended up sleeping with you! That's probably what you do. Manipulate people. I'm probably just like another dog for you to train.'

'Abraham isn't trained. Camille, please, wait—'

'Fils de pute!'

She walks out of the park. I could follow her. Every atom of me wants to follow her. I could talk to her and explain about Hendrich. I could quite possibly make everything all right. But I stay standing there, on the grass, under a purple sky, with the day dying around me. I calculate that pissing her off is better than endangering her. It is a total conundrum. The only way to protect her is to have as little to do with her as possible.

I know I have already done too much damage. Hendrich has heard her voice. He could have detected a French accent.

Shit. This is what happens when you drink wine. And when you try to get close to someone. You get trapped. But it is the same trap I've been in since 1891. As always, it is Hendrich's trap. I feel literally immobilised. I will never have a life. And now I have upset the first new person I have really cared about in what feels like eternity. *Shit. Shit. Shit.*

'Shit.' I tell it to Abraham too.

Abraham looks up, panting his confusion.

For centuries I have thought all my despair is grief. But people get over grief. They get over even the most serious grief in a matter of years. If not *get over* then at least *live beside.* And the way they do this is by investing in other people, through friendship, through family, through teaching, through love. I have been approaching this realisation for some time now.

But it is all a farce. I am not going to be able to make a difference to anyone else. I should stop being a teacher now. I should stop all attempts at conversation. I should have nothing to do with anyone. I should live in total isolation. I should go back to Iceland, doing nothing except the tasks Hendrich asks of me.

It doesn't seem possible for me to exist and not cause pain – my own, or other people's.

Abraham whimpers a little beside me, as if feeling my pain.

'It's all right, boy. Let's go home.'

I put some biscuits out for Abraham and drink some vodka and sing Carly Simon's 'Coming Around Again', repeating the title of the song until I think I'm going insane.

Seeing there is ten minutes before I must call Hendrich I click on YouTube and type in 'Sol Davis'. I find footage of waves and a man in a wetsuit on a board, carving his way across the water.

It cuts to this same man coming out of the water and walking over the sand, addressing the camera, with a smile but also a frown, and he shakes his head.

'Hey, man, don't do anything with that,' he says. He has an Australian accent and his head is shaven and he looks, in normal terms, nearly twenty years older but there is no doubt about it: it is Omai. I freeze the frame. His eyes stare straight at me, his forehead beaded with saltwater.

I pick up the phone, cradle it in my hand, go into 'Recents' and press my thumb on 'H'.

Hendrich answers.

'All right, Hendrich. I'll do it.'

PART FIVE

The Return

Plymouth, England, 1768

The story of how I met Omai began on a rainy Tuesday in March on the cobbles of Plymouth harbour. I was hungover. I was always hungover in Plymouth. Well, either hungover or drunk. It was a wet place. Rain, sea, ale. It felt like everyone was slowly drowning.

When I found Captain Samuel Wallis, I recognised him from the portrait I had seen hanging in the Guildhall. He was wearing his fine royal blue coat and walking along the jetty, deep in conversation with another man.

I had arrived in Plymouth only a month before. At this time my hope seemed to ebb ever further out to sea. I had stopped believing in ever finding my daughter and instead I found myself trying to solve the riddle that plagued me: what is the point of living when you have no one to live for? I still had no answer to that. I think, looking back, I was suffering from a kind of depression.

I ran over to him, to Wallis, and stood in front of his path, walking backwards as he walked forwards.

'I heard you were a man short,' I said. 'For the voyage. On the *Dolphin.*'

The men carried on walking. Captain Wallis looked at me. He was, like so many of the men made large by history, rather mediocre in the flesh, the fine tailoring highlighting rather than hiding his physical shortcomings. Short, pudgy, purple-cheeked. A man made more for grand dinners than seafaring. And yet he was only two years away from having an island named after him. In the meantime, his small green eyes viewed me with disdain.

'Who are you?' he asked, in a deep snorting kind of voice.

'John Frears.' It was the first time I had ever said that name.

Captain Wallis' companion lightly touched his arm. A quiet gesture but one which did its purpose. This man seemed very different to Mr Wallis. Sharp-eyed but with a kind mouth, his lips curling at their edges with interest. He was wearing a coal-black coat despite the weather. This was Tobias Furneaux, a man I would get to know quite well over the years. Both men now stopped still amid the busy harbour, near crates of speckled grey freshly killed fish, shining in the June sunlight. 'And why should we have you on our vessel?'

'I have skills, good sirs, that might be wanting elsewhere.'

'Like what?' asked Mr Furneaux.

I dug deep into my bag and took out my black wooden three-holed galoubet and put it to my lips. I began to play a few notes of a folk tune, 'The Bay of Biscay'.

'You play the pipe well,' said Mr Furneaux, suppressing a smile.

'I can also play the mandolin.' I didn't mention the lute, obviously. It would have been like, these days, saying you could use a fax machine in a job interview. It simply wasn't something people did any more.

Mr Furneaux was impressed, and said something along those lines.

'Hmm,' said Mr Wallis, humming a more doubtful tune and turning to his companion. 'We are not arranging a concert, Mr Furneaux.'

Mr Furneaux inhaled the damp air sharply. 'If I may be so bold, Mr Wallis, I would like to proffer that musical ability is an invaluable skill on long voyages such as ours.'

'I have other skills too, sir,' I said, addressing Mr Wallis.

He gave me a quizzical look.

'I can hook a sail and oil the masts and repair the rigging. I can read both words and maps. I can load a gun with powder, and fire it with reasonable aim. I can speak in the French tongue, sir. And the Dutch, though with less proficiency. I am sound on a night watch. I could go on, sir.'

Mr Furneaux was suppressing a laugh by now. Captain Wallis looked no happier than he had a minute before. In fact, he looked like he seriously didn't like me now. He began walking away, his velvet coat flapping in the breeze like the sail of a retreating ship.

'We sail early. Six of the clock, tomorrow morning. We'll see you harbourside.'

'Aye, sir, six of the clock. I'll be there. Thank you. Thank you very much.'

London, now

I am teaching more social history to the class of year nines when Camille walks past the window, like a tormenting dream.

'In Elizabethan England, no one carried bank notes in their pocket. It was all coins until the establishment of the Bank of England . . .'

I raise my hand instinctively, but Camille doesn't respond, even though she sees me. Anton watches as my hand falls.

It stays that way the whole week. I am invisible to Camille. Her eyes never meet mine in the staff room. She never says hello when we pass each other outside. I have hurt her. I know that. So I make no attempt to make it worse by talking to her. My plan is simply to see the week out, go to Australia, and then ask to go somewhere far away from here.

Once, though, crossing diagonal paths across the school hall, seeing her looking sad, I can't help but say, 'Camille, I'm sorry . . . I'm sorry.' And she gives a nod so small it might not have been there at all, and carries on walking.

That evening, as Abraham tries to shake off a Maltese terrier a quarter of his size, I stare over at the empty bench and remember putting my arm around Camille. The bench exudes a sadness, almost as if it remembers too.

The following Saturday is the start of the half-term break. I am due to fly to Australia and drop Abraham off at the dog sitter's the following day but right now I am in the supermarket. I am chucking a travel-size tube of toothpaste in my basket when I notice Daphne, bright-bloused and wide-eyed, behind her trolley.

I don't want her to know I am going away, so I hide the toothpaste and a bottle of sun tan lotion under a copy of *New Scientist*.

'Hey, Mr Hazard!' she says, laughing.

'Mrs Bello, hi!'

Unfortunately, we get talking. She says she has just seen Camille on her way to Columbia Road flower market.

Daphne's eyes dance a little mischievously. 'If I wasn't your boss – *which I am* – if I was just your next-door neighbour – *which I am not* – I would say that, well, Madame Guerin has, for some crazy reason, a bit of a *thing* for a certain new history teacher.'

I feel the unnatural brightness of the supermarket.

'But obviously *I* wouldn't say that, because I am a headteacher and headteachers shouldn't say that sort of thing. It would be totally unprofessional to encourage inter-staff romances. It's just . . . she's been very quiet this last week. Have you noticed?'

I force a smile. 'Fake news, I'm afraid.'

'I just thought that maybe you're the person to cheer her up.'

'I think I may be the last person for that job.'

There is an awkward silence. Well, it is awkward for me. I don't think Daphne does awkward. I notice a bottle of rum lying in her trolley, next to a bag of pasta.

'Having a party?' I ask, trying to initiate a new topic.

She sighs. 'I wish. No, no, the bottle of Bacardi is for my mum.'

'She isn't going to share it?'

'Ha! No. Bless her. She's quite a hog with her rum. She's in an old folk's home in Surbiton – her choice, she likes the company – and she always gets me to sneak in a bottle of the good stuff. She's a bit naughty, my mum. I always feel like a bootlegger or something, like in America during Prohibition, you know . . .'

I remember playing ragtime tunes on the piano in Arizona, a bottle of moonshine on the dusty floor beside me.

259

'She's had a bit of kidney trouble and has had a stroke so she should be off the booze completely, but she always says she's here for a good time not a long time, though she has been here for a long time, because she's eighty-seven and she's a right tough old bird. Ha!'

'She sounds great.' I try my hardest to engage in the conversation, but my painful, overactive hippocampus is now making me think of Camille at school. How pale she'd been looking. How she had deliberately placed herself at the opposite end of the staff room to me.

But then Daphne says something that snaps me out of my despair.

'Yeah, she's a good chick, my mum. Mind you, she's with a right motley crew in the home. There's one woman there who reckons she's so old she was born in the reign of William the Conqueror! She should be in a psychiatric ward, really.'

I stop in my tracks. My first thought is Marion. This is irrational. If Marion was alive she wouldn't look like an old person. She'd look younger than me. And she was born in the reign of King James, not William the Conqueror.

'Poor Mary Peters. Mad as a box of frogs. Gets scared of the TV. But a lovely old dear.'

Mary Peters.

I shake my head at Daphne, even as I remember the gossip that surrounded the disappearance of the Mary Peters we knew in Hackney. The one who Rose knew at the market. Who used to get Hell-turded by Old Mrs Adams and had arrived 'from nowhere'.

'Oh. Oh really? Poor woman.'

When Daphne has gone I leave my trolley in the aisle and walk with brisk determination out of the supermarket. I get out my phone and start looking up train times to Surbiton.

The care home is set back from the road. There are trees crowding out the whole front of the place. I stand outside on the pavement and wonder what I should do. There is a postman on the other side of the road, but other than that – no one. I inhale. Life has a strange rhythm. It takes a while to fully be aware of this. Decades. Centuries, even. It's not a simple rhythm. But the rhythm is there. The tempo shifts and fluctuates; there are structures within structures, patterns within patterns. It's baffling. Like when you first hear John Coltrane on the saxophone. But if you stick with it, the elements of familiarity become clear. The current rhythm is speeding up. I am approaching a crescendo. Everything is happening all at once. That is one of the patterns: when nothing is happening, nothing continues to happen, but after a while the lull becomes too much and the drums need to kick in. Something has to happen. Often that need comes from yourself. You make a phone call. You say, 'I can't do this life any more, I need to change.' And one thing happens that you are in control of. And then another happens which you have no say over. Newton's third law of motion. Actions create reactions. When things start to happen, other things start to happen. But sometimes it seems there is no explanation as to why the things are happening – why all the buses are coming along at once – why life's moments of luck and pain arrive in clusters. All we can do is observe the pattern, the rhythm, and then live it.

I take a deep breath, inhale the air.

Ash Grange Residential Care Home. The logo is a falling leaf. A generic leaf. The sign is pastel-yellow and blue. It is one of the most depressing things I have ever seen. The building itself is nearly as bad. Probably only twenty years old. Light orange brick and tinted windows and a muted quality. The whole place feels like a polite euphemism for death.

I go inside.

'Hello,' I say to the woman in the office after she has slid the Perspex window open for me to speak. 'I'm here to see Mary Peters.'

She looks at me and smiles in that brisk efficient way. A modern professional smile. The kind of smile that never existed before, say, the telephone.

'Oh yes, you called a short while ago, didn't you?'

'Yes. That was me. Tom Hazard. I knew her when she was younger, in Hackney.'

She stares at her computer screen and clicks the mouse. 'Oh yes. She wants to see you. Through there.'

'Oh good,' I say, and as I walk over the carpet tiles I almost feel like I am walking backwards through time.

Mary Peters looks at me with eyes made pink and weak by time. Her grey hair is as frail as dandelion seeds and the veins under her skin like routes on a secret map, but she is recognisably the woman I met in Hackney, four centuries ago.

'I remember you,' she says. 'The day you came into the market. The fight you had with that slimy bastard.'

'Mr Willow,' I say, remembering him disappear in a cloud of spice.

'Yes.'

There is a rattle to her breath. A kind of scraping sound on every in-breath. She winces a little, and her crooked fingers faintly caress her brow.

'I get headaches. It's what happens.'

'I'm starting to get them too.'

'They come and go. Mine have come back recently.'

I marvel at her. How she can still care enough to speak. She must have been an old woman for two hundred years now.

'I don't have long,' she says, as if reading my thoughts. 'That is why I came here. There is no risk for me.'

'No risk?'

'I only have about two years left.'

'You don't know that. You could have another fifty.'

She shakes her head. 'I hope not.'

'How are you feeling?'

She smiles as if I have told a joke.

'Near the end. See, I've had a variety of ailments. When the doctor told me I only had a matter of weeks I realised I . . . I only have two more years. Three at the most. So I knew it was safe, you know, to come here. Safer . . .'

It doesn't make sense. If she is still bothered about safety, then why did she talk openly to people here about her age?

There are other people in the room. Mainly sitting in chairs, lost in crosswords or memories.

'You were Rose's love. She spoke of nothing else but you. I had a flower stand next to where she and her little sister used to sell fruit. Tom this. Tom that. Tom everything. She came alive after she met you. She was a different girl.'

'I loved her so much,' I tell her. 'She was so strong. She was the greatest person I ever knew.'

She smiles in faint sympathy. 'I was a sad old thing in them days. Suffered my own heartache.'

She stares around the room. Someone switches on the TV. The opening credits of a show called *A New Life in the Sun* start to play. Then images of a couple inside their Spanish restaurant, the Blue Marlin, looking stressed as they rinse mussels in a pot.

When Mary's face returns to mine she is pensive, almost trembling with thought. And then she tells me: 'I met your daughter.'

It is so out of context that I don't really understand what she has said.

'What did you say?'

'Your child, Marion.'

'Marion?'

'Quite recent. We were in hospital together.'

My mind is racing to understand. This is so often the way with life. You spend so much time waiting for something – a person, a feeling, a piece of information – that you can't quite absorb it when it is in front of you. The hole is so used to being a hole it doesn't know how to close itself.

'What?'

'The psychiatric hospital in Southall. I was a day patient, just a mad old bird crying in a chair. She was there all the time. I came to know her. I had left before she had been born, hadn't I?'

'So how did you know it was my daughter?'

She looks at me as if it is a silly question. 'She told me. She told everyone. That was one of the reasons she was there in the first place. No one believed her of course. She was mad. That's what they thought . . . She used to talk in French sometimes, and she sang a lot.'

'What did she sing?'

'Old songs. Old, *old* songs. She used to cry when she sang.'

'Is she still there?'

She shakes her head. 'She left. It was strange, how it happened—'

'Strange? How do you mean?'

'One night she just went. People who were there said there was a lot of noise and commotion . . . Then, when I came in the next day she was gone.'

'Where? *Where?*'

Mary sighs. She takes a moment. Looks sad and confused as she thinks about it. 'No one knew. No one said. They just told us she'd been discharged. But we never knew for sure. That sounds strange, but we didn't always know what was going on. That was the nature of the place.'

I can't let go. For so long I have been waiting for hope, and then hope has come along for ten seconds only to be dashed again. 'Where would she have gone? Did she ever give you any clues as to where she might end up? She must have.'

'I don't know. Honestly, I just don't know.'

'Did she talk about places?'

'She'd travelled. She talked about places she'd been. She'd been to Canada.'

'Canada? Where? Toronto? I was in Toronto.'

'I don't know. I don't think so. She'd also spent a lot of time in Scotland, I think. Her voice was very Scottish. I think she'd travelled around, though. Through Europe.'

'Do you think she's in London?'

'I honestly don't know.'

I sit back. Try to think. I am simultaneously relieved that Marion is still alive – or had been until recently – and worried for whatever torments she has known.

I wonder if the society has caught up with her. I wonder if someone has tried to silence her. I wonder if Hendrich knows about this and hasn't told me. I wonder if someone has taken her. The institute in Berlin. Or someone else.

'Listen, Mary,' I say, before I leave, 'I think it's important that you don't talk about the past any more. It may have been dangerous for Marion, and it is dangerous for you. You can think about it. But it's dangerous to talk about your age.'

She winces at some invisible pain as she shifts, with careful effort, in her seat. A minute goes by. She is mulling my words, and dismissing them.

'I loved someone once. A woman. I loved her madly. Do you understand? We were together, in secret, for nearly twenty years. And we were told we couldn't talk about that love . . . because it was dangerous. It was dangerous to love.'

I nod. I understand.

'There comes a time when the only way to start living is to tell the truth. To be who you really are, even if it is dangerous.'

I hold Mary's hand. 'You have helped me more than you know.'

One of the nurses comes over and asks if I want a cup of tea and I say I am fine.

And then I ask Mary, in a low voice, 'Have you ever heard of the Albatross Society?'

'No. Can't say I have.'

'Well, just be careful. Please, don't talk about, you know . . .'

I look at the clock on the wall. It is a quarter to three. In three hours' time I need to be on a plane to Dubai, en route to Sydney.

'Be careful,' I tell Mary.

She shakes her head. Closes her eyes. Her sigh sounds closer to a cat's hiss. 'I am too old to be scared any more. I am too old to lie.' She leans forward in her chair, and clasps her walking stick until her knuckles whiten. 'And so are you.'

I step outside and phone Hendrich.

'Tom? How are things?'

'Did you know she was alive?'

'Who?'

'Marion. *Marion.* Have you found her? Did you know?'

'Tom, calm down. No, Tom. Have you got a lead?'

'She is alive. She was at a hospital in Southall. And then she disappeared.'

'Disappeared? As in, taken?'

'I don't know. She might've run away.'

'From a hospital?'

'It was a mental hospital.'

A postman trundles along the pavement. 'I don't know where she is,' I whisper into the phone. 'But I can't go to Australia. I need to find her.'

'If she has been taken . . .'

'I don't know that.'

'If she has been taken you will not find her alone. Listen, listen. I will get Agnes to put her ear to the ground in Berlin. After Australia this will be our chief operation. We will find her. If she's been taken she'll probably be in Berlin, or Beijing, or Silicon Valley.

You won't find her alone. I mean, you've been in London and you haven't found her.'

'I haven't been looking. I mean, I've been side-tracked.'

'Yes, Tom. Yes. You finally see it. You've been side-tracked. That is exactly it. Now, we will sort this. But you have a flight to catch.'

'I can't. I can't.'

'If you want to find Marion, you need to focus again, Tom. You need to go and bring your friend in. Who knows? He himself might have information for us. You know how it is. Albas are the people to ask about albas. You need to get back on track, Tom. The truth is: you don't know where Marion is. But we know where your friend is. And so does Berlin. Marion has survived for over four hundred years. She'll still be alive for another week. Just do this in Australia and I swear – I *swear* – we will work together and we will find her. You have a lead, yes?'

I can't tell him about Mary Peters. I don't want to endanger a woman who clearly would never agree to be a part of the society. 'I, just, I need to find her.'

'We will, Tom,' he says, and I hate him almost as much as I believe him. I have doubted him many times, but the truth is, I feel it too. I feel every word as he says it. 'I can sense it. I have experienced so much past that I can sense the future. I know. I know. We are nearly there, Tom. You will see her again. But, first, if you want to save your friend, you really need to get to the airport. Omai needs you.'

And the conversation ends and, as always, I do what Hendrich wants me to do. Because he is the best hope I have.

Tahiti, 1767

I was meant to set fire to the village.

'Light it!' roared Wallis. 'If you ever want a trip home you will light the savage's hut, Frears! Then light the others!'

I held the flaming torch in my hand, my arm weak from the weight, my whole body weak from just standing up. It would have been easy to let it down, but I couldn't light the hut. I just stood there, in the black sand, as the islander stared at me. The young man said nothing. He did nothing. He just stood in front of the hut and stared at me. His eyes were wide, and he looked at me with a mixture of horror and defiance. He had long wispy hair, down to his chest, and was wearing more jewellery than most of the other islanders. Bracelets made with bone. Necklaces too. I would have said he was about twenty years old. But I also knew, better than most, that when it came to matters of age, appearances could be deceptive.

Centuries later, watching this same man step out of the ocean in a YouTube video, I would see those eyes stare out with a similar expression. Somewhere between defiance and bewilderment.

I was no saint. I saw no shame in the discovering of new lands or the forging of empire. I was thoroughly a man of a different age, even to the one I was then inhabiting. And yet, I could not set fire to the man's home. Whether it was the eyes, whether I could recognise in him a fellow outsider, or whether I knew the damage that was caused to the soul by the accumulation of sin in a long life, I still do not know.

But even as Wallis barked at me I walked away. I carried the torch to the smooth wet sand and let the sea take it. I walked back to the man whose hut was still standing and pulled out the pistol – given to me before treading onto the shore, by a scurvy-weakened officer – from my belt and placed it on the sand. I don't think the man understood the pistol, or what it was for, but he understood the knife, and I put that on the ground too.

I had a small mirror in my pocket and I showed it to him and he stared at it, at his own face, with fascination.

Wallis was now right at me.

'What the devil are you doing, Frears?'

I tried to stare at Wallis with the quiet dignity the islander had stared at me.

Luckily, Furneaux was also there. 'If we destroy their homes, we will never be welcome here. We need to tempt them, not scare them any more than we have. Sometimes the beast only needs to roar.'

And Wallis just mumbled and looked at me and said, 'Don't make me regret having brought you,' and the huts were burned to the ground anyway. And so it was that the island that would one day be known as Tahiti was first witnessed by Europeans. A mere two years later it would be used by Captain James Cook on his first voyage as the site on which he and his astronomer would observe the transit of Venus as it crossed the sun. It was indeed this reason – the convenient positioning of the island from which to observe something – that would advance not only scientific knowledge but the calculation of longitude.

While the village was ablaze the only two naturalists to survive the voyage, along with the artist Joe Webber, set about exploring the rainforest. We weren't there to take over, we were there, in our own minds, to *discover.*

And yet we had done what so often happened in the proud history of geographic discovery. We had found paradise. And then we had set it on fire.

Dubai, now

The airport in Dubai is very bright, even though it is the middle of the night. I wander through a shop where a woman wants to spray aftershave on me.

'I'm all right, thanks,' I say. But the woman doesn't believe me. She sprays the scent – *Sauvage* – onto a thin and perfectly rectangular strip of card and hands it to me. She smiles so forcefully I find myself taking the piece of card and walking away with it. I smell the paper. I imagine all those plants where the scent comes from. Think of how detached we are from nature. How we have to do so much to it before we can bottle it and put the name 'wild' on it. The smell does nothing for my head. I walk on and find myself in the airport bookshop. Some of the books are in Arabic but most are in English.

I look for something to read but at first see nothing but business books. I stare at the cover of one of them. It has the author on the front. He is wearing a suit and an unnatural pseudo-presidential smile. His teeth have an Arctic glare. He is called Dave Sanderson. The book, *The Wealth Within You*, has a subtitle: *How to Harness Your Inner Billionaire*.

I stare at it for quite some time, in a kind of trance. It is a popular modern idea. That the inner us is something different to the outer us. That there is an authentic realer and better and richer version of ourselves which we can only tap into by buying a solution. This idea that we are separate from our nature, as separate as a bottle of Dior perfume is from the plants of a forest.

As far as I can see, this is a problem with living in the twenty-first century. Many of us have every material thing we need, so the job of marketing is now to tie the economy to our emotions, to make us feel like we need more by making us want things we never needed before. We are made to feel poor on thirty thousand pounds a year. To feel poorly travelled if we have been to only ten other countries. To feel too old if we have a wrinkle. To feel ugly if we aren't photo-shopped and filtered.

No one I knew in the 1600s wanted to find their inner billionaire. They just wanted to live to see adolescence and avoid body lice.

Ah.

I am, I realise, in a bad mood.

My eyes are dry from tiredness and from seven hours on an aeroplane. I don't like flying. It isn't so much the being in the air that bothers me. It is the arriving in a different country, with a wholly different culture and weather system, just a few hours after you have left Gatwick. Maybe it is because I still remember the size of things. No one understands that any more. People didn't feel the enormity of the world or their own smallness within it. When I first travelled around the globe, it took over a year, on a boat full of men, who were lucky if they made it. Now, the world is just *there*. All of it. In an hour I will be on a flight to Sydney, and by lunchtime I will have arrived. It makes me feel claustro-phobic, as if the world is literally shrinking, like a balloon losing air.

I move to a different section in the bookshop. The section, mainly books in English or English translation, is titled 'Thought'. It is a much smaller area than the one for business books. Confucius. The ancient Greeks. Then I see a book, face out, with a simple academic cover.

Michel de Montaigne's *Essays*.

It nearly turns me to ash. I even say my daughter's name out loud, to myself, as if I am close to her again, as if a part of us is contained in every book we've loved. I pick it up and turn to a random page and read a sentence – 'Nothing fixes a thing so firmly in the memory as the wish to forget it' – and I begin to feel the onset of potential tears.

My phone beeps. I hastily put the book down. I check my phone. A text message. It is from Omai: 'Been too long. Can't wait to catch up. Have booked us in for dinner at a place called the Fig Tree restaurant at 8. Should give you time to nap off your jetlag a bit.'

Jetlag.

It seems funny him writing the word. He belongs, in my mind, to a time when the idea of humans flying was as fantastical as, to us now, humans living on Neptune. Maybe even more so.

I text back: 'See you there.'

I leave Montaigne and the airport bookshop and head over to a large window and wait for them to announce my flight. I lean my head against the glass and stare out beyond my reflection at the infinite darkness of the desert.

Plymouth, England, 1772

After our return I stayed around Plymouth. I liked it there. As with London, it was an easy place to disappear into. A town of seafarers, ragamuffins, criminals, runaways, drifters, musicians, artists, dreamers, loners, and I was, at various points, any and all of those things.

One morning I left my lodgings at the Minerva Inn and went to the new dockyard. There was a large naval warship sitting high on the water.

'Impressive, ain't she?' said a man on the dockside, seeing my awe.

'Yes. Yes, she is.'

'Set to find new worlds.'

'New worlds?'

'Aye. That's Cook's ship.'

'Cook?'

Then I heard footsteps behind me. A hand fell on my shoulder. I jumped.

'My goodness, Mr Frears, you seem a little shaken.'

I turned to see a tall lean finely dressed gentleman, smiling kindly at me.

'Oh, Mr Furneaux . . . it is a pleasure, sir.'

His astute eyes studied me a moment. 'You never look a day older, Frears.'

'Sea air, sir.'

'Fancy more of it? Want to go back out there?'

He gestured towards the horizon beyond the harbour. 'It will be different this time. Cook has prepared things a little better than Wallis.'

'Are you sailing on Cook's boat?'

'Not exactly. I am accompanying him,' he told me. 'On the voyage. As a commander on the *Adventure*. I am assembling a crew. Would you like to be part of it?'

Somewhere above Australia, now

I am on a connecting flight between Sydney and the Gold Coast, feeling tired. I have spent most of the last two days either in aeroplanes or at airports. There is a baby crying at the back of the plane. It makes me think, momentarily, of Marion, when she was teething, and how worried Rose had been, imagining the pain could be fatal. In the same way every dog is similar to every other dog, every baby's cry echoes every crying baby there has ever been.

And, on that note, there is a young couple in front of me. A head sleeping on a shoulder. A man's head on a man's shoulder, the way you never used to see. It is a touching sight, I suppose, but makes me jealous. I want a head on my shoulder, like Camille's had been on mine, just before Hendrich's call. Is this how I had once felt about Rose, at the beginning? Or is this something different? Maybe *this is* a different kind of love. Did it matter?

I think about how we have barely spoken a word to each other during the last week at school. I think about an awkward moment near the kettle in the staff room. She was rummaging through the teas, looking for chamomile. The silence screamed.

My mother had told me to live. After she had gone, I had to live. It was easy for her to say, but of course she was right. And it was an understandable wish. When you die the last thing you want is for your death to leak out and infect those left behind, for those loved ones to become a kind of living dead. And yet, inevitably, that often happens. It has happened to me.

But I sense it is getting closer. Life. I sense it, just inches ahead of me. Marion is part of it. The suddenly very real idea of finding her. I sleep and I dream of Omai. I dream of seeing him standing on a South Pacific beach staring out at sunset. And when I get to him I grab his arm and he crumbles away like sand and there is someone else, someone smaller, there beneath him, like a Russian doll. A child. A child with a long braid in her hair and wearing a green cotton dress.

'Marion,' I say.

And then she, too, crumbles into sand, into the beach itself, and I try to keep her intact even as the water washes her away.

And when I wake up, the baby is no longer crying and I am there – here. The plane has landed, and I know that in a matter of hours I will be seeing someone I haven't seen for centuries. And I can't help but feel terrified.

Huahine, Society Islands, 1773

Arthur Flynn, second lieutenant of the *Adventure*, sunburnt, sweltering in his once white shirt, knelt on the sand, holding bright red and white ribbons in his hands and, in clumsy, emphatic sign language, mimed tying them in his hair. He smiled an imitation of a pretty girl, quite a reach given his scorched face and scalp and untamed beard.

But still, his audience of little children seemed impressed. I had travelled enough to understand that laughter was pretty universal, at least among children. Even the older islanders, standing a little more po-faced behind, were suddenly smiling at this strange red-skinned Englishman playing the fool. Arthur handed a ribbon to the long-haired girl nearest to him – she could have been no more than six years old – and, after confirmation from her mother, she took it.

Then Arthur turned, and said to me, in a voice softer than his usual, 'Frears, do you have the beads?'

Behind them, the two ships sat like inanimate elegant beasts transferred from another reality.

As we stayed there, giving out gifts and peace-brokering with ribbons, I saw a face in the crowd that I recognised. It was a man I had seen before.

He was holding a wooden board and he was wet from the sea. I had seen similar wooden boards on my last visit to the Pacific Islands. They were used by fishermen to go out to sea. They would stand up on them, riding waves. Sometimes they had seemed to do this wave riding simply for fun. But none of this explained how

I could know this man. How could this be? I had never visited this island before. I tried to think. It didn't take long before it came to me. It was the man whose hut I had refused to torch. The handsome one with the long hair and wide eyes. But that had been on Tahiti. It wasn't a vast stretch of ocean he had travelled over, but it seemed ridiculous to imagine he'd done it on nothing but a board of wood. And in Tahiti he had been bedecked with neck-laces and bracelets, denoting a status his unadorned chest and arms would suggest he no longer had.

He looked exactly as I had remembered him. I supposed four years wasn't that long. His face looked at me with a kind of longing, a desperate need to communicate something.

I looked around, at Arthur and some of the other men, hoping perhaps that the man's attention might be diverted elsewhere. But no. It stayed solely on me. He spoke words I couldn't understand. Then, with his right hand, he pinched the ends of his fingers together and brought them to his chest. The fingers beat against his chest in rapid staccato succession. I understood the mime.

I.

Me.

Him.

Then he pointed to the sea, to the boats, then beyond to the horizon. Then he looked down at the sand and gave a look of either fear or disgust. He kept that expression as he turned to look behind him, towards the breadfruit trees and lush green jungle beyond the beach, before looking again to the boats and the ocean. He did this a few times until I was clear about what he was saying.

I heard boots in sand walking towards me. I saw Captain Cook and Commander Furneaux, together, sharing a mutual frown.

'What is happening here, Fines?' asked Cook.

'Frears,' corrected Furneaux, with soft authority.

Cook shook the correction away as if it were a midge-fly. 'Tell

us. There seems to be some sort of minor commotion with this
. . . gentleman.'

'Yes, Captain.'

'Well?'

'I believe he wants to come with us.'

Pacific Ocean, 1773

His name was Omai.

We later learned, when his English was better, that his name was actually Mai, and what he had been saying was 'I am Mai' in Tahitian. Anyway, the name stuck, and he never corrected us.

When we stopped off at other islands he would try to get me to stand on his board. The use of 'surf' as a verb was still a long way away, but that is what he was doing, and he could stay upright for as long as he seemed to want to, whatever size the wave. Unlike myself, of course, who fell off to great laughter every time I tried to stand up on it. Still, I often like to think I was the first European ever to use a surfboard.

Omai was a quick learner. He grasped English with remarkable speed. I liked him, not least because he enabled me to escape the more mundane duties on deck. We would sit in the shade, or find a quiet corner below deck, and run through nouns and verbs and share a jar of pickled cabbage.

I talked to him a little about Rose and Marion. I showed him Marion's coin. Taught him the word 'money'.

He educated me about the world as he saw it.

Everything contained something called *mana* – every tree, every animal, every human.

Mana was a special power. A supernatural power. It could be good or evil but it always had to be respected.

One fine day we were out on deck and he pointed at the boards. 'What is this called?' he asked.

I followed the line of his finger. 'That is called a shadow,' I told him.

He told me mana lives in shadows and that there are lots of rules about shadows.

'Rules? What kind of rules?'

'It is very bad to stand on the shadow of a . . .' He looked around, as if the word he was searching for was somewhere in the air. Then he saw Furneaux heading sternwards over the poop deck and pointed to him.

I understood. 'Commander? Leader? Chief?'

He nodded. 'When I first saw you, you did not stand on my shadow. You came near. But you did not stand on it. This was a sign that I could trust you. The mana inside you respected the mana inside me.'

I found it interesting that this seemed of more significance to him than my decision not to set fire to his home. I shifted a little distance away from him.

He laughed at me. Put a hand on my shoulder. 'It is not bad when you know someone, just when you first meet them.'

'Were you a chief?'

He nodded. 'On Tahiti.'

'But not on Huahine?'

'No.'

'So why did you move from Tahiti to live on Huahine?'

He was generally quite a light-hearted person, and remarkably relaxed for a man heading away from all he had ever known, but when I asked this his brow creased and he chewed on his top lip and he seemed almost hurt by it.

'It is all right,' I assured him. 'You don't have to tell me.'

This is when he told me.

'I know I can trust you,' he said. 'I know it as much as I know anything. You have been a good teacher. And you are a good friend.

I also sense something about you. The way you talk about the past. The look in your eyes. The penny you have which you tell is old. All the knowledge you have. I think you are like me. You are a good friend.' He kept saying it, as if needing confirmation.

'Yes. We are good friends.'

'Muruuru. Thank you.'

There was some understanding that passed between us then – a confidence to move out into the open.

Hollamby walked by. Hollamby, who I slept next to, had already told me that he thought it was a bad idea to have Omai on board: 'He is a burden, eating the rations and bringing unknown curses with him.' He gave us a sideways look, but let his eyebrows do the talking and walked on by.

'I am older than other men,' he said. 'And I think you are too. Your face has not changed in five years. Not one bit.'

'Yes,' I said, lowering my voice to a whisper. I was too shocked to say anything else. It felt like the most terrifying and wonderful release, a century before seeing Dr Hutchinson, to find someone like me, and to be able to tell the truth. It was like being shipwrecked on an island for decades and then finding another survivor.

He stared at me and he was smiling. There was more relief than fear with him now. 'You are like me. I am like you. I knew it.' He laughed with relief. 'I knew it.'

He hugged me. Our shadows merged. 'It does not matter! Our mana is the same. Our shadows are one.'

I cannot express the magnitude of that moment enough. Yes, Marion was like me but I still hadn't found her. And so Omai made me feel less alone. He made me feel normal. And I imme-diately wanted to know *everything*. Looking around, making sure the other crew were below deck or elsewhere, we began to talk.

'Is this why you came? Is this why you wanted to leave the islands?'

He nodded. Nodding, it seemed, was universal. So was superstition. 'Yes. It was difficult. At the beginning when in Tahiti it was good. They saw me as . . . as the special One. That is why I became a . . . a *chief*. They saw it as . . . proof that the mana inside me was good. That *I* was good. That I was half a man and half a god. No one ever dared come too close to me in the daylight in case they stepped on my shadow.' He laughed, and stared out to sea, as if the memory was something he could almost see on the horizon. 'And I did my best and I think I was a good chief but after many, many moons had passed things changed. Other men. They wanted to be chief. And I could not stop being chief. The only way to stop being a chief was to die. So I was . . .'

He mimed claustrophobia. Hands throbbing in the air near his head.

'Trapped.'

'Yes, I was trapped. So I had to go. I had to begin like the dawn. But a day is only meant to last so long and then they want the night. I had run out of places to go. I just wanted to live.'

I told him what had happened to my mother. About Manning. About Marion, being like us. I told him how Rose had been in danger because of me. I told him how much I missed her.

He smiled softly. 'People you love never die.'

I had no idea of the sense of his words, but they stayed with me for centuries.

People you love never die.

'In England they do not accept us either,' I told him, returning to our topic. 'You can tell no one on this ship about your condition. When I return to England, I must become someone else again. Already Mr Furneaux is a little suspicious.'

Omai looked a little worried. Touched his face. He was probably wondering how on earth he was going to hide.

'Don't worry,' I said. 'You are exotic.'

'Exotic? What is that word?'

'Different. From far away. Far. Far. Like a pine-apple.'

'A pine-apple? You don't have pine-apples in England?'

'There are probably about thirty in England. On mantelpieces.'

He looked confused. The sea splashed gently against the bow of the boat. 'What is a mantelpiece?'

Byron Bay, Australia, now

We sit out on a veranda, surrounded by fairy lights and the indistinct buzz of happy conversation.

The last time I saw Omai, Australia was, to my mind, a new discovery. And yet Omai is still so recognisably the same. His face has broadened slightly – not fattened, just that broadening that happens with age – and there are a few lines around his eyes that stay there even when he stops smiling, but I think an innocent bystander would put his age at thirty-six. He's wearing a faded T-shirt with a print of a Frida Kahlo self-portrait, advertising an exhibition of her art at the Art Gallery of New South Wales, Sydney.

'It has been a long time,' Omai says wistfully. 'I missed you, dude.'

'I've missed you too. Wow. And you say dude now? Suits you.'

'Since the sixties. It's kind of compulsory here. Surf thing.'

We are kicking things off with coconut chilli Martinis which Omai has tried before and insists I try too. I can see the sea from here, beyond the stubby palms and the vast beach, glimmering softly under the half moon.

'I've never had a coconut chilli Martini before,' I tell him. 'That's the thing with getting older. You run out of new things to try.'

'Oh, I don't know,' he says, still the optimist. 'I have lived beside one ocean or another most of my life and I have yet to see the same wave twice. It's the mana, you see. It's everywhere. It's never still. It keeps the world new. The whole planet is a coconut chilli Martini.'

I laugh.

'So how long have you been Sol Davis?'

'Seventeen years, I guess. That's when I came to Byron.'

I look around at all the happy Australians enjoying their Friday evening. A birthday is being celebrated. A collective roar of excitement erupts as the cake arrives with three sparklers sticking out of it. There is a shower of applause as the cake lands in front of a woman at the end of the table. She has an oversized badge pinned to her vest top. She is turning forty.

'Just a baby,' I say.

'Forty,' says Omai wryly. 'Remember that?'

I nod. 'Yes,' I say sadly. 'I remember. You?'

A sorrow on his face too. 'Yeah, that was the year I had to leave Tahiti.'

He looks off into the distance, as if that other time and space could be seen somewhere in the darkness beyond the veranda. 'I was a man god. The sun shone because of me. I was in league with the weather and the ocean and the fruit in the trees. And you've got to remember, back then, before the people of Europe came to Christianise us, well, men gods weren't so uncommon. God wasn't something up in the clouds. I mean, look at me, I could pass for a god, right?'

'These Martinis are strong,' I offer.

'I have probably told you all this before.'

'Probably. A long time ago.'

'Long, long, long, long, long, long.'

A waitress comes over. I order a pumpkin salad to start and red snapper for main and Omai goes for dishes which, according to the waitress, 'both have pork belly in them'.

'I know,' he says, flashing his smile. He is still the best-looking man I have ever seen.

'Just thought I'd point it out, in case you want some variety.'

'It's still variety. Two different dishes.'

'All right, sir.'

'And two more of these,' he says, raising his glass.

'Gotcha.'

He holds the waitress's gaze. She holds it back.

'I know you,' she says. 'You're the surfer, aren't you?'

Omai laughs. 'It's Byron Bay. Everyone's a surfer.'

'No. Not like you. You're Sol Davis, aren't you?'

He nods, looks at me sheepishly. 'For my sins.'

'Wow. You're pretty famous around here.'

'I wouldn't say that.'

'No, sure you are. I saw you surf that tube. It was *amazing*. It's on the internet.'

Omai smiles politely, but I can sense his awkwardness. After the waitress has gone he stares down at his right hand. He spreads the fingers wide, as if miming a starfish, then closes them together, makes a fist, turns his hand over. His skin is smooth and caramel and young-looking. Ocean-preserved. Anageria-preserved.

We chat some more.

Our starters arrive.

He begins to tuck in. He closes his eyes on the first mouthful and makes appreciative noises. I envy his easy access to pleasure.

'So,' he says, 'what have you been up to?'

I tell him. About my life as a teacher. About my life before. Recent history. Iceland, Canada. Germany. Hong Kong. India. America. Then I talk about 1891. About Hendrich. The Albatross Society.

'It's people like us. There are lots of us. Well, maybe not lots.'

I explain about the help you're given. About the Eight-Year Rule. About albas and mayflies. Omai stares at me, wide-eyed and baffled.

'So what do you do?' he asks. 'I mean you?'

'I go where Hendrich, the boss, tells me to go. I do *assignments*. I bring people in. Even that isn't so bad. I recently went to Sri Lanka. It's a comfortable life.'

Even to my ears 'comfortable' sounds like a euphemism.

287

He laughs, concerned. 'Bring them in where?'

'It's not a particular place. What I mean is: I make people members.'

'Make? How?'

'Well, normally it's a no-brainer. I explain how the society can protect them, handle identity switches – Hendrich has *all* kinds of contacts. It's like a union. Insurance. Except we get paid, just for living.'

'You're quite the salesman. You really move with the times, don't you?'

'Listen, Omai. This isn't a joke. We're as unsafe now as we've ever been.'

'Yeah. And yet, here we still are. Still breathing. In and out.'

'There are dangers. You – right now – are in danger. There is an institute in Berlin. It knows about you. It has, over the years, taken people.'

Omai laughs. He is actually *laughing*. I think of Marion, missing, possibly, for all I know, taken, and I feel angry. I feel like he is challenging me, like an atheist in front of a Catholic. 'Taken people? Wow.'

'It's true. And it's not just them these days. There are biotech firms in Silicon Valley and elsewhere who want the ultimate competitive advantage, and we could give it them. We're not human to them. We're lab rats.'

He rubs his eyes. He looks tired, suddenly. I am tiring him.

'Okay. So what do you do for this "protection"? What's the catch?'

'The catch is, there are certain obligations.'

He laughs, rubbing his eyes, as if my words are sleep to be shaken off. 'Obligations?'

'Once in a while you have to do something for the Albatross Society.'

He laughs louder. 'That *name.*'

288

'Yeah, it is a bit antiquated.'

'What kind of things do you have to do?'

'Different things. Things like this. Talk to people. Try to get them to sign up.'

'Sign up? Are there pieces of paper?'

'No, no, there's no paper. Just good faith. Trust. The oldest kind of contract.' I realise how like Hendrich I sound. The last time I had that feeling was Arizona, and that didn't end well.

'And what happens when people say no?'

'They don't, generally. It's a good deal.' I close my eyes. I remember firing the gun in the desert. 'Listen, Omai, I am telling you. You are not safe.'

'So what do I have to do?'

'Well, the whole idea is for people not to gather moss. Hendrich, he's always on about not getting too attached to people. And it makes sense for people to move on every eight years. Start somewhere new. Become someone else. And you've been here more than—'

'I can't do that. The moving thing.'

He looks pretty adamant. I know I have to be straight.

'There is no choice. All members of the society have—'

'But I haven't chosen to become a member of the society.'

'You become a member automatically. As soon as an alba is located they become a member.'

'Alba, alba, alba . . . yada, yada, yada . . .'

'To know of the existence of the society is to be part of it.'

'A bit like life.'

'I suppose.'

'And what precisely does happen if I say no? If I refuse?'

I wait too long with the answer.

He leans back in his chair and shakes his head at me. 'Wow, dude. It's like the mafia. You've joined the mafia.'

'I never opted in,' I tell him. 'That's the whole point. But trust me, it makes sense . . . You see, if one alba is exposed, it endangers *all* albas. But you know you have to hide. You've been hiding. You told me . . .'

He shakes his head. 'For thirty years I've been in Australia.'

I contemplate that.

For thirty years I've been in Australia.

'I was told it was twenty.'

His face hardens a little. This isn't good. None of this is good. I think of us on the ship, laughing. I think of afterwards, at the Royal Society in London, when Omai insisted I stay there with him. The fun we had. Drinking gin and telling lies to Samuel Johnson and the celebrities of the day. 'Told? Who by? Have I been watched?'

'I just don't understand how you managed thirty years. Have you been moving around?'

'Was in Sydney for thirteen years but been in Byron seventeen. Travelled the coast a little. Went up the Blue Mountains. Mainly, though, I've been in the same house.'

'And no one's been suspicious?'

He stares at me. I can see his nostrils expand and contract with the intensity of his breath.

'People generally see what they want to see.'

'But you're on the internet, the waitress has even seen it. Someone filmed you. You're attracting too much interest.'

'You. You still think you have the fire in your hand. I am still the "Other" you want to steer to your will. Well, you can take that fire and put it in the ocean.'

Steady thyself.

'Jesus, Omai. I'm trying to help you. This isn't me. I'm just the middle man here. It's Hendrich. He knows things. He can stop terrible things happening, but he can also' – the terrible truth of it occurs to me – 'he can also make very terrible things happen.'

'Do you know what?' He pulls out his wallet and delves inside and places some notes on the table and stands up. 'If it's not really you I'm talking to, this won't be rude, will it?'

And I just sit there after he has walked away. The food comes and I tell the waitress I think he is coming back. But, of course, he doesn't.

In honesty, I thought it was going to go differently. I thought we were going to catch up on old times and talk about all the good and horrifying things that had happened that we could once never have imagined. I thought we were going to talk about bicycles or cars or aeroplanes. Trains, telephones, photographs, electric lightbulbs, TV shows, computers, rockets to the moon. Skyscrapers. Einstein. Gandhi. Napoleon. Hitler. Civil rights. Tchaikovsky. Rock. Jazz. *Kind of Blue. Revolver.* Does he like 'The Boys of Summer'? Hip-hop. Sushi bars. Picasso. Frida Kahlo. Climate change. Climate denial. *Star Wars.* The Cuban Missile Crisis. Beyoncé. Twitter. Emojis. Reality TV. Fake news. Donald Trump. The continual rise and fall of empathy. What we did in the wars. Our reasons to carry on.

But, no, we talked about none of that.

I had blown it.

I was, in short, a fucking idiot. And a friendless one.

People you love never die.

That is what Omai had said, all those years ago.

And he was right. They don't die. Not completely. They live in your mind, the way they always lived inside you. You keep their light alive. If you remember them well enough, they can still guide you, like the shine of long-extinguished stars could guide ships in unfamiliar waters. If you stop mourning them, and start listening to them, they still have the power to change your life. They can, in short, be salvation.

Omai lives on the edge of town, at 352 Broken Head Road. A one-storey clapboard house.

You can see the sea from here. Of course you can. Omai would have lived *in* the sea if he could have done.

I wait a couple of minutes after knocking. My head is a dull ache. I hear soft noises from inside the house. The door opens a little. An old woman with short white hair peers out from behind the latch chain. Late eighties, I would have said. Face as lined as a map. Standing asymmetrically from arthritis and osteoporosis. Worried, cataract-infested eyes. Luminous yellow cardigan. She is holding an electric tin opener.

'Yes?'

'Oh, I'm sorry. I think I might have the wrong address. Sorry for bothering you so late.'

'Don't worry. I never sleep these days.'

She is closing the door. Hastily I say it: 'I'm looking for Sol. Sol Davis. Is this the right address? I'm an old friend. I was having a meal with him tonight and I'm worried I've upset him.'

She hesitates a moment.

'Tom. My name is Tom.'

She nods. She has heard of me. 'He's gone surfing.'

'In the dark?'

'It's his favourite time to do it. The ocean never goes home. That's what he always says.'

'Where does he surf?'

She thinks. Looks down at the cement path in front of her door, as if there is some kind of clue there. 'Damn my old brain . . . Tallow Beach.'

'Thank you. Thank you very much.'

I sit on the sand and watch him, lit by the full moon. A small shadow rising up a wave. And then I feel my phone vibrate in my pocket.

Hendrich.

To not answer it would only make him suspicious.

'Is he with you?'

'No.'

'I can hear the sea.'

'He's surfing.'

'So you can talk?'

'I won't have long. I'm meeting him later.'

'Is he sold?'

'He will be.'

'Have you explained everything?'

'In the process. Not everything.'

'The film of him on YouTube now has four hundred thousand views. He needs to disappear.'

Omai vanishes under a wave. The head rises up again. It seems the perfect way to live. Riding a wave, falling off, getting back on. So much of life seems to be based around the idea of *rising*, of building something up – income or status or power – of living a kind of upward life, as vertical as a skyscraper. But Omai's existence seems as natural as the ocean itself, as wide and open as the horizon. He is on his board again, on his front, paddling with his arms over the swell of the water.

'He will, I'm sure.'

'Oh, I know he will. For all our sakes. It's not just Berlin. There's a biotech research firm in Beijing and they're—'

I have heard this stuff for over a century. I know I should be concerned, especially with Marion out there somewhere, but it is just another noise in the world. Like water against sand.

'Yes. Listen, Hendrich, I'd better go. I think he's coming out of the water.'

'Plan A. That's all you are, Tom. Remember, there's always a Plan B.'

'I hear you.'

'You'd better.'

After the call I just sit there, on the sand. From here the waves sound like breath. Inhale. Exhale.

Twenty minutes later Omai is out of the water.

He sees me and keeps walking, carrying his board.

'Hey!' I follow him up the beach. 'Listen, I'm your friend. I'm trying to protect you.'

'I don't need your protection.'

'Who is the woman, Omai? The woman in your house?'

'That's none of your business. And stay away from my house.'

'Omai. Jesus, Omai. Fuck. This is important.'

He stops on the rough grass at the fringe of the beach. 'I have a good life. I don't want to hide any more. I just want to be myself. I want to live a life of integrity.'

'You can move anywhere in the world. Hawaii. Indonesia. Anywhere you want. They have good surf in a lot of places. The thing with the ocean is it all joins up. It's all the same mass of water.' I try to think. I try to find something in our shared past that will break through the stubborn walls of his mind. 'Can you remember what Dr Johnson told us, that first week after the voyage? At that meal they did for you, at the Royal Society. About *integrity*?'

Omai shrugs. 'It was a long time ago.'

'Come on, don't you remember? We ate partridge. He told us that you always had to be ready for new knowledge. *While knowledge without integrity is dangerous, integrity without knowledge is weak and useless.* I'm trying to give you knowledge and all you are giving me back is integrity. Integrity that is going to get you killed and risk everything.'

'And do you want some knowledge, Tom?'

I gesture a 'go ahead'.

He closes his eyes, as if taking a shard of glass from his foot. 'All right, I will give you some information. I have been like you. I moved around. All over the Pacific. Anywhere questions wouldn't be asked. Samoa. The Solomon Islands. Lautoka in Fiji. Sugar City. New Zealand. Even went back to Tahiti. Hopping around. Where necessary I formed the right connections. Found little ways into the underground. Got fake documents. Always starting afresh. Wiping the slate twice a decade. Then things started to change.'

'How?'

A man walks by, a late middle-aged man in a faded Quiksilver T-shirt and frayed cut-off jeans and flip-flops. He is on the beach path, heading onto the sand with a joint and can of Coke. He is mumble-singing a sad but indiscernible tune. He is a peaceful, oblivious stoned drunk who wants nothing to do with us. He sits heavily on the sand, to smoke and watch the waves, well out of earshot.

Omai sits down too, placing his wet board on the sandy grass and sitting cross-legged on it. I join him.

He stares out at the sea with sad fondness, as if it is a memory. Moments pass, unregistered. 'I fell in love.'

Obviously this raises questions but I keep them silent for now.

'You used to tell me about love, didn't you? You used to tell me about that girl you fell in love with. The one you married. The mother of Marion. What was she called?'

'Rose.' To say her name, on a beach in Australia in the twenty-first century, makes me feel a strange and dizzy sensation. The distance of time and place fuses with the closeness of emotion. I place my hands on the grass and the sand, as if needing to feel something solid, as if there are elemental traces of her there.

'Well, I found my Rose. She was beautiful. Her name was Hoku. I get headaches, nowadays, when I think of her.'

I nod. 'Memory headaches. I've been getting a lot of them too, recently.'

I wonder, for a moment, if Hoku is the old woman with the tin opener that I had seen in the house, though this idea is quickly put to rest.

'We were only together seven years. She died in the war . . .'

I wonder which one. And where. Second World War, I assume, and I'm right.

'That was when I moved to New Zealand and got some fake

papers and signed up to fight. There was never an easier time to fake your identity. They accepted anyone then. They didn't pry too deeply. Not that I did much fighting. Was sent to Syria and sat and baked there for a bit. Then Tunisia, for more baking with a bit of actual action thrown in. Saw some things. It was intense. What about you? Did you fight in that one?'

I sigh. 'I wasn't allowed. Hendrich thought the combination of science and ideology was the most dangerous thing for us. And he was right, but there were the Nazis, with all their deluded obsessions about creating the perfect race. Their pseudo-science eugenics people were onto us. They'd taken over the Institute for Experimental Research in Berlin and discovered their research into us, into albas, and they were after as many of us as possible . . . Anyway, Hendrich was going through a paranoid phase. He didn't want any of us involved in the war. And, yes, while you were saving civilisation I was being a short-sighted asthmatic librarian in Boston. I still hate myself for that. I suppose I have tried to avoid love the way Hendrich has wanted us to avoid war. To try to stay alive without any more pain.'

A distant siren wails on a road somewhere beyond.

Omai strokes water off his board. 'No. Not for me. Love is where you find the meaning. Those seven years I was with her contained more than anything else. Do you understand? You can take all the years before and since and weigh them next to those, and they wouldn't stand a chance. That's the thing with time, isn't it? It's not all the same. Some days – some years – some *decades* – are empty. There is nothing to them. It's just flat water. And then you come across a year, or even a day, or an afternoon. And it is everything. It is the whole thing.' I think of Camille, sitting on the bench in the park, reading *Tender Is the Night*, as Omai continues. 'I've been trying to find the point of it all. I used to believe in mana. Everyone did in those days, on the islands. I think I still do, you know, in a sense. Not as a superstition but as an idea of *something*. Something

296

inside us. Something still not explained that doesn't come from the sky or the clouds or some palace in Heaven but from inside here.' He pats his chest. 'You simply can't fall in love and not think there is something bigger ruling us. Something, you know, *not quite us.* Something that lives inside us, caged in us, ready to help us or fuck us over. We are mysteries to ourselves. Even science knows that. We have no fucking idea how our own minds work.'

We fall quiet after that.

The drunk man is now lying down, staring up at the stars. He stubs his joint out on the sand.

A minute passes. Maybe two. Then Omai feels ready to say it.

'We had a baby.' His voice rolls as soft as the sea. 'We called her Anna.'

I try to absorb this. The significance of it. I think of Marion. Then it clicks.

'That was her, wasn't it? The woman in your house is . . .'

The smallest of nods.

'She's not like your daughter. She aged. In real time. She got married. But her husband, my son-in-law, he died of cancer thirty years ago. She's lived with me ever since.'

'So she knows about you?'

He laughs. It is, admittedly, a stupid question, but I still find it such an alien idea, that a mayfly could know such a thing about a loved one, and be fine with that, and not feel the risk. Of course, Rose knew about me, and my mother too, but that knowledge was torment, and drove me apart from both of them. 'She knows. She knows. Her husband knew too.'

'And the secret didn't get out?'

'Who would believe a secret like that?'

'Some people. Dangerous people.'

The way he looks at me right then makes me feel weak, pathetic. A coward on the run.

'A wave can kill you. Or you can ride it. It's sometimes more

297

dangerous to shy away. You can't live your life in fear, Tom. You have to be prepared to get on your board and stand on your feet. If you are in the barrel of a wave you have to ignore the fear. You have to be in that moment. You have to carve on through. You get scared, and the next thing you know you are off your board and smashing your head on a rock. I'm never going to live in fear. I can't do it for you, Tom, I just can't. I have run away too often. I feel at home now. I love you, man, I do, but I don't care if Captain Furneaux's ghost comes walking along the sand, I'm not going anywhere with you.'

And then he stands up, and takes the board with him.

'I'm going to put this right,' I find myself saying. '*I'm going to put this right.*'

He nods but keeps walking, his bare feet now on the concrete path, and I turn to see the stoner on the beach raising his hand at me and I give a small wave back. I lie back in the sand and think of the war Omai fought in that I didn't, because of Hendrich. I sense it is nearing my time to fight again. My phone starts to vibrate, buzzing against my thigh like something alive, and I just let it ring and wonder what the hell I am going to do.

I fall asleep on the beach. When I wake up, the morning light is bleeding into the sky and I go back to the hotel and eat and check my messages and find it weird that Hendrich only tried to call once. I go back to the room and have a little trouble with the wi-fi but eventually get online and go on Facebook and see that Camille hasn't updated. I want to talk to her. I want to message her. But know I can't. I am dangerous. While I am still a part of the Albatross Society I am the thing I need to protect her from.

I curl up into a foetal ball on the bed and cry shuddering tears and wonder if I am having a breakdown.

'Fuck you, Hendrich,' I whisper up to the ceiling. 'Fuck this.'

I leave the hotel on foot and I keep walking around trying to pace away my tears, and think. I need to think. I walk along the clifftop and along the beach. I head to the Cape Byron lighthouse and stare out at the sea.

I remember staring out at the Antarctic Ocean from the deck of the *Adventure*, caught up in Cook's foolish greedy quest for a land larger than Australia.

There comes a moment in every life when we realise there is no land beyond the ice. There is just more ice. And then the world we know continues again.

You sometimes have to look at what you know is there and discover the things right in front of you. The people you love.

I think of Camille. I think of her voice. I think of her head tilting up to the sun. I think of the fear as she fell off her chair.

I suddenly realise it doesn't matter. It doesn't matter that we age differently. It doesn't matter that there is no way of resisting the laws of time. The time ahead of you is like the land beyond the ice. You can guess what it could be like but you can never know. All you know is the moment you are in.

I walk inland and find a lagoon. The water is a deep delicious green with rocks and lush vegetation all around. I have lived a long time but I don't know the names of most of the plants. Nor do I know the name of the lagoon itself. It is so nice to be somewhere I don't know. To be somewhere new, when the world has felt so stale and familiar. Two small waterfalls pour into the lagoon, cancelling all other noise. I look at the falling water until it seems like a bride's veil.

I have no wi-fi. No phone reception. It is calm here. The air fragrant. Even the water sounds like a shush to the world. I sit down on a log and notice something. My head stays painless.

I know something absolutely.

There is no way I am going to convert Omai. And there is also no way I am going to kill him. I inhale the fresh flower-scented air and close my eyes.

I hear a noise that isn't water.

A rustle, from a bush near the narrow path behind me. Maybe it is an animal. But, no, I get the sense of someone approaching. Someone human. A tourist, maybe.

I turn around.

I see a woman and she is holding a gun and she is pointing it at me. I feel a pulse of shock.

The shock is not from the sight of the gun.

The shock is from the sight of *her.*

On the face of it she looks so different. Her hair is dyed blue, for one thing. She is tall. Taller than I thought she would ever be. She has tattoos on her arms. She looks entirely twenty-first century, with her T-shirt ('People Scare Me') and jeans and lip-ring and orange plastic watch and her anger. She looks, also, like a woman in her late thirties, and not the girl I said goodbye to four hundred years ago. But it is her. Eyes are their own proof.

'Marion.'

'Don't say that name.'

'It's me.'

'Look back at the water.'

'No, Marion, I'm not going to.'

I stand up and keep looking at her. The shock is immense. I try so hard not to think of the gun that is inches in front of my face or the death that could be seconds away. I try to see nothing except my daughter.

'You are the reason I am still alive. Your mother told me to find you. And I knew you were somewhere. I knew it.'

'You left us.'

'Yes, I did. I left you and I regret it. I left you to save your life. To save your mother's life. She wanted me to go. It was the only way. We'd escaped London but we couldn't escape the reality. I had watched my mother *drown* because of me. Do you know what it's like, to have that guilt inside you, Marion? You don't want it.

You don't want to kill me for the same reason. Is this Hendrich? Did he tell you to do this? Has he recruited you? Has he brainwashed you? Because that's what he does, Marion, he brainwashes people. He can be persuasive. He's been around for nearly a thousand years. He knows how to manipulate.'

'You never wanted me. That's what you told Hendrich. You never wanted to be a father.'

This is shock on top of shock. Hendrich had found Marion and he hadn't told me. The one thing he knew I desperately wanted to know – where she was – he had hidden. How long had we been in the same society, without my knowing?

I could hardly get the air required to speak.

'No, no, that's not the truth. Marion, listen, I've been trying to find you. Please? When was . . . when did?'

The gun is still there. I contemplate grabbing her arm and seizing it. But this is my daughter, this is Marion, this is the absence I have always felt. I can talk to her. If Hendrich can talk to her so can I.

'You wanted to find me because I was the one person in this world who knew about you who you didn't trust. You didn't care about me, you hadn't seen me for centuries. You just wanted to protect yourself and you asked the Albatross Society to find me and get rid of me.'

'That is the exact opposite of the case.'

'I saw the letter you wrote to Hendrich decades ago.'

'What letter?'

'I saw it. In your own handwriting. I saw the envelope. I saw what you said. I saw your conditions of joining the society. It killed me inside. It sent me fucking insane. Depression. Panic disorder. Psychosis. I've had it fucking all because I found out my own father who I loved more than anything in the world wanted me dead. You see, I wanted to find you too. *You* were the thing that kept *me* going. To know that the one thing that kept me going wanted to kill me was too much. I don't owe you a fucking thing, *Dad*.'

She is crying now. Her face is steel but she is crying, and I love her so much I feel the force of it like the ever-flowing waterfalls and I want everything to be okay. I want her to know that it could be.

'Hendrich lies. He fakes things. Gets other people to fake things. Sometimes that works for us and sometimes it works against us. He has connections and money, Marion. Got rich by hyping up the tulip trade and never lost it.'

'Agnes verified it. Agnes told me it was true. She said that I was the reason you had to leave and you hated me for it. You fuck.'

'I have never said I hated you. Agnes is so deep inside his pocket she can't see daylight. Marion, I love you. I am not a perfect person. I wasn't a perfect father. But I have always loved you. I have been searching for you for ever. For ever, Marion. You were such an amazing child. I have looked for you for ever. Every day I have missed you.'

I picture her, close to the window, grabbing the last light of the day so she could finish reading *The Faerie Queene*. I picture her sitting up in her bed, playing the pipe, determined to get the notes right.

She is still crying, but the gun stays targeted at me. 'You said you were coming back. You never came back.'

'I know, I know. Because I was the danger, remember? The signs and words they scratched on the door? The witchfinder? The gossip? You knew what was happening. You knew what had happened to my own mother. I was the problem. So I had to go away. Like you had to go away.'

She clenches her eyes closed, as if making a fist with her face. '*Motherfucker*,' she says.

I could make an easy grab for the gun now, but I don't.

For centuries she has been my only reason to go on living. But now, I realise, I actively want to live. For the sake of life itself. For the sake of possibility and the future and the possibility of something new.

'I remember you playing "Under the Greenwood Tree",' I tell her. 'On that little pipe. The one I got from Eastcheap market. Can you remember? Can you remember when I taught you to play that thing? You struggled at first. You never seemed to be able to cover the holes with your fingers, not fully, but then one day you just got it. And you played the pipe in the street, even though your mother didn't want you to . . . She never wanted attention. For reasons you can probably now understand.'

She says nothing. I stare out at the water, and at the trees on the other side of the lagoon. I can hear her breathing.

I put my hand in my pocket.

'What are you doing?' she asks, her voice so quiet it is almost drowned by the water.

I take my wallet out. 'Just wait one second.' I pull the small sealed polythene bag out and hold it in the air. She looks at the thin dark fragile coin inside.

'What is that?'

'Can't you remember that day in Canterbury? The sun was shining. You were playing the pipe and someone placed this in your hand. And you gave it to me that last day and said I had to think of you. This here, this penny, it gave me hope. It kept me *alive*. I wanted one day to return it to you. So here. Here you go.'

I hold it out for her. Slowly she raises the arm not holding the pistol. I place the coin on her palm. Uncertainly she lowers the gun. Her fingers curl around the coin, slowly, like a lotus flower closing its petals.

She looks dazed. She says something which I don't hear, as she leans into me, and then before I know it she is crying in spasms on my shoulder and I hold her and want to press away all the lost centuries between us.

I want to know everything. I want to spend the next four hundred years hearing about her life to now in real time. But when she pulls away and wipes her eyes she has an anxious look to her.

'He's here,' she says, staring at me with her mother's green eyes. 'Hendrich. He's here.'

Hendrich had decided to escort Marion to Australia. He had booked into the same hotel as her, the Byron Sands. He had been worried, from when he first asked me, that I wouldn't be able to do the Omai job. He had – and in truth I knew this – been worried about me for a while. Ever since Sri Lanka, and the moment I had decided I wanted to return to London.

Marion had been told to follow me unseen. She wasn't expected to kill me which was the one thing we had on our side.

'It's going to be fine, Marion,' I had told her, petrified I was telling her another lie. 'All of it. It's all going to be fine.'

It is evening now. Marion and Hendrich are eating dinner together in the Byron Sands.

'You must not even flicker,' I told her. 'You must be the person you were an hour ago. In front of him you must absolutely believe you want me dead.'

I stay out. I am walking along a coastal road near the Byron Sands, in case Marion needs me, with the evening calm of grass and beach and sea juxtaposing with the intensity of my mind, roaming beyond the streetlamps into darkness.

I am on the phone. I am trying to call Camille. Hendrich had heard her voice, that day when I was drunk in the park. For all I know he might have an alba on assignment in London now – Agnes or another – ready to kill her and mask her death as a suicide.

'Pick up,' I say, uselessly into the air. 'Pick up, pick up . . .'

But she doesn't. So I send her a text.

'I'm sorry about the way I was. There is more I need to explain.

And I will. I just want to tell you that you should get away. You might be in danger. Leave your flat. Go somewhere. Somewhere public.'

I send the text.

My heart beats wildly.

All my life, I realise, I have been dogged by fear. Hendrich had promised to be an end to those fears but all he had done was accentuate them. He controlled people by fear. He had controlled me by fear and he controlled Marion by fear. When it was just me, it was hard to see, but seeing how he had manipulated Marion, lying to her and me in the process, had made me realise the Albatross Society ran on secrets and the manipulation of its members, all to serve Hendrich's increasing paranoia about external threats. Biotech companies aiming to stop the ageing process were his latest area of concern: one called GeneControl Therapies and another called StopTime that were both investing in stem cell technology that could one day prevent humans ageing.

Hendrich held on to the idea that those scientists at the Berlin institute had been killers, and he always had some new conspiracy theory to work with. Albas knew it was hard to be their true selves, and often had memories of horrific injustices, as I did. But I was no longer prepared to let the long shadow of William Manning shroud my judgement. The more I thought about the threat, the more I realised the threat was Hendrich himself.

He had tainted everything. Even the reunion with Marion.

I get a text from Camille. The text says: '????'

A taxi rolls by. The only car on the road.

Then my phone vibrates.

It is not Camille, but Marion.

'He's going to see Omai.'

'What?'

'He's just leaving the restaurant. He's going. He's just got in a taxi. He'll be at the house in ten minutes.'

A large yellow-striped lizard scuttles amid palm trees.

'I just saw the taxi. What's he going to do?'

'He didn't say. He told me to wait. I couldn't push it. He was suspicious enough.'

'Marion, has he got a gun?'

'I don't know. But—'

I am already running north to Broken Head Road before she finishes her sentence.

'Father.'

Marion was looking up at me from her pillow. Her eyes were heavy with worry. She sighed. I'd been telling her about the birds that disappeared to the moon and lived there, on the side we couldn't see.

'Yes, Marion?'

'I wish we were on the moon.'

'Why is that, Marion?'

She frowned, deeply. As deep as only she could frown. 'Someone spat at Mother. He came up to the stall and he stood there. He was wearing nice gloves. But he made a face like a gargoyle, and said no more words than a gargoyle, and he gave Ma the most horrid look, and then he gave me the same eyes and Ma didn't like the way he was looking at me so she said, "Do you want any flowers, mister?" And I suppose she asked it a little harshly but that was because she felt nervous.'

'So he spat at her?'

Marion nodded. 'Yes. He waited a moment more and then he spat in her face.' She clenched her jaw so tight I could see the muscles shift beneath her face.

I took this in. 'And did the man say anything more? Did he explain himself?'

Marion frowned. The anguish in her eyes made her look older. I could easily picture the woman she would become. 'He said nothing. He left Ma wiping herself, with all the hawkers and folk from town staring at us.'

'And did he act peculiar to anyone else?'

'No. Only to us.'

I kissed her forehead. I pulled the blanket up.

'Sometimes,' I told her, 'the world is not how we wish it to be. Sometimes people can disappoint us. Sometimes people can do terrible things to others. You must be careful in this life. You see, I am different. You know that, don't you? The rest of the world ages forwards and I age to the side, it appears.'

Her face sharpened. She was lost in violent imaginings. 'I hope that man gets sick. I hope he dies in agony for shaming Ma like that. I'd like to see him hanging and his legs kicking wild and have him sliced into quarters and his innards slip out. I'd like to pull out his eyes and feed them to a dog.'

I looked at her. The fury was a force that you could almost feel in the air.

'Marion, you are still a child. You must not think this way.'

She calmed a little. 'I was scared.'

'But what is it that Montaigne teaches us? About fear?'

She nodded slowly, as if Montaigne himself was also in the room. '"He who fears he shall suffer, already suffers what he fears."'

I nod. 'Now, hear me, Marion. If anything were to happen to you, if you were ever to become like me, if you were different, you must learn to build a shell around yourself. A shell as hard as a walnut. A shell no one else can see, but one you know is there. Do you understand what I am saying?'

'I think I might.'

'Be a walnut.'

'People crack walnuts. And eat them.'

I suppressed a smile. There was nothing I could say to Marion sometimes.

A little later, after a jar of ale, I lay beside Rose, fearing for a future I already knew was against us. And I felt sick, knowing the time would arrive when I'd have to leave them. When I'd have to

308

run away, and keep running, for however much life I had been given. Away from Canterbury. Away from Rose. Away from Marion. Away from myself. I was already feeling a kind of homesickness for a present I was still living. And I lay there, trying to find a route to a far distant future, where things might be better. Where somehow the course of my life had re-routed and headed homewards once more.

Byron Bay, Australia, now

You can hear the crashing of waves quite clearly on Broken Head Road. Where they break against the side of the cliff. It is quite easy for the sound of petrol splashing against timber to be disguised. I smell it before I see what he is doing.

'Hendrich,' I say, 'stop!'

In the dark he almost looks his age. Stooped and thin and withered, like a Giacometti sculpture in jeans and a Hawaiian shirt. One of his arms hangs down, crooked, struggling awkwardly with the weight of the petrol can. But there is an urgent energy to his movement.

He stops for a second and looks at me with blank eyes. He isn't smiling. I note this because I have rarely seen Hendrich without a smile.

'You told me you couldn't be the one to burn his house down in Tahiti. You were never really a finisher, were you, Tom? Well, history has a way of correcting its mistakes.'

'Don't do this. Omai isn't a danger.'

'As you get older you not only get a certain aptitude for people, Tom, you also get an insight into time itself. You're probably not quite there yet but there are moments where the understanding is so profound that you see time both ways. Forwards and back. When they say "to understand the future you must understand the past", I don't think they know the real truth of it, Tom. You can actually see the future. Not the whole of it. Just pieces. Flashes. Like reverse memories. We forget some of our future just as we forget some of our past, it seems. But I've seen enough. I knew you weren't to be trusted any more to finish a job. I've sensed it for some time. I knew where this was going.'

'It doesn't matter. None of this matters.'

'Of course it matters. We need to protect ourselves.'

'Fuck, Hendrich. That's bullshit. You mean protect *yourself*. That's all you've ever meant. The society is a society of one. Come on, Hendrich. It's not the eighteen hundreds any more. You knew about Marion. You lied to me.'

He shakes his head. 'I did something you find hard. I kept my promise. I told you I would find her and I found her. Something you were unable to do. I keep people safe.'

'By setting fire to their homes?'

'You have your nose against the canvas, Tom. Stand back and see the whole picture. We are under threat like never before. Berlin, biotech, everything. Things don't get better. Look at the world, Tom. It's all fucked. Mayflies don't live long enough to learn. They are born, they grow up, they make the same mistakes, over and over. It's all a big circle, spinning around, creating more destruction every time. Look at America. Look at Europe. Look at the internet. Civilisation never stays around for long before the Roman Empire is falling again. Superstition is back. Lies are back. Witch hunts are back. We're dipping back into the Dark Ages, Tom. Not that we ever really left them. We need to stay a secret.'

'But all you've done is replace superstition with more superstition. You lie. You found my daughter and you sent her to kill me.'

'I'm not the only one who lies, Tom, am I now?'

He pulls a chrome lighter from his pocket. It was the same lighter he'd had the first time I met him, back in the Dakota. 'Gave up smoking years ago. They lynch you in LA for less. But I kept this memento. You know, like you with that stupid penny. The petrol, though, the petrol I had to buy.'

He flicks a flame into life. Suddenly, I understand this is real. There is no surprise, really, that Hendrich is willing to kill Omai,

311

or me, or that he kept Marion's whereabouts secret. Ever since I joined the society I have known what he is capable of. The surprise is that he is willing to expose himself like this, endanger himself, be this close to the *heat*.

'Omai!' I shout. 'Omai! Omai! Get out of the house!'

And then it happens.

The peak of the crescendo. A cascade of everything. All the paths of my life intersecting in one spot.

As I begin to run towards Hendrich, a voice rings out, puncturing the night: 'Stop!'

It is, of course, Marion.

And then Hendrich stops, for a moment, and seems suddenly weak and vulnerable, like a little boy lost in the woods. He glances from Marion to me and back again. Simultaneously, Omai steps barefoot out of the house, carrying his aged daughter in his arms.

'Look at this. Isn't it so sweet? A father and daughter get-together. That's your weakness, you see. That's what separates you from me. This desire to be like them. The mayflies. I never had that. I knew, before I acquired my first fortune, *years* before I sold my first tulip, that the only way to be free was to have no one at all.'

A shot rings out. The noise of it shakes from the sky. Marion's face looks hard – yes, hard as a walnut – but her eyes are now filled with tears and her hands are shaking.

She's hit her target. Black lines of blood trickle from his shoulder down his arm. But he is raising the can of petrol and tilting it, pouring the fluid over himself.

'In the end, it turns out *I* was Icarus after all.'

He drops the can as he brings the flame close to his chest. I think, or imagine, I see a small smile, a faint signal of contented acceptance, the moment before he violently blooms into fire. His flaming body staggers away from the house. He keeps walking across the grass towards the sea. The cliff.

He is heading to the edge, his feet pushing through the grass that grows wilder nearer to the edge. The grass smokes and singes and glows at its tips, like a hundred tiny fireflies. He keeps walking; there is no moment of pause or reflection, but nor is there a scream of pain. Just a continued staggering momentum. A determination, a last act of control.

'Hendrich?' I say. I don't know why his name comes out as a question. I suppose because, even in his last moments, he is a collection of mysteries. I have lived a long life but it is never long enough to be entirely free from surprise.

'Oh, man,' Omai keeps saying. 'Oh, man, oh, man . . .'

And his instinct, as a good person, is to go over to him. So he places his daughter down on the grass.

'No!' Marion says. Still holding the gun. I sense now that Hendrich is not only the man who wanted her to kill me, but the man who spat on her mother's face, the one whose guts she'd wanted to see. He is the unavenged William Manning. He is every single person who has hurt her in the space between, and I sense there have been a lot. 'Leave him. The motherfucker. Stand back. Stay where you are. Leave him.'

So we leave him. And all is silent. No cars pass by, no one sees a thing. The only witness is our side of the gape-mouthed moon, as always. And the vertical fire of Hendrich walks and walks and then isn't walking at all. He is gone. The ground that had been glowing and shifting from the light of the fire is now in sudden darkness. He has fallen. The temporal distance between him walking and him not being there is so minute it is imperceptible.

There is a world in which he lives and there is a world in which he is dead. And the move between the two happens with no greater ricochet than the whisper of waves crashing onto distant rocks.

And, just as it only takes a moment to die, it only takes a moment to live. You just close your eyes and let every futile fear slip away. And then, in this new state, free from fear, you ask yourself: who am I? If I could live without doubt what would I do? If I could be kind without the fear of being fucked over? If I could love without fear of being hurt? If I could taste the sweetness of today without thinking of how I will miss that taste tomorrow? If I could not fear the passing of time and the people it will steal? Yes. What would I do? Who would I care for? What battle would I fight? Which paths would I step down? What joys would I allow myself? What internal mysteries would I solve? How, in short, would I live?

London, now

Marion.

My daughter. Rose's daughter.

She's still the same little girl.

That's what people say, isn't it? About children grown up. Well, in truth, I can't say it about Marion. She is not the same little girl.

Yes, the intensity had always been there. The sensitive intelligence. The bookishness. The desire – once no more than a child's fantasy – to exact bloody vengeance on those who wronged her.

But there are a thousand new things there now.

After all, we aren't just who we are born. We are who we become. We are what life does to us. And she, born four hundred years ago, has had a lot of it, has done a lot of living.

For instance, she is scared of Abraham. She now has 'a thing about dogs'. I daren't ask her what happened.

Abraham likes her straight away, from the moment we pick him up from the dog sitter, but Marion sits well away from him, casting nervous glances in his direction.

She is very open about the things she has done.

She tells me some of the places she has lived, other than London and Heidelberg and LA. Rouen, that had been her first trip overseas. Then Bordeaux. She knew the language, and both had strong Montaigne associations, so that had guided her. But there had been other places in more recent times: Amsterdam, Vancouver, Scotland. She had lived in Scotland for about a hundred years, apparently, from the 1840s onwards. She had moved around. The Highlands. The East

Neuk of Fife. Shetland. Edinburgh. She had been a weaver. She'd had a loom. 'A travelling loom,' she says, and laughs a little, which is rare.

She is on Citalopram for depression. 'It spaces me out, but I need that.' She says she gets strange dreams all the time, and often has panic attacks. Sometimes she has panic attacks about having panic attacks. Vicious circles. She had one on the plane, coming back from Australia, but I hardly even noticed, except she became quite still.

We had left Australia with no problems at all. She had not flown there with Hendrich, and his body hadn't yet been discovered, so no questions were asked. He had changed his identity, of course, to arrive in Australia, so in a sense he didn't exist at all. He had disguised his life so well his death became, like every other aspect of him, one more secret.

I had said goodbye to Omai. I had told him that at some point it might be a good idea to move and he said he'd think about it and that was that. He wasn't going to move. He was going to stay still and, well, only the future knows what that means.

I write an email. I type it out and keep very nearly pressing 'send'. The email is to Kristen Curial, who heads up StopTime, the leading part-government-funded biotech company that is investigating ways to halt the cellular damage behind illness and ageing. One of the ones Hendrich was paranoid about.

Dear Kristen,
  I am 439 years old. And I can prove it. I believe I can help you with your research.
  Tom

And then I attach the Ciro's picture and a selfie of me now, complete with arm scar. I stare at the email and see how ridiculous it looks and then save it in drafts. Maybe later.

316

Marion does not talk much. But when she does talk she swears a lot more. There is a joy she takes in swearing which I suspect she inherited from her aunt Grace. She likes the word 'motherfucker' in particular (not that this particular one was around in her aunt's day). Everything is a motherfucker. For instance, the TV is a motherfucker. (There is 'never anything on the motherfucker'.) Her shoes are motherfuckers. The American president is a motherfucker. Weaving yarn through a loom is a motherfucker. Bertrand Russell's *History of Western Philosophy* is a motherfucker.

She also tells me that she had a 'short spell' on hard drugs from 1963 to 1999.

'Oh,' I say, feeling like fatherhood is something I have lost the knack of. 'That's . . . uh . . .'

She is staying with me for a little while. Right now she is sitting on the chair, away from Abraham, vaping, and humming an old tune. Very old. 'Flow My Tears' by John Dowland. A tune I used to play on the lute when she was a little girl, before she ever played the pipe. She doesn't say anything about it, and nor do I. There is a vibration to her voice. A softness. There is still a soft nut beneath the shell.

'Do you miss Ma?' she asks me.

'I miss her every day. Even after all these years. It's ridiculous, isn't it?'

She smiles sadly, then sucks on her e-cigarette. 'Has there been anyone else?'

'No . . . mainly.'

'Mainly?'

'Well, there hasn't been. For centuries. But there is someone at school. Camille. I like her. But I feel like I might have messed it up.'

'Love is a motherfucker.'

I sigh. 'Of course it is.'

'You should just shoot for it. Tell her you messed up. Tell her why you messed up. Be honest. Honesty works. Well, honesty gets you locked up in a psych ward. But sometimes it works.'

'Honesty is a motherfucker,' I say, and she laughs.

She goes quiet for a little while. Remembers something. '"I speak the truth not so much as I would, but as much as I dare, and I dare a little more as I grow older."'

'Is that . . .?'

'Montaigne himself.'

'Wow. You still like him?'

'Some of it's a bit dodgy nowadays, but yeah. He was a wise man.'

'What about you? Has there been anyone?'

'There was. Yes. There have been a few. But I'm fine on my own. I'm happier on my own. It always got too complicated. You know, the age thing. I have generally found men to be quite a disappointment. Montaigne said that the point of life is to give yourself to yourself. I am working on that. Reading, painting, playing the piano. Shooting nine-hundred-year-old men.'

'You play the piano?'

'I find it offers more than the tin pipe.'

'Me too.' I am enjoying this. This is our first real proper conversation since Australia. 'When did you get your lip pierced?'

'About thirty years ago. Before it was a thing everyone had.'

'Does it ever hurt?'

'No. Are you judging me?'

'I'm your father. That's what I'm here for.'

'I also have tattoos.'

'I can see.'

'I have one on my shoulder. Want to see it?' She pulls down her jumper and shows me a tree. Beneath it are the words: 'Under the Greenwood Tree'. 'I got it to remember you. You taught me the song, remember.'

I smile. 'I remember.'

She is a bit jetlagged, still. So am I. I want her to stay but she says London gives her panic attacks and she doesn't want to go back to hospital. She says there's a house on Fetlar, one of the Shetland Islands where she had lived in the 1920s, which is still there and abandoned. She says she wants to go back. She says she has some cash. And that by next weekend – after my week back at school – she will go. It saddens me, but I understand, and promise to visit as soon as I can.

'Time doesn't move there,' she says. 'On the islands. It used to make me feel normal. Being surrounded by all that unchanging nature. The city is harder work. Things happen in cities.'

Her hands have a slight tremble to them. I wonder at the horrors she has been through. The stuff she has blocked out. I wonder about the future, about what will happen to her, and to me, now that the secret of the albas is likely to be revealed. Now that we, or Omai, might be the ones to reveal it.

But the thing is: you cannot know the future. You look at the news and it looks terrifying. But you can never be sure. That is the whole thing with the future. You don't know. At some point you have to accept that you don't know. You have to stop flicking ahead and just concentrate on the page you are on.

Abraham slides off the sofa and slopes off into the kitchen. Marion comes and sits next to me. I want to put my arm around her, like a father would a daughter. I don't think she wants me to, but then she places her head on my shoulder and says nothing. I remember that same head resting on that same shoulder, when she was ten years old, that night in the coach. That had felt, then, like the end of everything. This, now, feels like a beginning.

Time can surprise you sometimes.

I cycle to school.

I see Anton walking into the main building on his own. He has his headphones in and he is reading a book. I can't see what the book is called but it is a book. Whenever I see someone reading a book, especially if it is someone I don't expect, I feel civilisation has become a little safer. He looks up. Sees me. Raises his hand.

I like this job. I can't right now think of a better purpose in life than to be a teacher. To teach feels like you are a guardian of time itself, protecting the future happiness of the world via the minds that are yet to shape it. It isn't playing the lute for Shakespeare, or the piano at Ciro's, but it's something as good. And goodness has its own kind of harmony.

Sure, I have no idea how long I will stay as one, once I go public about who I am. I might have the job for a week or a month or a decade. I don't know. But it doesn't matter. Everything in life is uncertain. That is how you know you are existing in the world, the uncertainty. Of course, this is why we sometimes want to return to the past, because we know it, or we think we do. It's a song we've heard.

And it's good to think of the past.

Those who cannot remember the past, observed the philosopher George Santayana in 1905, are condemned to repeat it. And you only need to switch on the news to see the dreadful repetitions, the terrible unlearned lessons, the twenty-first century slowly becoming a crude cover version of the twentieth.

But, although you can gaze at the past, you can't visit it. Not really. I can't sit by a tree in a forest and have my mother sing to me. I can't walk along Fairfield Road and see Rose and her sister again, selling fruit out of a basket. I can't cross the old London Bridge and enter Elizabethan Southwark. I can't go back and offer more words of comfort to Rose in that dark house on Chapel Street. *I can't ever see Marion as a little girl again.* I can't go back to a time when the world's map wasn't known. I can't walk snowy streets lined with beautiful Victorian streetlamps and choose not to visit Dr Hutchinson. I can't go back to 1891 and tell myself not to follow Agnes onto the *Etruria*.

The yellow bird sits on a windowsill for a while and then it flies away. That is nature. There are things I have experienced that I will never again be able to experience for the first time: love, a kiss, Tchaikovsky, a Tahitian sunset, jazz, a hot dog, a Bloody Mary. That is the nature of things. History was – *is* – a one-way street. You have to keep walking forwards. But you don't always need to look ahead. Sometimes you can just look around and be happy right where you are.

I no longer have my headache. I haven't had it since Australia. And yet, I am still worried.

I can see Camille staring at me through the staff-room window. She is smiling and then she notices me and suddenly she looks cross, or scared; it's hard to tell. I stand there and wait. I will speak to her. I will explain things. I will tell her who I was on the phone to. I will tell her about Hendrich. I will tell her about Marion. Maybe someday soon we can try another park bench. I don't know. I can't know.

But from now on, I am going to exist in the open. I am not going to let secrets hurt people any more.

Yes.

It is about time.

It is about time I *lived*.

So I inhale the east London air, which feels purer than usual, and I walk, among the teenagers, into the rather uninspiring 1960s school building with a strange and long-forgotten feeling.

I feel at the beginning of something.

I feel ready to care and be hurt and take a risk on living.

And within two minutes I see her. Camille.

'Hello,' she says. Business-like, polite.

I can see now from her eyes she wants me to say something. And I was going to. In the moment after this one, I am going to try to do what has always been so hard.

I am going to try to explain myself. And a peculiar feeling

321

happens when I am right in front of her. It is a sense of total understanding, as though inside this one moment I can see every other one. Not just the moments before but those lying ahead. The whole universe in a grain of sand. This is what Agnes had been talking about in Paris almost a century ago. And Mary Peters. I had finally had this experience of total understanding of time. What is and what was and what will be. It is just a single second, but inside it I feel as though, just staring into Camille's eyes, I can see for ever.

La Forêt de Pons, France, the future

Two years from that moment in the school corridor.

France.

The forest near Pons that still remains. The one I once knew.

Abraham is old now. He had a kidney stone removed last month, but still isn't exactly in great shape. Today, though, he seems happy sniffing a thousand new scents.

'I'm still scared,' I say, as we walk Abraham among the beech trees.

'Of?' Camille asks.

'Time.'

'Why are you the one scared of time? You're going to live for ever.'

'Exactly. And one day you won't be with me.'

She stops. 'It's strange.'

'What's strange?'

'How much time you spend worrying about the future.'

'Why? It always happens. That's the thing with the future.'

'Yes, it always happens. But it's not always terrible. Look. Look right now. At us. Here. This is the future.'

She grabs my wrist and places my hand on her stomach. 'There. Can you feel her?'

I feel it – the strange movement – as you kick. You. Marion's little sister. 'I feel her.'

'Exactly.'

'And one day she might look older than me.'

She stops, right then. Points through the trees. There is a deer.

It turns and looks at us, holding our gaze for a moment, before darting away. Abraham tugs on the lead half-heartedly.

'I don't know what will happen,' Camille says, staring at the space where the creature had been. 'I don't know if I will make it through the afternoon without having a seizure. Who knows anything?'

'Yes. Who knows?'

I keep staring between the trees at the air that had been inhabited by the deer and realise it is true. The deer isn't there, but I know it had been there and so the space is different than it would otherwise have been. The memory made it different.

'"You are no longer insulated; but I suppose you must touch life in order to spring from it."'

'What's that? A quote?' I ask.

'Fitzgerald.'

We carry on walking. 'I met him, you know.'

'Yes, I know.'

'I knew Shakespeare too. And met Dr Johnson. And once saw Josephine Baker dance.'

'Name dropper.'

'It's true.'

'Speaking of names,' she says slowly, as if considering her words as carefully as her steps on this uneven path. 'I've been thinking. I don't know what you would say. Now we know it's going to be a girl I think we should call her Sophie. After my grandmother. Sophie Rose.'

'Rose?'

She holds my hand. Then, just so she is clear: 'I have always loved the name. The flower, but also the sense of having risen . . . Like you now, now you're free to be who you are. And yes, I know it's weird for someone to name their baby after, you know . . . But it's quite hard to be jealous of someone from four centuries ago. And, besides, I like her. She helped you become you. I think it would be nice. To have that thread through things.'

324

'Well, we'll see.'

We kiss. Just standing there, in the forest. I love her so much. I could not love her more. And the terror of not allowing myself to love her has beaten that fear of losing her. Omai is right. You have to choose to live.

'Everything is going to be all right. Or, if not, everything is going to *be*, so let's not worry.'

I see now how right she is. Sometimes I can see futures beyond this one. I can see her try and fail to remember my own face, even as I am there in front of her. I can see her holding my hand as Rose had done, pale and ill at the end of life. I can feel the fringes of a pain that will one day overwhelm me, after she has gone. She knows I know this. But she doesn't want me to tell her any more. She is right. Everything is going to be. And every moment lasts for ever. It lives on. Somewhere. Somehow. So, as we keep walking back down the path from where we came we are in a way staying there, kissing, just as I am also congratulating Anton on his exam results and drinking whisky with Marion in her Shetland home and shuddering from the sound of artillery fire and talking to Captain Furneaux in the rain and clutching a lucky coin and walking past the stables with Rose and listening to my mother sing as sycamore seeds spin and fall in this same forest.

There is only the present. Just as every object on earth contains similar and interchanging atoms, so every fragment of time contains aspects of every other.

Yes.

It is clear. In those moments that burst alive the present lasts for ever, and I know there are many more presents to live. I understand. I understand you can be free. I understand that the way you stop time is by stopping being ruled by it. I am no longer drowning in my past, or fearful of my future. How can I be?

The future is you.

325

Acknowledgements

Thank you for reading this book. That is the first acknowledgement to make. A book only becomes real by being read, so thank you for giving my daydream a reality. I wanted to write a book that you enjoyed reading and I enjoyed writing, and I guarantee I achieved at least the latter. I have never had as much fun writing a book. It was time travel and a therapy session in one, minus the psychiatrist's fees and the DeLorean.

I first had the idea of writing it as I was writing another novel, *The Humans*. That had been a book that was really about placing our small but wonderful human lives within the vast context of the universe. So whereas the perspective of that was space, I wanted the perspective of this one to be time. The way time can comfort us and terrify us, and the way it makes us appreciate the scale and precious texture of our lives.

Anyway, wanting to write something is not the same as writing it. And I am very lucky to have an editor like Francis Bickmore who always understands the essence of what I am trying to do, and helps me get there. Indeed, I am grateful to Jamie Byng and all at Canongate, for giving me the freedom to write the books I want to write and for publishing them so well. Particular mentions to Jenny Todd, Jenny Fry, Pete Adlington, Claire Maxwell, Jo Dingley, Neal Price, Andrea Joyce, Caroline Clarke, Jessica Neale, Alice Shortland, Alan Trotter, Rona Williamson and Megan Reid.

I am very lucky to have the most magnificent agent Clare Conville, who has somehow helped me turn my eclectic scribblings into something resembling a career.

Also, I would like to thank Katherine Boyle, Kirk McElhearn and Joanne Harris for help with making my French a bit more natural, and Greg Jenner for his emails packed with historical knowledge, firing my mind off in different directions through time. Of course, I must also thank Benedict Cumberbatch and all at StudioCanal and SunnyMarch for seeing the film potential.

Most of all, I must acknowledge my wife and best friend Andrea Semple, who is the first reader I write for, and the first one to tell me what is and isn't working, and who is a daily inspiration. The one I always want to stop time for.

Thank you.

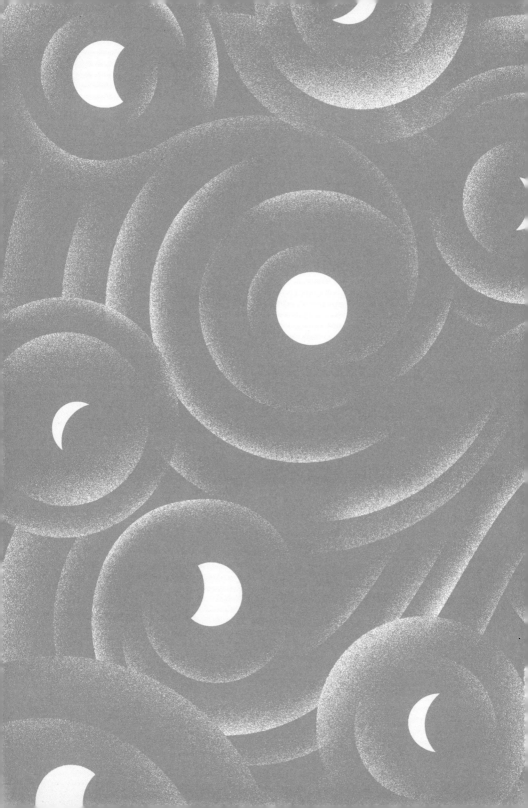